JEFFERSON COU
620 Cedar
Port Hadlock,
(360) 385-6544 w

MW00450644

DISCARD

JBM 12/19
:O

8-19
DATE DUE
Bws
SEP 1 8 2019
11/08
JAN 1 8

THE ENTANGLED CHASE

THE
ENTANGLED CHASE

CHASE FULTON NOVEL #6

CAP DANIELS

ANCHOR WATCH
PUBLISHING
** USA **

The Entangled Chase
Chase Fulton Novel #6
Cap Daniels

This is a work of fiction. Names, characters, places, historical events, and incidents are the product of the author's imagination or have been used fictitiously. Although many locations such as marinas, airports, hotels, restaurants, etc. used in this work actually exist, they are used fictitiously and may have been relocated, exaggerated, or otherwise modified by creative license for the purpose of this work. Although many characters are based on personalities, physical attributes, skills, or intellect of actual individuals, all of the characters in this work are products of the author's imagination.

Published by:

ANCHOR WATCH
—— PUBLISHING ——
** USA **

All rights reserved. No part of this book may be reproduced or transmitted in any form or by any means, electronic or mechanical, including information storage and retrieval systems without written permission from the publisher, except by a reviewer who may quote brief passages in a review.

13-Digit ISBN: 978-1-7323024-8-8
Library of Congress Control Number: 2019943157
Copyright © 2019 Cap Daniels – All Rights Reserved

Cover Design: German Creative

Printed in the United States of America

Dedication

This book is dedicated to…

Wayne Stinnett,
a brilliant storyteller, author, marine, sailor, and friend. Just like Captain Stinnett, the fictional master of the Research Vessel Lori Danielle in this novel, Wayne has been a source of enormous inspiration and encouragement for me. Without his guidance, mentorship, faith, and support, I would not be a successful novelist, and this Chase Fulton Series would not exist. I owe Wayne a debt I will never have the ability to repay, but because of his character and selfless desire to see other writers succeed, he refuses to consider it a debt at all. I treasure not only the invaluable lessons he has taught me on my journey to becoming a novelist, but also his friendship.

May fate grant you not only boundless success, but also immeasurable happiness as long as the sun continues to rise over the South Carolina Lowcountry you call home and love so much.

Special Thanks To:

My Astonishing Editor:
Sarah Flores – Write Down the Line, LLC
www.WriteDowntheLine.com

Sarah devotes countless hours not only editing my work, but also teaching and encouraging me to continually hone my craft and become a better writer, communicator, and storyteller. Her incredible mastery of language never fails to fascinate and impress me. Her involvement in this series has progressed far beyond her tireless work as an editor. She has now become an integral part of the entire process, managing the incredibly complex details of promotion, advertising, publication, communications, graphic arts, and a thousand other things I'm not smart enough to accomplish. Without her, this series would not exist. I am eternally grateful for her dedication, professionalism, devotion, patience, emotional and intellectual investment, and most of all, for her friendship.

Table of Contents

Also by Cap Daniels

Book One: *The Opening Chase*
Book Two: *The Broken Chase*
Book Three: *The Stronger Chase*
Book Four: *The Unending Chase*
Book Five: *The Distant Chase*
Book Six: *The Entangled Chase*
Book Seven: *The Devil's Chase* (Autumn 2019)

I Am Gypsy

The Entangled Chase

CAP DANIELS

Chapter 1

My Rights

I watched Penny Thomas—the woman I loved, the woman I decided would be the only Mrs. Fulton of my life—stand with tears in her eyes and shock on her beautiful face as I was handcuffed, searched, and Mirandized on the dock of the St. Augustine Municipal Marina.

"Mr. Fulton, you have the right to remain silent. Anything you say can and will..."

The detective droned on, but I wasn't listening. I was staring into Penny's tear-drenched eyes. "Listen to me. Call Clark and tell him what's happening. Tell no one else. Do you understand?"

She nodded. "Yes, Chase. I understand."

I offered no resistance to the detectives who were simply doing their jobs as I tried to stay calm and think clearly. Dr. Richter, and even Dominic had warned me this would happen sooner or later. I would follow the protocol I was taught—to the letter.

"Penny, get my credentials from the top shelf of the safe, and give them to the detective."

The older of the two detectives stepped forward. "If you'd like, Mr. Fulton, we can allow you to go aboard your boat to retrieve your identification."

"No, thank you. Penny can retrieve my credentials and give them to you before you take me away."

"I'll go with her," said the younger cop.

I locked eyes with the detective. "Is she under arrest?"

"No, not at this time."

"Then she'll retrieve my credentials without you, and you may not follow her aboard my boat."

In his practiced, overconfident tone, the cop said, "We have the right to search your boat incident to your arrest, Mr. Fulton."

"No, you don't," I said. "You'd have the right to search my boat incident to my arrest if you had made the arrest *aboard* my boat, but that isn't the case."

The younger cop licked his lips and growled. "Let's go."

Penny ran toward the boat with our black-lab puppy galloping after her as the two men led me back toward Avenida de Menendez. Before we'd reached the ramp leading up to the street, Penny caught up with us and thrust my black leather credential pack toward the younger cop. He reached toward the cred pack and swatted it from her hand, sending it flying through the air and into the Matanzas River.

Penny's eyes narrowed as she glared at the cop. The puppy, who did his best to keep up with Penny as she ran up the dock, did precisely what hundreds of years of genetics had programmed his marble-sized brain to do. He clumsily leapt from the dock and plunged into the brackish water of the river. His webbed feet powered his pudgy body far more gracefully than they'd allowed him to run, and he clamped his tiny teeth into the leather of my cred pack before it began to sink.

All of us, especially the cops, watched in amazement as the puppy climbed from the river onto the muddy bank, shook wildly, and stumbled his way back onto the dock. He ran between my feet and laid his chin on Penny's bare foot with the dripping wallet still clenched in his jaw.

She patted his head, pulled the wallet from his mouth, and glared at the officers. "I'll follow you to the station and bring these credentials with me."

I began to doubt the two men who'd read me my rights were what they claimed to be. "I'd like to see some identification if you guys wouldn't mind."

"We ain't showing you shit." The younger man turned to face Penny. "And you ain't following us nowhere if you know what's good for you."

A familiar voice yelled from the sidewalk above. "Hey, Chase! What's going on?"

I looked up to see Officer Kevin O'Malley peering down at us with that inquisitive look cops are so good at. "These detectives are arresting me, Officer. Why don't you come down here and give them a hand?"

The two men holding my elbows froze and looked around frantically.

O'Malley's size disguised his athleticism. The two-hundred-fifty-pound beat cop drew his pistol, keyed his radio mic, reported the incident, and closed the seventy-five feet that separated him from us.

I didn't know who these guys were, but I was confident O'Malley and I were about to find out. The younger of the two men at my side quickly rolled behind me and wrapped a muscled arm beneath my chin, pulling me backward in the typical hostage position. The older man released his vice-like grip on my elbow and ran up the opposite ramp.

I yelled, "Get him, O'Malley! I can handle this one."

I pressed my chin into my captor's forearm, preparing to thrust my head backward and crush his nose with the back of my head, but that's when I heard the crack and felt the blood spatter. The man's arm fell limp, and he melted away toward my left side. I ducked to one knee and pivoted to see Penny standing over him in a perfect follow-through position, a wooden boat hook clenched in her fists like a six-foot-long baseball bat. The man was lying motionless on his side with blood pooling beneath his right ear.

"Get his keys and unhook me."

Penny dug at the man's pockets and came up with a single hand-cuff key. She unlocked the cuffs just as a pair of shots rang out from the street above.

"Take the dog! Get back to the boat!"

I grabbed the man's pistol from his holster and ran toward the gunfire. As I rounded the marina office, three more shots rang out, and I slammed my body against the wall. The shots sounded like a significantly larger caliber than the first pair I'd heard.

I realized the pistol in my hand was a .38 revolver, and I tried to remember what the butt of the other man's gun looked like. I couldn't picture it, but I knew O'Malley would be firing a nine millimeter and would have no shortage of ammunition. As I peered around the corner of the building, I prayed he hadn't been hit.

O'Malley was on lying on his back with his pistol pointed between his feet. I followed his line of sight in the direction he was aiming and saw the older of the two men who'd tried to abduct me lying facedown on the grass beside the sidewalk.

"O'Malley!" I yelled. "Are you hit?"

"Yeah, the son of a bitch got off two shots. Is your guy down?"

I kept my eyes on the man in the grass as I slowly approached my friend. "Yeah, Penny clocked him with a boat hook. If he's still alive, he won't be getting up anytime soon. Where are you hit?"

He rocked as if he were trying to determine the entry point. "Make sure that bastard's dead before you worry about me, lad."

I cautiously approached the supine form and discovered exit wounds in his back: two through the center, and one high above his left shoulder blade. O'Malley had put three rounds in the man's chest after taking at least one, and maybe two rounds himself. There was no doubt the man in the grass was standing in line to meet Saint Peter.

I picked up his revolver with a stick I found and returned to O'Malley's side. A pair of black-and-white St. Augustine police cruisers screeched to a stop at the curb as I knelt by my friend's side. A trickle of blood seeped from a wound on his left shoulder, and his gold badge had a perfect hole directly through the center.

"It looks like he put one in your shield and the other in your left shoulder," I said. "How about telling your buddies up there not to shoot me?"

O'Malley holstered his Glock and keyed his radio mic. "One-six-seven to base. Shots fired, officer down, two suspects down, scene secure. One friendly civilian on scene providing aid. We're going to need the coroner and forensics. One-six-seven, out."

One of the approaching officers had his gun drawn, but he wasn't pointing it at me. "Hands up where we can see 'em!"

I raised both hands above my head just as O'Malley said, "Relax. He's the good guy."

The officer holstered his weapon and rushed to O'Malley's side. He ripped open his uniform shirt to find a pair of holes high on the left side of O'Malley's bulletproof vest. The vest had stopped only one of the bullets, while the second left a small entry wound beneath the front of O'Malley's shoulder. He would spend the night in the hospital after the doctors cut the bullet out of him, but he'd survive.

The street was soon full of every imaginable emergency vehicle. Looky-loos gathered in mass trying to get a peek at what was happening. A dozen officers attempted to control the crowd, but they weren't having much success. EMS arrived and bagged the body of the man who'd chosen to start a gunfight with an Irish-Catholic-linebacker-turned-beat-cop.

O'Malley fought off another team of paramedics who thought they'd put the big man on a gurney. He made it abundantly clear he was going to walk to the ambulance under his own power, and they were welcome to try catching him if he fell.

"You can shoot me if you want, but I'm going to check on Stud Muffin, so you'd better get out of my way!" Earl from the End plowed her way past the officers attempting crowd control. The five-foot-tall tree stump of a woman ran up to me and bear-hugged me. "You ain't hurt, are you, Baby Boy?"

"No, Earl. I'm fine."

"How 'bout your boat? They didn't shoot your boat, did they? 'Cause if they did, I'll whoop somebody's—"

"Take it easy, Earl. The boat's fine, and I'm fine. The bad guys... not so much."

O'Malley's ambulance drove away, and I headed for the dock where two paramedics were leaning over the man Penny had clubbed. They were working feverishly on him and had already strapped a C-collar around his neck. Apparently, he was still alive.

Chapter 2
Holiday Road

"Mr. Fulton, I'm Detective Holiday. I'm a *real* detective with the St. Augustine Police Department. Here are my credentials." The man handed me his cred pack instead of flashing his badge.

I handed the wallet back to him. "It's nice to meet you, Detective Holiday. Please call me Chase. And this is Penny Thomas."

The man let his gaze linger on Penny a moment longer than I liked, but then asked, "Is there someplace we can sit and talk? I have a few questions about what happened here this afternoon."

I pointed toward a pair of dock boxes. "You can have a seat there, and I'll be right back. I have to make a call."

Without a word, Penny turned and headed for the boat with our puppy still in her arms.

The detective withdrew his pad and watched me turn toward my boat. "Okay, but we have to get a statement."

"I understand."

As I followed Penny back to the boat, she whispered, "This is going to get nasty, isn't it?"

I sighed. "It's already nasty."

"Do you have any idea who those guys were?"

"We'll talk about it on the boat. I don't want the detective to think we're conspiring."

The puppy converted his squirming motion into a climbing effort and leapt across Penny's shoulder. I spun and caught him in midair just as the marina cat rocketed past. I had no idea how I would ever break him from chasing that cat. Perhaps I never would.

Back aboard *Aegis*, my fifty-foot custom sailing catamaran, I dialed Dominic's number. Although the organization for which I worked had no apparent formal rank structure, I believed anything as serious as a shootout on American soil, a few hundred feet from my boat, was something my handler needed to know.

"Hey, Chase. Welcome home. We've got a lot to talk about."

I knew he probably wasn't particularly happy about the mission I'd just completed without official sanction, but we had more pressing issues to deal with.

"Thanks, Dominic. Listen, there's a bit of a situation going on up here. Two guys dressed like cops cuffed me and read me my rights. They said I was under arrest for the murder of Salvatore D'Angelo. I didn't resist until it became obvious they weren't real cops. Anyway, it turned into a shootout. One local cop, a buddy of mine, took out one of the bad guys, but he caught a couple rounds in the vest. He'll be okay."

Dominic jumped in. "What about the other guy?"

"Penny took care of him with a boat hook."

"Way to go, Penny," he said.

"Yeah, exactly. So, needless to say, the real cops now have a bunch of questions for me. I need to stay clean."

I could almost hear Dominic's wheels turning inside his head.

"Let me talk with the lead detective," he said.

"Are you sure? Do you really want to get wrapped up in this?"

"I don't have any choice. I have to keep you clean. Now, put me on with the top cop on the scene. I'll hold."

"Yes, sir." I headed back onto the dock and approached Detective Holiday. "Are you the senior detective on the scene?"

"Yeah, I am."

I handed the phone to him. "It's for you."

I pretended to ignore the conversation while I watched the crime scene techs comb through the grass where victim number one had taken his final breath. I could only hear Holiday's side of the conversation.

"Detective Lieutenant James D. Holiday, assistant chief of detectives…I see… Well, that certainly is a unique set of circumstances… Yes, but… How can I reach you if I have more questions?… But there's… Somebody will have to… Yes, I understand, but… Okay, here he is."

I took the phone from Holiday. "Hello?"

"Walk away, and don't look back," Dominic said. "Do you understand?"

"I do."

"Good. Call me in an hour."

The line went dead, and as he said to do, I ignored Holiday and headed back for my boat.

Women, in my experience, have an inherent need to know everything that's going on around them, but Penny was the best in the world at hiding that need. When I stepped aboard the boat, she handed me my Secret Service credentials that were inside the wallet, which, I discovered, had become the pup's favorite new chew toy.

I shoved the identification into my pocket and sat on the deck. Penny took turns watching the puppy and smiling at me. "I love him already, Chase. Thank you!" She leaned against me and kissed me gently. "Are you all right?"

"Never better." I ruffled the pup's fur with my bare toes. He took the gesture as an invitation and climbed onto my lap, slobbering and wagging his tail. "I guess you'd like to know what's going on, huh?"

Penny ran her fingers through my hair and stared into my eyes. "That's the thing I love most about you."

"What's that?"

"I never have to worry. I always know you're going to take care of whatever comes up."

"I'm afraid this one may be harder to take care of." I looked up the docks, toward the hordes of police officers still working the scene.

"What do you mean?"

"This is going to turn into a mess. There's no question about who's behind it, but I don't know if I can just turn it over to the cops and walk away."

"What did Dominic say?"

"I'm not sure what he told the detective, but from what I could hear, Dominic told him to butt out."

"I didn't know that was something he could do," she said, tracing her finger down the puppy's spine as he slept on my leg.

"I didn't either," I admitted, "but I've still got a lot to learn."

"Life's never going to be dull with you, Chase Fulton, so I guess I should embrace the adventure."

"I've actually been giving that a lot of thought. Maybe I'll go back to school."

"Back to school?" she said with obvious surprise in her voice.

"Yeah, maybe. I might like to work on my master's instead of chasing bad guys all over the world."

She grinned. "You'd lose your mind if you weren't playing James Bond, and you know it."

I shrugged. "I don't know. It's something I've been thinking about, but it doesn't matter right now. Whatever that was with the fake cops and the shootout is serious business. I need to figure out what's going on and stop it."

"Who do you think it was?"

I'd been trained to avoid jumping to the obvious conclusion, but there was no doubt in my mind who was behind my bogus arrest. "It has to be the congresswoman. Who else could it be?"

Before I'd left for Europe to trade one Russian spy for another, I played a game with Salvatore D'Angelo, the son of Florida's newest congresswoman. Sal had apparently developed a need to mess with kids, specifically elementary school children from the Catholic school in St. Augustine. I intervened when he pulled a knife on a nun, and I left him devoid of the knife and consciousness. After I'd learned about his propensity for misconduct with children, Penny and I snatched him off the beach in front of his house and dangled him over Red Snapper Sink, a bottomless pit thirty miles off the coast of St. Augustine. I didn't kill him. I merely encouraged him to make a rather sizable donation to the Catholic school and find a new place to live outside of Florida. When we dropped him off back on the beach, I believed the episode was over, but it seemed as if the congresswoman had other ideas.

Penny furrowed her brow. "But why would a congresswoman use fake cops? Couldn't she get real cops, like the FBI or something, to arrest you for real?"

"Not if Sal's not dead. Arresting someone for the murder of someone who's still alive isn't something the FBI does."

"How do you know he's still alive?"

"I don't," I admitted, "but the fact that the cops weren't real is a pretty good indication."

"Who do you think they were?"

I considered her question, but I didn't have a good answer. "I don't know yet, but I'm going to find out. There's a good chance there's some mafia ties, but that's supposition at this point."

"Mafia?" She said it loud enough to rouse the slobbering puppy from his slumber.

I picked him up just as his bladder reached its limit. Penny giggled, but I did not.

"Do you have any idea how to housebreak, or, in this case, boat-break a puppy?"

"No." She was still giggling at the puddle on my lap. "I've never had an inside dog."

"Here." I handed her the black furball. "I'm going to change clothes. Do something with him."

She cuddled him against her chest, and he started his twisting again.

"He needs a name, you know."

"I've been thinking about that," she said. "I like the name Charleston, and we can call him Charlie. If you remember, we met in Charleston."

"Oh, I remember. How could I ever forget the beautiful woman who wanted me to read her screenplay?"

She smiled. "Did you ever actually read it?"

"Not only did I read it, I loved it. Have you finished yet?"

She sighed. "No, I've been a bit busy kidnapping a child molester with you, but I plan to finish it and maybe find an agent."

"You should, but right now, I need to find some clean pants and call Dominic."

* * *

He answered on the third ring and said, "Are you alone?"

"No, Penny's here with me, but no one else."

"Great, listen. Here's what I did. I told Detective Holiday you're a Treasury agent on assignment, and then I called the chief of police and the mayor. They're not going to be asking you any more questions."

Even though I'd been on the job for almost five years, it was still difficult for me to fathom the fact that I could simply pretend to be a Treasury agent and everybody would buy it. I had the credentials and a number to an office where some official-sounding voice would confirm that I was, in fact, an agent of the Federal Government. I suppose that was partially true. The work I did was mostly done for the government, but I'd occasionally leave the reservation and strike out on my own.

"So what should I do now?" I asked.

"It's really up to you, Chase. If you want to take Penny to an island somewhere and drink piña coladas on the beach, that wouldn't be a bad plan."

"I'm not sure that'll solve the problem," I said. "Whoever those guys are, they aren't going to stop coming, so running away is just going to delay the inevitable."

"Yeah, you're probably right, but it wouldn't be a bad idea to get Penny out of harm's way."

I shot a glance at Penny, who seemed to be dancing from the waist down while staring out the window at Detective Holiday. "I'm not sure she'd go."

"Well, I'm not sure you should give her another choice."

I laughed. "Have you met Penny Thomas? She's not exactly the personality who would take orders from me or anyone else."

"But in this case," he said, "it would certainly be in her best interest to spend time someplace safe while we resolve this issue."

"I'll talk with her about it, but I can't promise she's going to hop on a plane and head for the Caymans."

He sighed. "So what do you need from me?"

I thought for a moment. "I need to know who the fake cops were. Can you get me that information from the local cops?"

"Probably, but if you have any friends in the department, you might have more luck working that source."

"My local source is the cop who took two rounds in the chest. I suspect he'll be spending at least the night in the hospital. He may be out of the loop for a while."

"Okay, then. I'll see what I can find out. What else?"

"Is Ginger tasked on anything right now?"

"Not that I know of," he said, "but she doesn't work exclusively for me."

"Can I use her if she's available?"

"Of course, but feel free to make contact yourself. There's no reason for me to be involved."

"You know she's training Skipper, right?"

"Yes, I know, and from what I hear, she's doing exceptionally well."

A sense of pride sent a smile to my face. "She does everything exceptionally well."

"You're the reason she's alive," Dominic said. "You should be proud of that."

I swallowed hard. "Anya is the reason she's alive."

He cleared his throat. "Yes, well, that's something we'll have to discuss. We need to debrief you on your jaunt through Europe."

My mouth went dry. "Yeah, I know. But first, let me get to the bottom of this mess here."

Chapter 3
I Need You

Penny stood with her hands on her hips. "Let me guess. He said you should send me away until all of this blows over."

I lifted her hands and draped them across my shoulders. "No, not exactly. He actually suggested that both of us go away until this blows over."

Anticipation replaced the defiance in her eyes. "Now, that sounds like an idea I could fall in love with."

I held her face in my hands and tried to picture how she would look one day when the lines around her eyes began to form and the golden blonde of her hair slowly gave way to gray. She was more beauty than the world deserved, and she was incapable of subduing the emotions behind her eyes. "You know, one day I'm going to be a crazy old man, and I'll probably get fat and might even go bald."

She ran her fingers through my hair. "Yeah, well, then you'll be *my* bald, fat, crazy old man, and I'll love you even more than I do now."

I loved the way she saw me and especially how she accepted the harsh realities of what I am.

I sat on the cabin sole beside her and Charlie. "I can't run away from this situation."

She closed her eyes. "I know. Running isn't what you do."

I flashed back to the night when Clark said something similar after I told him I was going to help Sister Mary Robicheaux. He'd warned me, and I probably should've listened, but I'd never been very good at doing what I should have done.

"Do you want me to go away?" Sadness weighed heavily on her face as the corners of her mouth slowly turned downward.

I gently kissed her nose. "I want you to be safe."

I thought I'd loved Anya, but I never looked into her eyes and pictured growing old with her, and she'd never looked at me with the tenderness and devotion Penny showed so effortlessly. I'd never forget Anya's passionate touch, but Penny's desire to entangle her life, her mind, and even the depths of her soul with mine was purer and stronger than a thousand nights of passion in the arms of another.

"I'll do whatever you think is best as long as you'll promise to come for me when this is all over."

I thought it must have been fear driving her offer to go away, but I couldn't have been more wrong.

"I want to be with you," she said, "but I know you'd die to protect me from a hangnail. If you're going to find these people and end whatever this is, you'll need to be focused on nothing else, including protecting me."

I'd never understand how she could possess such wisdom and fortitude in the face of the unknown. Most people would crumble under the pressure of living with a man like me. In the past two hours of my life, I'd knelt before her, on the verge of asking her to be my wife, only to be interrupted by a pair of thugs pretending to be cops. She'd not only kept her wits about her, but she'd also temporarily sent one of my would-be abductors into the spirit world with a well-placed boat hook shot beneath his ear. She'd witnessed a foot pursuit morph into a gunfight and then listened as I discussed the whole thing with a man who'd lied to the lead detective and bought me a reprieve from hours of questions I could never answer honestly. She was a rock, and she was mine. I'd never deserve her, and I'd never let myself forget that.

"I think it's best if you pick a beach a thousand miles from here and reclaim that summer tan I love so much."

She tried to smile. "Promise?"

I furrowed my brow. "Promise what?"

She traced my jawline with her fingertips. "Promise you'll come find me when you get to the bottom of this, and then finish what you started on the dock two hours ago."

I bit at my lip. "I promise."

"Then I promise to say yes every day for the rest of our lives."

We wordlessly held each other for several minutes, feeling the boat rock gently beneath our feet and listening to the puppy continue his relentless attack on my leather cred pack.

I kissed the top of her head and looked into her perfect face. "I have to make some calls while you decide where you're going and how you'll get there."

She peered through the portlight. "It looks like the crime scene techs are finishing up."

I leaned down so I could look across her shoulder. "Looks like it, but I doubt they'll have any real answers for a while."

* * *

Clark answered on the second ring, but there was no cheerful greeting. "I'm on my way."

"I take it you've spoken with your dad."

My handler, Dominic, was Clark's father, although they didn't share surnames. Dominic's dedication to his work over the past thirty years had taken him far away from his two sons, Clark and Tony, and their mother in Tennessee. If there was lingering resentment, I'd never detected it.

Clark said, "Yeah, he called me as soon as he hung up with you. So, should I bring lawyers, guns, and money—or just guns?"

"This isn't your fight, Clark. I got myself into this one, and you warned me not to do it. I'm not asking for your help. I'm calling to brief you on what's going on."

He huffed. "Your fights are my fights. You screwed up and didn't listen to me. So what? This isn't the first time, and it won't be the last. You can brief me when I get there."

The line went dead before I could put up an argument.

As Penny sat on the countertop eating a peach, I tried to think of anything she could do that I wouldn't find sexy. I was envious of both the peach and the countertop.

She wiped her mouth with the back of her hand. "He's coming, isn't he?"

"He is, and I should've known."

She offered me a bite of the peach, and I gladly accepted. The psychologist in me wanted to call it a fetish, but I preferred to think of it simply as enjoying Penny feeding me with her fingers.

"Oh, that's good. Thank you."

"The peach, or my fingers?"

"Both," I said, wrapping my arms around her waist.

She draped her arms across my shoulders and cocked her head. "It's really nice."

"What's nice?"

"Knowing that you're completely mine and I don't have to share any part of you with *her*."

"You've never had to share any part of me."

She lowered her head and looked at me from beneath raised eyebrows. "Anya has had one corner of your brain since long before you met me."

"Brains don't have corners."

She rubbed the juicy peach all over my face and tried not to laugh. "You know what I mean."

"Yeah, I know what you mean, but I'm all yours, Penny—including *every* corner of my brain."

She wrapped her legs around my waist. "I love your brain, but that's not the part of you I'm particularly interested in at the moment."

I carried her down the companionway and into our stateroom. Something tumbled down the steps behind us, and I turned to see the puppy flipping head over heels until he finally thudded to a stop on the cabin sole.

"Oh, Chase! He's—"

But it was too late. The puddle had already formed beneath him, and he began tracking wet paw prints everywhere he stepped.

Penny unraveled from my arms, and she was swabbing the deck in an instant. She scooped up the puppy and pointed her finger in his face. "Charlie, this is going to be a problem."

When I bought him, I hadn't given much thought to the reality of a puppy on a boat, but Penny was right.

She held Charlie in front of her face as if he were on the verge of his first scolding. "Listen to me, and listen good, Charlie. I don't mind cleaning up your pee, but you can't be interrupting when I'm being carried to bed by that beautiful man." She spun him around to face me.

I held up my hands in surrender. "I can't help you here, buddy. She won't let me pee on the floor."

"Ahoy, Stud Muffin! Is anybody home?"

Earl's unmistakable voice carried throughout the boat, and un-doubtedly, the entire marina. Charlie's ears perked up, and he stared up the stairs, eyes wide, and then made the first real sound I'd ever heard him make: He barked. It was more of a shrill yelp that I hoped would one day become a bark, but maybe he'd become a watchdog after all.

I galloped up the stairs. "Hey, Earl. What's going on?"

She was standing in the cockpit with a wooden contraption about three feet square and four inches thick. Her natural inclina-tion to make herself at home on my boat had become something I'd learned to accept. Besides, there was nothing I could do to stop her. She was coming aboard when she wanted, regardless of what I had to say about it.

"What on earth is that thing, Earl?"

She thrust the box toward me. "It ain't for you. It's for that puppy of yours. I'm bettin' you didn't think he was gonna need somewhere to poop and pee, did you?"

I looked back through the main salon and saw Charlie bouncing through the space, still making that sound.

"Actually, we had our first clean-up on aisle five," I said as the pup ran straight to Earl.

I took the box from her, and she hefted Charlie into her arms. "Have you named him yet?"

Penny emerged from the interior. "We're going with Charlie. What do you think?"

Earl held him up in front of her face. "Yeah, Charlie fits him just fine." He licked her face, and the barking ceased. "I made you something, Charlie."

It was odd watching Earl talk to a dog, but it wasn't the weirdest thing I'd ever seen her do.

I examined the contraption Earl had built and discovered it was a litterbox of sorts, with strips of rubber on the bottom to keep it from sliding across the deck and real grass sod inside. I set it down, and Earl placed Charlie in the center. He sniffed and scratched at the sod and then produced exactly what the box was made to receive.

In her best Vanna White impersonation, Earl motioned toward the box with both hands. "Ta-da!"

I hugged her, and of course, she grabbed my butt. "Thank you, Earl. You're the best."

She stepped back and looked up at me. Her challenges vertically were more than outweighed by her width. She probably would've been taller lying down than standing up, but she was one of the most kind-hearted people I'd ever known.

"Let me know if you need anything else. I guess you'll be heading out for a while after what happened here, huh?"

Earl had an insight that seemed to allow her to predict human behavior—especially my behavior before it happened.

"Yeah, I think we'll get away for a few days and let the police sort this out."

She laughed. "Yeah, right. Like you're gonna leave this to those idiots. I know you better than that, Baby Boy. You're gonna shake some trees and stomp what falls out. You ain't foolin' old Earl. What time's that good-lookin', baby-faced partner of yours gettin' here?"

I shook my head, unable to suppress a smile. "He's on his way now. He's a pretty good tree shaker, too."

She looked at her watch. "Yeah, and I bet he ain't bad at stompin' what falls out, neither."

I looked down at Charlie, who was still inspecting Earl's gift. "Thank you for the litter box, Earl. You're too good to me."

"Like I said, it ain't for you, Baby Boy. It's for Charlie. And he's welcome."

Earl peered around me. "Bye, Miss Sugar Britches. You take good care of *our* man. You hear me?"

Penny laughed. "You know I will, Earl, but if anything happens to me, you know I want you to have him, right?"

Earl huffed. "Ha! What makes you believe I'm gonna wait for something to happen to you?"

She winked at me and waddled off the boat and back onto the dock.

"She's hilarious. Is she that way with everybody?"

"I don't know," I said. "I suspect she rarely changes. I doubt she gives much thought to what other people think of her."

* * *

We made a provisioning trip into town for groceries, dog food, and other necessities we'd need, regardless of what decisions we made about where we'd go in the coming days.

We were quickly learning how dramatic the effects of having a puppy were. We couldn't pop into the Columbia for dinner while we were out. We couldn't leave him in the car while we made even a brief stop at some place that didn't allow pets. That may have been an early taste of what parenthood might be like someday. Nothing about my life was ready for that step.

When we made it back to the boat, Clark had arrived and made himself at home. He was having a sandwich on the upper deck and watching the sun set across the oldest city in America.

He came sliding down the ladder and helped us haul the provisions aboard. "Hey, who's this little guy?"

"That's Charlie." Penny offered Clark a welcome-home hug.

He flinched when she wrapped her arms around his waist. "What's wrong, Clark? Are you hurt?"

He raised his shirt, revealing the wound on his left side. "Your boyfriend got me shot, and it's not healing as well as I'd like."

"Chase! Why didn't you tell me you got Clark hurt?"

"I didn't get him hurt. He got himself hurt."

Penny knelt by his side. "Let me take a look."

Clark eyed me with a look of a sibling who had just successfully gotten his brother in trouble.

"Oh, Clark. It looks infected to me. You need to see a doctor."

He lowered his shirt. "It'll be fine. I needed to give Chase a hard time. Besides, I can't show up in the walk-in clinic and say I was shot by a Russian oligarch in Moscow last week."

Penny frowned. "Clark, I'm serious. You need to see a doctor."

He raised his shirt again and twisted to take a look at the wound. Penny was right. It was red and swollen—much worse than it had been while we were still overseas.

"I've got an idea. I'll be right back." I headed for the main salon and made a couple of calls before returning to the cockpit. "I talked to Fred, and he gave me the name of a local doctor who's sympathetic to our cause. I called him up, and he's on his way."

"You shouldn't have done that," Clark said. "It's fine. I was just bustin' your chops."

"No, Penny's right. It looks nasty. I'm going to need you at your best. We've got a mess on our hands."

I filled him in on the events of the day, and he listened intently.

"So," he began, "it has to be D'Angelo behind it, right?"

"Yeah, that's how I see it, but what do you think they were going to do with me if they'd actually nabbed me?"

Clark laughed. "Oh, there's no doubt about what they were going to do. You pissed off a powerful family, and they were going to drop you in that hole you threatened to sink Salvatore in."

"Maybe, but that's pretty gutsy to grab me right out in the open like that."

"Yeah, it's ballsy, all right, but you cost them a million bucks and embarrassed their boy pretty good."

I gave in. "Fine, let's start with that theory and work from there, but we're going to need some more help." I pulled my phone from my pocket. "I'll call Ginger. You call your dad."

Chapter 4
Take Two of These

The doctor arrived with a bag that looked like it should've contained a bowling ball and an ugly pair of shoes. He was the most unremarkable person I'd ever seen—neither tall nor short, thin nor fat, and average in every detail. I envied his look. No one could ever adequately describe him, and he wouldn't stand out in any crowd. At nearly six-and-a-half feet and over two hundred pounds, I stood out everywhere except on a basketball court.

He earned his first bit of respect from me when he asked, "Permission to come aboard?"

"Of course, come aboard. And thanks for asking. You'd be amazed how many people don't."

He shook my hand. "I'm Chris."

"It's nice to meet you, Doctor. Thanks for coming. Clark's inside."

"It's just Chris," he said with no inflection or obvious accent.

Chris followed me into the main salon and eyed every inch of the space. He didn't appear intimidated, just perfectly aware of his surroundings. Chalk up another mark of respect for Dr. Chris.

Chris's eyes finally settled on Clark. "You must be the patient."

My partner stuck out his hand. "I'm Clark Johnson."

Chris shook the offered hand and then perched on the table in front of Clark. "Tell me about your injury."

Clark raised his shirt and turned so Chris could see the gunshot wound.

"No, I said tell me about it. Don't show it to me."

Clark raised his eyebrows and slowly lowered his shirt. "Okay, then. It's a small-caliber GSW to the lower left side of my abdomen—a through-and-through. It didn't produce much blood, but it hurt like a...well, like something that hurts a lot."

Chris stuck his thumbs beneath the lenses of his glasses and pushed them atop his head. "I see. And when did this happen?"

Clark glanced at the ceiling and closed one eye. "Seven or eight days ago."

"And I'm going to need a brief medical history."

Clark stood, removed his shirt, and let his pants fall to the cabin sole. His body was all the medical history Chris needed to know. Scars were scattered about his chest and back from nearly twenty years living the life of a soldier and covert operator. An eleven-inch scar from the back of his knee up his thigh told the tale of a knife fight gone horribly wrong, and several quarter-sized scars punctuated his gunfight history.

Chris showed no reaction. "Okay, lie on your side and let me have a look."

Clark did as he was told but flinched every time Chris prodded the wound.

"I'm going to give you an anesthetic. Have you had anything to drink in the last six hours?"

"Water and Gatorade. Why are you giving me an anesthetic?"

"There's a small piece of the bullet lodged beneath the skin, and you'll scream like a little bitch if I don't numb it up before I cut it out."

That brought a round of laughter.

Chris opened his bag and removed what he needed for the procedure. "Would you mind taking the dog outside?"

Penny picked Charlie up and hurried through the door to the cockpit. "Thank God," she said. "I was praying for an excuse to avoid watching what's about to happen in here."

Chris placed an absorbent cloth beneath Clark and then cocked his head my way. "I wouldn't want to get blood on your upholstery." He injected the anesthetic into the flesh around the wound. "Would you happen to have any good bourbon?"

"I have some Bookers. Is that good enough?"

"It is," he answered. "May I have one over seven cubes of ice?"

I wasn't crazy about the doctor having a cocktail while performing surgery on my partner, and I'd been reduced from deadly covert operative to bartender...but that was fine with me. I poured the bourbon over ice and set it on the table beside Chris.

He ignored both me and the drink and went to work. I watched him make a small incision and flush the wound with saline solution. A few seconds later, a tiny sliver of black metal appeared in the pink flesh. Chris removed it with a pair of forceps and closed the wound with three stitches. He drew off several syringes of yellow puss and thoroughly cleaned the area, then finally taped a sterile dressing in place.

He nodded. "That should do it. It was good of you to call. This would've gotten out of control." He placed a brown plastic pill bottle in Clark's hand. "Take two of these every day until they're gone. Do not skip a dose, and do not stop taking them before they are all gone. Do you understand?"

Clark shook the bottle, rattling the pills inside. "Sure. Take them til they're gone. I understand."

Chris wrapped the tools he'd use in the absorbent pad and placed them back into his bag. He lifted the glass of bourbon from the table beside him and handed it to Clark. "Cheers. I'll buy you a proper drink some time, but for now, this will have to do. Thank you for what you do."

With that, he was gone. He never asked for payment and offered no small talk. He was simply gone.

Penny came through the door. "Well, that was weird."

"What was weird?" Clark and I asked in unison.

"He gave me the name of a local veterinarian for Charlie and said, 'The tall one loves you, and the other one respects you. Never take either for granted.'"

"That *is* weird," Clark said. "I don't like being called 'the other one.'"

We poured cocktails of our own and joined Clark.

Penny cleared her throat. "You know…you can put your clothes back on now."

Clark looked down, suddenly realizing he was still in nothing but his boxers.

Penny stretched her neck and scanned Clark's body. "Why don't you have any tattoos?"

He pulled on his shirt. "Tattoos tie their bearers to people and things. They give away tiny details about our lives. I don't necessarily want people to know details about my life. Especially people who might be interrogating me."

"Interesting," she said.

I changed the subject. "What did your dad have to say?"

Clark took another sip of the bourbon. "He said there's an old guy in Saint Marys, Georgia, we need to talk with."

"What's this 'old guy' supposed to tell us?"

Clark cocked his head. "He didn't say. He was cryptic about the whole thing, to be honest, but I got the impression we really need to talk to the guy. Did you get in touch with Ginger?"

"Yeah, she and Skipper are in Silver Springs, Maryland. She says they can support the op from there, and I think that's a good idea. There's no need to expose them to the dangers they might face down here."

Clark nodded his agreement and then looked at Penny.

She rubbed Charlie's head and bit at her bottom lip. "Are you going to need the boat?"

Clark shook his head. "No, probably not, but what do you have in mind?"

She put Charlie on the cabin sole, and he immediately trotted toward the cockpit. I followed to see where he was going. I didn't want him in the water at night.

"What's he doing?" Penny asked.

"You'll never believe it," I said, "but he's in his box. It looks like he won't be so hard to train after all."

Charlie finished and ran back inside to plop down on Penny's feet. "He's so cute, Chase. Thank you."

I smiled. "The things you want are important to me. Now, what did you have in mind for the boat?"

She ducked her chin as if she were afraid to tell me what she was thinking. "I don't know. I thought maybe I could take Charlie to the Keys while you and Clark do whatever it is you're going to do here."

"That's a great idea," I said. "That'll get you out of the middle of this mess in case it gets ugly, and it'll give Charlie a chance to get his sea legs."

She picked up the puppy and nuzzled his nose. "Did you hear that, Charlie? We're going to the Keys…just you and me."

We spent the rest of the night packing and making sure the boat was ready for the trip south. Penny was a better sailor than I'd ever be, so I didn't worry about the five-hundred-mile trip to the Keys. She and Charlie could handle it.

I made arrangements for lodging at the Kings Bay Naval Submarine Base for Clark and me. I was secretly excited about meeting another mysterious old guy, as I'd grown quite fond of them and learned they always had something to teach me. I just hoped this one could point me in the direction of some much-needed answers.

Taking on the family of a U.S. congresswoman wasn't something I was particularly looking forward to doing. I wanted answers, but meddling in political issues wasn't my idea of a good time.

The stairs into the hulls of my catamaran were challenging for Charlie, so Clark built five small boxes from cardboard to act as intermediate stairs, making it easier for the ten-pound ball of fur to climb. He wouldn't need the boxes for long, but they'd make the next few weeks of his life a little easier.

Clark and I loaded the car with all the gear we thought we'd need, and I kissed Penny goodbye as the sun was coming up the following morning.

She draped her arms across my shoulders and stared up at me. "I'm going to miss you, Stud Muffin."

I laughed. "I'll miss you, too—and Charlie—but try not to worry. Clark and I can handle this. We'll have some answers, and hopefully, some solutions in a few days, and I'll join you in the Keys."

"You know, it's a waste of time to tell me not to worry."

"Yeah, I know, but compared to sunken freighters in the Panama Canal and Russian prison breaks, this is a piece of cake."

She forced a smile. "Be careful, will you? I still owe you an answer to a question you never finished asking."

I had no doubt she was the woman with whom I'd spend the rest of my life. That life would never be normal, and we may never have a white picket fence, but we'd always have each other, no matter how crazy that life became.

"I love you, Penny Thomas. The weather looks great for your trip, and the boat is in shipshape. I'll see you in a few days."

"I love you, too, Chase. Please be careful."

I kissed her again and headed up the dock to meet Clark at the car.

Looking back, I saw the Bridge of Lions drawbridge opening up, allowing *Aegis* to motor through. The ornate old bridge was one of my favorite parts of Saint Augustine. Another favorite was the most unforgettable woman I'd ever meet, and she was standing at the helm of *Aegis*, my beloved boat. Watching her motor northward toward the pass into the North Atlantic was enough to solidify my resolve to get to the bottom of the mystery of the D'Angelo family, and to put an end to whatever they had planned for me.

Chapter 5
The Judge

The old man's house didn't have a street address. In fact, it wasn't even on a street. The antebellum plantation house sat on the western bank of the North River with a half-mile winding driveway lined by century-old pecan trees. Had the overhead powerlines running to the house not been visible, it would've been easy to believe we'd been transported back into the pre-Civil War South.

When we pulled to a stop in front of the grand old mansion, I noticed a man of perhaps seventy, in bib overalls and a sweat-stained straw hat, raking leaves near the base of the stairs. He propped his rake against the railing of the stairs, removed his hat, and wiped at his brow with a red bandana. Dusting off his hands, he approached my car.

I had misjudged his age. He was well into his eighties but still stood erect, the muscles in his arms sinewy and well-defined. "Mornin' to you both. I 'spect you're here to see the judge."

I shot a look at Clark, but he offered no help at all.

"I'm Chase Fulton, and this is—"

The old man interrupted. "Clark Johnson, yes, I know. I know quite well who you both are. Come on 'round back."

We followed him around the house, and he motioned us into a gazebo situated near the river. "Judge, these are the two boys from St. Augustine—Mr. Fulton and Mr. Johnson."

A character straight out of *Gone with the Wind* rose from his seat, removed his felt hat, and stuck out his meaty hand. "Good mornin', gentlemen. I'm Bernard Henry Huntsinger, but you can call me Judge. Everybody does. Won't you have a seat?"

The judge raised his eyes to the old man who showed us in. "Arthur, have Maebelle send out some breakfast for us. These boys look like they could use a plate."

"Thank you, Judge, but we've already eaten," I said.

As if he'd never heard me say a word, he continued pointing toward the house. "That's right, Arthur. Three plates and coffee."

Clark and I sat on floral print cushions on the bench of the gazebo and joined the judge in surveying the river.

"Just look at that river, boys. It's been flowing right there longer than us white men have been on this side of the Earth. Now, isn't that somethin'?"

"You have a beautiful home, Judge, and we appreciate you seeing us this morning. We understand you may have some information that—"

The judge held up his hand. "Slow down, son. This is the South, and neither of you boys strikes me as being a Yankee, so have some manners about you. Visit with me. Eat a plate of Maebelle's cookin', and take in the beauty of the world around you. This old world goes by fast enough without us rushin' it."

Twenty minutes later, a young teenage girl and two mid-twenties men dressed in navy blue suits arrived.

"Ah, our breakfast is here," the judge said as the two men began setting a table in the center of the gazebo.

"And this lovely young lady is my great-granddaughter, Maebelle. Maebelle says she's going to be a chef when she grows up, but I say she already is."

Maebelle kissed the judge on the cheek, and he bloomed with pride.

What the judge had called breakfast plates turned out to be a feast. Steak and eggs adorned the plates while a basket of steaming biscuits rested in the center of the table. A large bowl of white gravy sat beside the biscuits, and piping hot cups of coffee landed beside our plates. Jellies, jams, and preserves of every imaginable kind in pint-sized Mason jars rested in a carousel.

Clark took in the contents of the table. "This is quite a spread, Judge. Thank you."

"This is no spread, son. This is breakfast at Bonaventure Plantation. Now, eat up, and I'll tell you about the place."

We dug into the steak and eggs, and they practically melted in our mouths. The fast-food biscuits we ate in St. Augustine didn't deserve to be called biscuits compared to the three-inch-thick, golden-brown pieces of Heaven Maebelle made.

The judge wiped the corners of his mouth with a white linen napkin. "My thrice great-grandfather, Mathias Huntsinger, came to these United States, such as they were back then, in seventeen ninety-five, as an indentured servant to a tobacco farmer in Virginia named Davenport, on a five-year contract. After twelve months, Mathias renegotiated the terms of that contract with Davenport. It included a tiny percentage of the sale of his tobacco and an agreement that if the price of his tobacco didn't increase at least three percent per year, Mathias would tack an extra year of servitude onto his contract for every percentage point below the promised three percent."

Clark and I were mesmerized. The judge was either the greatest historical liar of all time, or his story was brilliantly true. The judge loaded a fork with steak and eggs and savored the combination. Although I wanted more of everything on the table, I was leaning in, hoping for the rest of the judge's story.

Apparently, Clark felt the same. He placed his fork on the plate and stared at the judge. "So, how did it work out?"

The judge cocked his head and stared back at Clark. "How did *what* work out?"

"The contract with the tobacco farmer."

"Oh, that. Mathias married the farmer's oldest daughter, Maebelle Davenport, and inherited the whole darned thing. You see, Mathias was quite the salesman. He convinced the buyers that Davenport tobacco was the best tobacco that had ever been grown anywhere in the world. He sold the tobacco farm to the remaining indentured servants and slaves on a fifty-year note and terminated all the indentured contracts, freeing the black slaves. It was the first cooperative farm in the newborn United States."

"That's an astonishing story," I said, still unsure I completely believed it.

"Oh, that's just the beginning of the story, son. Eat, eat, or else it'll get cold and you'll hurt Miss Maebelle's feelings."

Clark and I reclaimed our forks and continued the feast.

"Sometime around eighteen ten, or thereabouts, Mathias and Maebelle moved south to get away from those miserable Virginia winters and ended up here in St Marys. They bought the piece of ground you're having breakfast on and planted pecan trees. Except for the ones the hurricanes and blights got over the years, those original pecan trees are still here and still bearing fruit."

He paused to finish his breakfast and call for another pot of coffee, which was delivered by one of the young men who'd set up the table.

"Is he a grandson?" I asked.

The judge laughed. "I suppose he's *somebody's* grandson, but not mine. He's my law clerk. You see, I sat on the federal bench in the eleventh circuit for thirty-seven years. Then, one day, I remembered how much I used to enjoy practicing law before I abandoned that noble pursuit to become a judicial referee. I still get a couple of young, ambitious, soon-to-be barristers out here every year. They don't learn much about the practice of law, but when I'm done with 'em, they can clean a catfish, shoot a rifle, and recite the Constitution by heart. The way I see it, those three things can keep Old Glory flying over that courthouse long after they sink my old bones in one of these marshes around here."

He pushed back from the table and ambled toward the riverside. Clark and I wasted no time giving chase, and soon, his history lesson continued.

"In January of eighteen fifteen, a Red Coat admiral named Sir George Cockburn showed up with fifteen hundred Royal Marines and camped out right over there on Cumberland Island. After he'd fed, watered, and allowed his marines to sleep a spell, they took to shelling the hell out of a place you've never heard of called Fort Peter on Point Peter." He pointed his long, crooked index finger out over the river. "The Red Coats killed nearly everybody at the fort and then marched into town, where they came toe to toe with an old boy named Captain Abraham Massias. Massias was twenty-seven years old and in command of the Forty-third Infantry Regiment and the Rifle Corps—somewhere around a hundred and fifty men. The Forty-third put up a good fight—the best they could—but a hundred and fifty musketeers against ten times as many British Royal Marines...well, those aren't good odds. Being a man of good sense, Massias had his bugler blow retreat, and they turned tail and ran. Now that may sound cowardly to you fellows, but wait'll you hear what happened next."

The judge led us onto a pier over the river and into a twenty-six-foot Carolina Skiff with a pair of one-hundred-fifty horsepower engines on the back. Being on a boat, a boat of any kind, made me feel right at home.

The engines fired up at the touch of the keys, and Clark and I cast off the dock lines. Despite the boat's ability to make fifty knots, we idled along the bank of the river, occasionally stopping to pull on a line tied to a floating plastic jug. The third pull produced a ten-pound catfish that had fallen victim to the hook hidden beneath the chicken liver bait. The judge freed the catfish from the hook and tossed it into the live well, no doubt to later be cleaned by one of his clerks.

We continued down the river until we reached the south end of Cumberland Island, where SVR Captain Ekaterina Norikova had killed her fellow Russian, Michael Anderson, in front of Skipper. The universe seemed to keep bringing me back to the lowlands of coastal Georgia.

The judge cut the engines in the middle of Cumberland Sound and pointed toward the island. "Picture this, boys. Enough British ships to carry fifteen hundred marines, two American gunboats, plus twelve merchantmen, including an East Indiaman, *The Countess of Harcourt*, a two-decker merchant ship that was captured, first by us—the U.S.—and then by the damned Red Coats again. This whole sound was full of boats, and every living soul there was to guard those boats was over there." He pointed toward the town of St. Marys.

"They were pillaging the town, stealing everything from silverware to underwear, and good ol' Captain Abraham Massias had snuck around the Royal Marines in what they believed was a retreat. Massias came knockin' on the door of Bonaventure Plantation and begging to borrow every boat my ancestors had. Dear old thrice great-granddaddy Mathias Huntsinger not only offered every boat he owned, but he also asked for volunteers from the plantation to help with whatever Captain Massias was doing. Every man who worked for Mathias raised his hand and volunteered, including Mathias himself. Do you know that rag-tag bunch of shot-up Americans and plantation workers rowed those boats right here where we're sittin' this morning and sank nearly half the ships in this sound? They tell me if you root around in the mud deep enough, you'll still find a heap of cannons and balls down there." The judge stared across the docile water as if he could somehow see those British ships ablaze. "I'm too old for that kind of thing, but I'd sure like to have one of those old cannons."

I never loved the history classes I was forced to take in school, but if the judge had taught them, I would've never missed a lecture.

Clark and I sat in awe, trying to picture what the scene must've looked like two hundred years before, as the judge started the engines again and headed back up the river at top speed. We tied up at the dock, and I retrieved the catfish from the live well, but the judge didn't move. From behind the wheel of the boat, he silently stared at his home.

"When Mathias and his men rowed back up here after sinking those ships, they found every woman they'd left behind had been slaughtered. Not a living soul existed on the plantation except one nine-year-old boy, my twice great-granddaddy Nathen Henry Huntsinger, who was perched in the fork of that pecan tree right there.

"He had a musket tucked under his left arm and blood pouring from his right shoulder. He'd climbed that tree and fought off the Red Coats the best he could with a musket that was taller than he was. The surgeon from Captain Massias's regiment dug the musket ball out of my great-great-granddaddy's shoulder and saved the life of the boy who'd be Mathias Huntsinger's only living heir. Later that year, Mathias died of grief over the loss of his five daughters and the beautiful wife he loved, Mary Bell Davenport Huntsinger, and this beautiful plantation fell to a ten-year-old boy who'd done exactly what you boys do now. He'd fought with everything he had to save his home and the people he loved."

Chapter 6
Practice to Deceive

The judge set his eyes on mine. "Now, I figure you're probably wondering what my pedigree has to do with you."

"Actually, Judge, I'm intrigued by your story, but I must admit, I'm looking forward to hearing what you have to tell us about the situation I'm in."

"Keep your shirt on, son. We'll get there. Maebelle's frying up yesterday's catch for lunch, so you won't be going anywhere til midafternoon. In the meantime, let's make ourselves comfortable on the porch."

We strolled up the ancient stone path toward the back porch of the mansion. The judge pulled a twisted length of tobacco from his hip pocket, cut off a chunk two inches long, and then held the twist toward Clark and me. I'd spent twelve years of my life playing baseball and chewing practically anything I could get in my mouth, but I'd never tried what the judge was offering.

Before I could reach for the leathery brown sinew, Clark lifted it from the judge's hand and cut off two one-inch sections. One landed in my palm and the other in Clark's jaw. Not wanting to offend the judge by refusing his tobacco, I slid the hunk between my molars and worked it into a soft, flavorful wad inside my cheek. Surprised by the mild, earthy taste, I was glad I'd accepted.

The judge measured my reaction beneath sunken eyebrows and smiled. "Remember that Virginia tobacco farm I told you about this morning? Well, you're chewing the direct descendants of the same seeds my great-great-great-granddaddy planted over two hundred years ago in those Virginia hills."

Flavors and aromas have a magical way of reanimating the emotion of times long passed. The last time I'd had tobacco in my mouth, other than a Cuban cigar, had been in Omaha, Nebraska, during the final game of the nineteen ninety-six College World Series, the game in which I'd broken my hand and wrist so badly that I'd never play ball again. I was a different man—better in some ways, and far worse in others—than I'd been back then, but who am I to say life would have been any better—or worse—in an Atlanta Braves uniform.

The judge spat a long stream of brown tobacco juice from his mouth. "Never trust a man who won't chew your tobacco. That's what I always say. Have a seat, boys, and we'll get somebody to bring us out a cold drink. How's that sound?"

For some reason, Adirondack chairs seemed out of place on the back porch of the plantation house, but we settled in.

The judge stomped his heavy foot on the painted gray boards of the porch, and one of his clerks materialized. "Which one are you?"

"I'm Jeff, Judge."

"Of course you are." Tobacco juice slowly leaked from the corner of his mouth. "And what's the other one's name?"

"Ben, Judge. He's Ben Hedgcock, and I'm Jeff Montgomery."

"Of course, of course, Ben. How about bringing us something cold to drink, and maybe a little something to spice it up?"

"Right away, Judge. But I'm Jeff."

The judge raised his gaze and surveyed the young lawyer who'd undoubtedly come to regret applying for a clerkship with Judge Huntsinger. Jeff vanished as quickly as he'd appeared.

"Those boys have been out here almost five weeks now, and I could tell you what color eyes their first puppy dogs had, but I can't let them believe I'm anything other than a senile old man. They'll both make fine litigators, but it's gonna take some time. I swear to my soul, I hope I was never that green."

A tray containing three ice-filled glasses, a pitcher of lemonade, and two bottles of whiskey arrived.

"Thank you, Billy," the judge said. "Now help me remember, if you will. The privilege of the writ of habeas corpus shall not be suspended, unless when in cases of rebellion or invasion the public safety may require it. Just where would a gentleman find such a passage in the founding documents of these United States?"

Ben donned the smile of a teacher's pet. "Why, Judge, that would be the second paragraph of section nine of article one of our great Constitution."

The judge looked at Clark. "There may be hope for this boy, yet. Don't you think?"

Clearly pleased with himself, Ben vanished.

"Help yourself to some lemonade, and make it as happy as you'd like." The judge motioned toward the tray and its contents.

I poured a glass two thirds full of the milky yellow lemonade and slid it toward the judge. He nodded and topped it off with Wild Turkey. The golden bourbon infiltrated the contents of the glass and seemed to claim it as its own. To help determine if the two whiskey choices were a test, I screwed the top from the Gentleman Jack and watched the Tennessee sipping whiskey cascade across the clear cubes of ice in my glass. The lemonade followed, and just like the bourbon the judge poured, the Jack held its own against the sugary liquid and lent its golden color to the drink.

The judge watched and then raised his glass. "Here's to Reverend Dan Call."

Ah, it was a test, I thought, and touched the rim of my glass to his. "To Reverend Call, without whom Jack Daniel would have never learned to turn Tennessee corn into Tennessee whiskey."

The judge smiled and spat the remains of his tobacco across the rail of the porch before savoring his first mouthful of the cocktail. I had no illusions about impressing a man who'd been on the planet almost four times as long I had, but I may have gained a morsel of respect with my knowledge of distilling history.

"So, fast-forward fifty years or so, and one of the youngest countries on the face of the Earth started tearing itself apart from the inside. Brothers shootin' brothers, and Americans killin' Americans—on purpose. All in the name of state's rights. This place belonged to my grandfather during the War of Northern Aggression." He paused, seemingly to allow me to react to the alternate moniker for the American Civil War, but I didn't react.

He had another swallow and looked out over the river. "Plantations don't run without slaves. Everybody knows that, right?"

Unsure what he expected me to say, I chose to say nothing, and he chuckled. "I like you, young man. I'm glad you came to see me this morning. Plantations, especially plantations of this size, are labor-intensive enterprises. Over four hundred slaves were bought specifically for labor on the land you see around you during the first sixty years of the nineteenth century, but not a single slave ever did a minute's work on this ground."

I was perplexed, and I'm certain the look on my face telegraphed my confusion.

The judge smiled. "You see, my family bought slaves and then treated them like the men they were. We offered them employment on our plantation. In return for their hard work—and make no mistake, it was back-breaking hard work—they would be fed, housed, educated, provided medical care, and paid a fair wage. In most cases, they were paid a percentage of the profits of the plantation. If they wanted to leave, they were free to do so anytime they wanted. Although this was, by no means, the typical method by which most plantations were run, it was the way this one and a few others operated back in those days."

The judge paused to enjoy a sip of his cocktail and watch a pair of squirrels frolicking in the yard. "I don't tell you these things to brag, you see. This is how we've always done things in my family—as far as the circumstances allow."

I caught myself leaning toward the judge and hanging on his every word. He was a captivating storyteller.

"Now, I suppose you'd like to know why your friend, Dominic, suggested that you come see me."

"I would."

The judge cleared his throat. "I've described for you, in great detail, the kind of men I descended from. I count myself quite fortunate to have that bloodline flowing through my veins, and I believe I am, by virtue of that bloodline, responsible to carry on the traditions the Huntsingers before me began, nurtured, and passed down. I'm sure you feel some of that same responsibility to your father and those who came before him."

He raised his eyebrows appraisingly, and I nodded but didn't speak.

"There are families who have passed down traditions and moral codes through the years who are less than admirable. In fact, some are, in my opinion, downright despicable. I believe you've gone and gotten yourself mixed up with one such family…namely the D'Angelo clan." He coughed and then spat across the railing of the porch. "A rotten bunch they are, those D'Angelos."

We'd finally arrived at the reason for our visit to Saint Marys and Judge Bernard Henry Huntsinger's Bonaventure Plantation. I sat back in my chair, crossed my right ankle over my left knee, and did my best to appear patient and relaxed. I hoped that was the demeanor my exterior displayed while my brain did backflips and my ears anticipated what was coming next.

The judge lowered his chin and stared into my eyes. "Tell me what you've done to get wrapped up with this bunch of scoundrels."

I spent the next twenty minutes detailing how I'd found Salvatore D'Angelo accosting a woman—who I later discovered to be a nun—and encouraged him to leave her alone by breaking his arm. And then I laid out how Penny and I had abducted Salvatore D'Angelo, carried him out to sea, scared a million-dollar donation out of him for the Catholic school in St. Augustine, and convinced him to leave the state.

I noticed the judge was as enthralled with my story as I'd been with his, so I continued. "His mother, the congresswoman, apparently has kept her baby boy out of prison most of his adult life—through political favors, or perhaps threats. It seems to be common knowledge that Sal has a penchant for messing with kids."

The judge made a guttural sound of utter disgust. "Yeah, that's how I heard the story as well, and even though you did the right thing, you've stuck your nose—or perhaps some other body part—in a hornet's nest. I can't save you from gettin' stung, but I can tell you what I know about those particular bees if you want an old man's two cents' worth."

"Judge," I said, "your two cents' worth is closer to a small fortune as far as I'm concerned. I want to know everything I can before I get any deeper in this mess."

His glasses had slid almost down to the tip of his nose, so he no longer had to lower his chin to look over the rim at me. "You may be a bit brighter than most young men your age, Mr. Fulton. Have another glass of lemonade, and take out your notepad."

Clark tossed a small spiral-bound pad onto my lap, knowing I didn't have one.

"It was nineteen seventy-eight when I first heard the name D'Angelo. I was hearing an appeal on a capital murder conviction. The crime, in that particular case, had taken place in a little bitty town called Chipley, Florida. There's nothin' in Chipley except a post office, a traffic light, and peanut farms as far as you can see."

I'd actually heard of Chipley. A set of identical twins showed up at UGA on matching baseball scholarships the year I graduated. I remembered one of them saying baseball was the only way either of them would ever get off the peanut farm, and it seemed to me their plan was working for them.

"They had some hotshot lawyer from Miami in a suit that cost more than my car, and enough gold jewelry to start a pretty fair pawn shop. It was a boy named Antonio D'Angelo who'd been convicted of plucking out the eyes and lopping off the tongue of a small-time car thief who'd agreed to testify against his brother, Paolo D'Angelo. The poor boy bled to death, so Antonio ended up gettin' himself convicted of capital murder."

I found myself, once again, listening to every syllable. I can't say I liked what I was learning about the D'Angelo family, but I was hanging on the judge's every word.

"So, I was leaning toward upholding the conviction 'cause that Miami lawyer hadn't presented a solitary shred of evidence or compelling testimony to give me any reason to believe the lower court had done anything wrong. Now, keep in mind that judges aren't supposed to give any hint as to which way we're leaning from the bench, but I've never been too good at hiding how I feel about anything, especially people who have no respect for human life. Do you understand what I'm telling you, son?"

"Yes, sir, I do. And I know that feeling well. I'm supposed to do what I do without emotion, too, but like you, that's not one of my strong suits."

The judge pulled a knife from his pocket, opened the well-worn blade, and began to scrape at his fingernails, probably more out of habit than the need for a manicure. "Yeah, I suspect your job and mine have a great many similarities. I reckon the biggest difference is that in your brand of judgment, there aren't any appeals."

I don't know how, or exactly what, the judge knew about my profession, but he'd hit the nail on the head with that comparison.

"I don't know," I said. "I've never thought of myself as a judge."

He inspected the tip of his pocketknife. "So, you're more of an executioner?"

I wasn't fond of that particular moniker, but I had to admit it may have been more appropriate. "Maybe."

"Let's consider what you did to young Salvatore D'Angelo. You roughed him up when you caught him pushing a nun around."

"I didn't know she was a nun at the time."

"Even more noble, then. You intervened when you saw a man pushing a woman around—nun or not. May chivalry never die. Then, when you learned that lady was a nun, you listened when she told you of D'Angelo's sins. If you were an executioner, boy, you'd have found that man and killed him where he stood. But is that what you did? No, it was not. You asked around. You gathered evidence and testimony from people you trust, and then you gave that man an opportunity to make amends for the wrongs he'd done. You could've easily killed him. Hell, you could've sent him to the bottom of the ocean, and the world would've been a better place, but you gave him a chance. Sure, you rattled his cage and put the fear of God in him, but did you execute him? No, sir, you did not. You sat in judgment of that animal, and you showed him mercy. When was the last time you saw an executioner show any mercy?"

He paused, but believing his question was rhetorical, I didn't say a word. He waved his hand dismissively and shook his head. "Never. That's when. Never. So anyway, back to the Antonio D'Angelo appeal. When I left the courtroom that afternoon and returned to my chambers, I found a typed message on a single sheet of blue-lined, schoolhouse notebook paper—you know the kind."

I nodded.

"Typed on that piece of paper were these words: Wouldn't it be a shame if Mildred had to pay for your poor judgment?"

I furrowed my brow. "Who's Mildred?"

"Mildred, I'll have you know, was the finest woman who ever walked this crusty earth, young man. Mildred was the love of my life, the mother of my children, and the only wife I'd ever have."

I stared at the judge in disbelief as he bowed his head and closed his eyes. A tear escaped the corner of his eye and traced the lines that age had cut into his weathered face.

His Adam's apple rose and fell. "I threw off my robe and stuck my Three-Fifty-Seven revolver in the waistband of my trousers, then headed straight to the jail where they were holdin' that son of a bitch. There must've been half a dozen guards who tried to stop me, but I got my hands on the collar of that sorry bastard's orange jailhouse shirt and yanked him against those iron bars as hard as an old pecan farmer can yank. Then I stuck the barrel of my revolver right square in his eye. I told him, 'So help me, God. If you or any part of your sorry clan lays so much as a finger on my wife, I'll drill a hole through you that a mule could jump through without touching the sides.'"

I held my breath, wordlessly begging him to continue.

"One of the guards grabbed my gun, and three or four others grabbed me. When I got home, Mildred was lying dead not thirty feet from where we're sittin' now. Raped and murdered in her own kitchen. A sixty-eight-year-old woman, mind you."

Clark dropped his drink, and the collision of glass against the oak planks of the hundred-fifty-year-old porch sounded like cannon fire, but the judge never flinched.

"That's what you're dealing with, son. That's the web you've become entangled in, and let me warn you…there's more than one hungry spider in that web. What you have to do now is figure out how to get those spiders to eat each other instead of eating you."

Chapter 7
Need to Know

Some conversations reach their natural end with no need for another word. I feared my conversation with the judge had come to such an ending. I had a few thousand questions, but none of them seemed appropriate at that moment. Nothing felt as important as what the judge had experienced and the violence that befell his wife, Mildred.

I soon found myself in the library of the antebellum mansion, sitting across the table from Jeff Montgomery, one of the judge's clerks. "I need to know the name of the lawyer who represented Antonio D'Angelo in his capital murder appeal in nineteen seventy-eight."

Jeff stared at me, a look of uncertainty on his face. "Why could you possibly need to know something like that about an appeal from twenty-three years ago?"

I placed both hands palms-down on the table and leaned forward. I wasn't trying to intimidate Jeff. I simply wanted him to understand that I wasn't asking. I was demanding.

"Look, Jeff. You don't know me. You don't know who, or even what I am, but I'm going to settle a few old scores that have been unearthed by a few new scores. Standing in my way isn't what you want to do. The judge sent me in here to get the information I need, and what I need is the name of Antonio D'Angelo's attorney from nineteen seventy-eight."

Jeff sat up straighter in his chair and clenched his fists. "You want me firing shots across your bow, Mr. Fulton."

I locked eyes with the man. "Rest assured, Mr. Montgomery, any shots fired across my bow will be answered with shots fired amidships. I'm quite certain you're not prepared for me to return fire."

I had to hand it to Jeff. He was holding his own against a man who'd been trained to tear the lives out of better men than him. He wasn't backing down, and I admired him for that.

"Give the man what he wants, Jeff."

The judge was standing in the library doorway. He locked eyes with me and offered one slow nod, and nothing more, before sauntering away.

Jeff pulled a set of keys from a drawer and unlocked a black filing cabinet that appeared to be almost as old as the house. Minutes later, a thick file was lying on the table in front of me, and Jeff had vanished.

I opened the overflowing file folder and thumbed through the contents. There were dozens of pages of legal filings, motions, and gobbledygook that I didn't understand, but I found what I needed. The attorney of record for Antonio D'Angelo was one Mario Righetti of Righetti, Capriati & Associates in Miami. I was about to learn everything there was to know about Mario Righetti, consigliere for the D'Angelo family.

I closed the file and slid it to the center of the table, then dialed Skipper's number. Seconds later, her voice filled my ear.

"Hey, Chase! I didn't expect to hear from you. What's up?"

"Hey, Skipper. Listen, I have an assignment for you. I need to know everything you can find out about a lawyer in Miami named Mario Righetti."

A barely audible gasp came through the earpiece.

"Are you all right?" I asked.

Her voice cracked. "Yeah, but why do you need to know about Mario Righetti?"

Something about that name triggered a reaction in her. "Skipper, what do you know about Righetti?"

"It's just that I never thought I'd hear his name again."

"What do you mean? How do you know him?"

I heard her take a long, deep breath, obviously trying to still herself. "He's a lawyer in Miami."

"Yeah, I know that," I said, "but how do you know him?"

"Chase, he's the lawyer for Giovani Minelli."

After my first successful mission as an American operative, I learned Skipper, the daughter of my former college baseball coach, had made some less-than-stellar life decisions. She ended up in South Florida, enslaved by Giovani Minelli, a porn producer in Miami. I'd promised my coach, Bobby Woodley, that I'd find and rescue Skipper no matter what it cost. I had done exactly that, but it cost a bullet in the back of Anya Burinkova, a former Russian SVR officer, and at the time, the woman I loved.

Giovani hadn't survived the encounter, but Clark and I did rescue Skipper, and she'd emerged in the months since. She was well on her way to becoming a top-notch operations analyst and an invaluable member of my team. The childlike fear in her tone reminded me of how close she'd come to destruction.

"Skipper, I'm sorry. I'm working on an assignment that involved Righetti in nineteen seventy-eight. I had no way to know he was tied to what happened to you."

The fear that had defined her voice moments before gave way to determination. "Are you going to kill him?"

I didn't expect that question. "No, I don't plan to kill him, but I do need to know everything I can about him. If you're not up for this one, I completely understand. I'll have Ginger do it."

Ginger was one of the best active analysts in the game, unrivaled in her mastery of database and computer knowledge. She could order up an airstrike or a meat lover's pizza with the same number of keystrokes. Her prowess as an analyst was undisputed, but that wasn't the most intriguing trait she possessed. Had she been eighteen inches taller, she would've never become an analyst. She would have walked the runways of Paris and New York, modeling for the most elite designers, but at several inches below five feet tall, her supermodel looks never caught the eye of the fashion world. The years of experience and headful of knowledge Ginger possessed was being handed down to Skipper, who was absorbing every drop like a thirsty sponge.

In her recovered, confident tone, Skipper said, "No. I've got this, and whatever he's done, I'm going to help you make him pay."

"We don't know that he's done anything yet," I said. "All I know right now is that he was Antonio D'Angelo's attorney back in the seventies. I'm also pretty sure it's the D'Angelos who tried to abduct me under the guise of an arrest yesterday in Saint Augustine."

I filled her in on the shootout at the marina and the two men masquerading as police detectives.

"Is it possible for you to stay out of trouble for more than a few days? I mean, my gosh, you just got back from Europe, and now, two days later, you're already knee-deep in another mess."

I chuckled. "I know…I know. It feels like I have a trouble magnet attached to my spine, but this one is personal."

She laughed. "When was the last time it wasn't personal?"

"You have a good point, but we'll save that discussion for another day. Are you sure you're okay digging up everything you can find on Righetti?"

"Oh, yeah. You bet I am. How soon do you need the information?"

"Yesterday, but tomorrow will have to do. I'll call you from Miami." I hung up and headed for the back porch where I'd hoped to find Clark.

Of course, he wasn't there. He was in the kitchen sampling appetizers Maebelle was continuously sliding in front of him.

Clark looked up from his arduous task with crumbs in his beard and down the front of his shirt. "Oh, hey, Chase. You've got to try these. Maebelle's catering a wedding and trying to decide on the appetizers. Here, try this crab dip. It's so good, you could put a spoonful on your head, and your tongue would beat your brains out trying to get to it."

I ignored the crab dip. "We've got work to do. I just put Skipper on the research for D'Angelo's attorney, Mario Righetti, and you'll never believe the connection."

Instead of responding, or even listening, he spooned a dollop of crab dip onto a toast point and shoved it in my mouth. Surprised by the culinary assault, I backed up, but not before the taste consumed my tongue.

"Wow! You're right. That's the best crab dip I've ever had."

Maebelle tried to suppress a shy, timid grin, but it was no use. "It's made from fresh crabs from right out there in the river. That's what makes it so good. Well, that and a few other things I can't tell you. It's my secret, you know."

I loaded two more toast points with Maebelle's amazing dip and took Clark by the arm. "Let's go. We have to get to Miami."

Maebelle slid a paper plate loaded with appetizers toward Clark. "Here, take these with you and call me later. Tell me what your favorite is."

Clark winked at the girl and lifted the plate.

We met Judge Huntsinger by the front steps of the house, and I met his eyes. "Judge, I can't thank you enough for the hospitality, and especially for the information. You have a beautiful home and a magnificent story. I'd love to come back and visit when all of this is over."

The judge looked appraisingly at me and then at the blue sky where a few cumulus clouds were starting to develop. "Looks like we might be headed for a storm."

I glanced at the sky, but I only saw a few harmless clouds.

The judge tossed a pebble at a lizard who was scurrying about on the steps. "Not that kind of storm, son. I'm talking about the storm you're about to walk into. I know what you're thinking, and you're wrong. You're not going to scare these people. Fear isn't an emotion they experience. They've been in the business of getting everything they want for a hundred years, and they're not gonna like some sorry pissant from Georgia stompin' around in their petunia patch. So you listen to me. You make damned sure you're not underestimating these people, and don't ever let a mad dog get behind you."

"Thank you, Judge, but I've seen fear in the eyes of at least one of these people. I put it there, and I intend to keep doing it, but I'll take your advice and proceed with caution."

"You'd better proceed with more than caution, son. These are dangerous people. I've seen first-hand how far they'll go to protect their own."

I stuck my hand in his and stared into the eyes of experience. "I'm sorry about what happened to your wife. I can't undo that, but you can sleep tight tonight, and every night to come, knowing Clark and I are going to make them regret *that* and every other unforgivable sin they've committed."

Chapter 8
Decisions...Decisions

As we merged onto Interstate Ninety-Five South, Clark drummed his fingers on the dash. "Well, that was an interesting morning."

When it occurred to me that it was the song "Wipeout" Clark was drumming, I made a pathetic effort to join in. The duo of chaotic beats echoed until neither of us could continue the absurd attempted percussion.

I laughed. "Well, rhythm may not be our strong suit, but at least we're not afraid to try."

He shook his head. "We have our strengths, but apparently, re-membering that we're booked at the Navy base at Kings Bay tonight isn't one of yours."

I set the cruise control on eighty-five. "I'm not interested in wasting another minute, let alone an entire night. We need to be in Miami."

"Agreed," he said. "Are we driving or flying?"

I looked at my watch. "The plane would cut the time in half, but we'll need a car when we get there."

He punched a number into his phone and stuck it to his ear. I listened as he instructed whoever was on the other end to leave a car for us at the FBO at Miami-Opa Locka Executive Airport.

When he hung up, he turned to me. "Dad's leaving either his Range Rover or the Porsche for us."

I secretly hoped for the Porsche, but the Range Rover was much more practical. We could haul any gear—or bodies—if it became necessary.

"I've got Skipper digging for everything she can find on Mario Righetti, Antonio D'Angelo's attorney."

Clark nodded. "That's great. I'm sure she'll have a file on him at least a foot thick by the time we make Miami."

"That's not all," I said. "You'll never believe this, but Righetti was also the attorney for Giovanni, the porn producer we took down when we rescued Skipper."

"What do you mean, *we* took down? I did the down-taking while you were out…" He paused when it hit him.

I swallowed hard and bit my lip. "Yeah, that's when it happened. That's when Anya took a bullet in the back."

He put his hand on my shoulder. "That's all behind us now, man. We did a good thing getting Elizabeth out of there. And we've done some good work since then. Look at what we've accomplished —sending Colonel Tornovich off into the next life, the Chinese freighter in Panama, and now this. And just think how much better things are for Skipper…I mean Elizabeth. Man, you saved that girl's life. Look at her now. She's gonna be a top-notch analyst. Hell, she practically is already. You gotta let that crap with Anya go, man."

I nodded. "Yeah, I know. It's just that I'll always believe I got her shot because I was too cocky to listen to her before I ran into that house. If I had listened to her, we still would've gotten Skipper out, and Anya would've never taken that bullet."

"There's no way you can know that. A thousand other things could've gone wrong, and it could've been you, or even Skipper, who took that bullet. It's in the past, and there's nothing we can do to change it. After our trip to Moscow, you settled any leftover moral debt you had to Anya. Thanks to you, she's rich and free— two things she never would've been without you."

"Without *us*," I corrected him. "I couldn't have done any of it without you."

He laughed. "Sure you could've. I was just there to bring the sexy and occasionally the badassery. You were the brains behind it all."

"If you say so."

"So, seriously? This Righetti dude was the lawyer for the porn guy?"

I nodded. "That's what Skipper said. And by the tone of her voice, I'm pretty sure she remembered him. That's enough to make me want to have a chat with him, regardless of what he knows about the D'Angelos."

Clark wrinkled his forehead. "Hmm, I have a plan to get him to talk to us...alone."

Clark had my full attention. "Let's hear this plan of yours."

He squinted as if he were still plotting out the details in his mind. "How would Righetti react if I called him up and said I knew who shot Giovanni?"

I locked eyes with him. "You can't be serious. If the judge is right, this dude's connected with some pretty serious guys. We don't need them knowing *we're* the ones who took out Giovanni."

"*We* aren't the guys," he said. "*I'm* the guy."

"My point is that I'd rather be a little covert at first and save the freight-train-on-Main-Street technique for later...if it becomes necessary."

Clark had described himself as a freight train on Main Street when he was comparing our styles of operation. According to him, I was a surgeon, cutting out cancer with an extremely sharp scalpel, removing pestilence from the Earth, one soul at a time, while he tended to be more like a freight train running over everyone who got in his way. Our techniques were quite different, but we complemented each other perfectly. When subtlety was the order of the day, I was quick to fill the order, but when it was time to turn the bull loose in the china shop, Clark was an excellent bull.

We made the drive back to the Saint Augustine Airport in under an hour, with no unwanted attention from the Florida Highway Patrol. As I watched the towering metal door of my hangar rise on its motorized tracks, I saw November-Six-Eight-Two-Charlie-Foxtrot, my Cessna 182, perched in her corner, taking up less than half the available space in the hangar. Seeing the void drove a dagger through my heart, reminding me how much I missed my beloved mentor and friend, Dr. Richter.

Clark broke up my self-pity party. "I think the Mustang will fit in there. Don't you?"

Dr. Richter left me his P-51D Mustang in his will. It was still securely locked away in his hangar at the Ben Epps Airport in Athens, not far from my alma mater, the University of Georgia. Although I had no idea what to do with them, I also owned the hangar and the professor's modest house near the University.

"Yeah, it'll fit, but neither of us can fly it yet. Have you talked with your guy up in Tennessee about coming down to do some training for us?"

Clark looked at his watch. I'd come to believe looking at his watch was a stalling tactic he used subconsciously. He rarely answered any question without giving it at least a few seconds' thought. "I did talk with him, and he said he'd love to come down whenever we're ready."

"Great. That'll be second on the agenda when we clean up this mess I've dropped in our laps."

He looked at me with a furrowed brow. "Second on the agenda? What's first?"

I smirked. "That's my secret for now, but trust me, you're going to love it."

He shrugged. "That's good enough for me. Let's get the old girl out of the barn. I'll do the preflight inspection while you file a flight plan."

I connected the tow bar to the nosewheel of the 182, and Clark gently pushed on the left wing strut. Hangar rash is what happens when people carelessly pull or shove an airplane around inside or near their hangar. I wasn't willing to let any of the paint on my pristine airplane rub off on the doorframe of the hangar. We slowly maneuvered the plane through the door and onto the ramp, and Clark set about conducting the preflight inspection. The plane's previous owner, retired Air Force fighter jock and airline pilot, Cliff Fowler, had kept it meticulously maintained. I considered it a sign that his initials and mine happened to be the same, and that he'd registered the plane as November six-eight-two C-F. Some grand universal force intended for me to own the beautiful flying machine.

I called the Flight Service Station to get a weather briefing and file our flight plan from Saint Augustine Airport direct to Miami-Opa Locka Executive. There was no chance the air traffic controllers would clear us direct to Opa Locka right through the middle of Fort Lauderdale and Miami International airspace, but there was no harm in trying.

"All right. If she'll start, I'm convinced she'll fly."

That was Clark's way of saying the preflight inspection had been successful. I drove my car into the hangar and closed the mammoth door. Minutes later, the propeller was spinning, and we were ready to taxi to the runway.

I keyed the mic. "Saint Augustine clearance delivery, this is Skylane Six-Eight-Two-Charlie-Fox instruments to Oscar-Poppa-Fox. Clearance on request."

Surprisingly, the controller didn't have any bad news. "Skylane Two-Charlie-Fox, Saint Augustine clearance delivery, good afternoon. You are cleared to the Miami-Opa Locka Airport direct. On departure, climb and maintain two thousand. Expect one-one thousand ten minutes after departure, frequency one-two-zero point seven-five, squawk five-four-seven one."

I read back the clearance, and we were soon climbing through a thin cloud layer on our way to eleven thousand feet. The autopilot could fly the airplane far more precisely than any human, but I enjoyed the feel of the controls in my hands. On top of the cloud layer, the visibility was unlimited in every direction. It was one of those days when God intended men to fly…even though He didn't give us feathered wings.

As much as Clark enjoyed joking around, he was an entirely different personality in the cockpit. I enjoyed his lighthearted way of dealing with life on the ground, but I respected the serious manner with which he flew. Even though I was technically the pilot in command, he monitored every aspect of our climb to altitude. From exhaust gas temperatures to oil pressure, he didn't miss a detail.

Leveling off in cruise flight, I set the autopilot and settled in for the one-hundred-five-minute remainder of the flight. The Lycoming IO-540 engine purred in a reassuring hum that was almost enough to induce a nap, but that wouldn't be happening. My mind was consumed with how to go about the task that lay ahead.

I occasionally noticed Clark scanning the panel and checking our GPS position against VOR radials. Having a pilot—and partner—with such devotion to detail made my life not only safer, but far easier than it would've otherwise been. I looked forward to having Penny in the front seat with me on future flights. I believed she would share Clark's penchant for perfection at the controls. I owed whatever force brought them into my life a debt of gratitude.

That's when it hit me. Things as fortuitous as Clark showing up in my life rarely happen accidently. I'd never considered the possibility before that moment, but I had to know. "Were you sent to babysit me?"

Clark looked over the rim of his sunglasses. "What? No, you asked me to come."

"No, not today. I mean back on Jekyll Island two years ago. Did someone—maybe your father—send you to babysit me? Am I an assignment for you?"

He removed his glasses. "Why has it taken you this long to ask that question?"

"That sounds a lot like a *yes* from where I'm sitting."

He did that trademark biting of his bottom lip as he constructed what he'd say next. "It's not that simple."

"It's *exactly* that simple. You were either sent to babysit or you weren't, so which is it?"

He scanned the panel again, perhaps as a stalling tactic, but more likely because it was time to do so. Even when lesser men would forget the importance of the details, Clark Johnson did not.

"If you're asking if I was sent to babysit you, the answer is an unequivocal no. But we both know that isn't the real question. The real question is am I still here on assignment to keep an eye on you?"

He may have never spent a day in a college classroom, but his understanding of how the human mind works was far greater than most of my classmates who held licenses to practice clinical psychology.

"I've never lied to you, Chase, and I'm not going to start now. You made everybody nervous back then. You were this wildcard kid out of nowhere, who was all of a sudden the hottest thing on the covert ops scene. I mean, you caught and killed Suslik, for God's sake—on your first mission, no less. Of course the shot-callers had their eye on you."

I shook my head. "It wasn't just that, though. Was it?"

He looked away. "You know it wasn't. Anya had them scared."

It was my turn to scan the panel. Everything was in the green except the pressure inside my skull. "And they were right to be scared," I admitted.

Clark sighed. "Yeah, I guess they were, but that still doesn't answer your question, so here's the whole truth. Ready?"

I didn't blink.

"I *was* sent to check on you. You were, and still are, the Tiger Woods of the black ops world. Somebody had to sneak a look inside to make sure you weren't on the verge of imploding. In a short period, you'd been through more than most people could handle in a lifetime. You were twenty-four years old, almost instantly a multimillionaire, and had a gorgeous Russian SVR officer in your bed every night. Surely, you can see the potential that had to be a volatile combination."

I stared straight ahead over the cowling, at the blur of the spinning propeller. "Yeah, I can see it now, but I didn't see it back then. It was all happening so fast."

"Yeah, I know. That's why they sent me." He paused as if he wanted to say something else but wasn't sure how to do it.

"What is it? I know there's more. Omission is the worst lie."

"No, it isn't," he said. "Sometimes, the worst lie is the truth we decide to believe."

"What is that supposed to mean?"

"I wasn't there to babysit you, Chase. I was there to kill you."

My soul shuttered inside my chest, and the world in front of me turned into an abstract painting of a sky melting and burning simultaneously. "Kill me?"

"Yeah. The order to eliminate you came down the chain and landed at my feet. Hell, I didn't know who you were. I'd never even heard your name. I was just supposed to fly the King Air to Jekyll Island and see for myself that you were about to crash and burn. Then I was supposed to give you a reason to let me in your room so I could stick a needle in your neck."

I was, for one of the few times in my life, completely speechless. Thousands of hours of video played instantly through my mind. I questioned everything I thought I'd known about Clark Johnson, and tried to understand why he hadn't done it.

I finally caught my breath. "But a needle in the neck isn't your style."

"It was more metaphorical than anything else," he said. "I was supposed to get you alone and do whatever was necessary to complete the mission."

"Why didn't you?"

Again, he bit his lip. "Because they were wrong."

"What do you mean they were wrong? We don't get to make those decisions."

"Yeah, sometimes we do, and it didn't take me fifteen minutes to realize how wrong they were about you."

I cocked my head and eyed Clark. "What do you mean?"

"You were cautious, but not rude to me. You tested me at every turn to make sure I was who I claimed to be. You did everything right—in spite of being fresh from the farm, so to speak. More than that, you weren't distracted by the supermodel-looking Russian chick. You were a real operator, even though you'd never worn a uniform—other than on a baseball field—and you had your shit together. I was impressed, and I'm not easily impressed. I made the right decision. If I hadn't, it might not have been you with a needle in his neck."

"What does that mean?" I was still unsure how my question led us to this discussion.

"I'm not sure I could've pulled it off. I never saw you unarmed, and on the few occasions when you weren't paying attention to everything going on around you, that Russian wasn't missing a thing. If I had tried anything, you would've put a pair of bullets in me, or if not you, Anya would've cut me to my spine with that knife of hers."

"So, that's why you didn't try? You were afraid of Anya 'gutting you like pig'?"

He almost smiled. "No, that wasn't it. I made the decision not to take you out when I helped you tie up your boat. I just realized over the next few days how badly it would've ended for me if I had tried. And I'm not trying to turn this into anything meaningful—God knows I don't do that. But there's never been a time since the day I met you that I haven't been thankful I stumbled into you. You're the best teammate I've ever had. And I've had some of the best."

I didn't know what to say. Part of me was furious that whoever the hell I worked for had given the order to put me down. I thought we were the good guys. Another part of me was thankful to have Clark on my team. He'd saved my life on more than one occasion, but he and I would never keep score.

I opened my mouth to say something meant to cut the tension, but I was silenced by a snapping sound my airplane was never designed to make.

Chapter 9
Mayday

Clark heard it, too, and immediately scanned the panel. We saw the oil pressure gauge fall to zero, and simultaneously, our hands landed on the throttle, pulling it closed, and our eyes shot to the oil temperature gauge. The temperature was rising out of control, and the engine rattled and shuddered. We'd either lost the oil pump or the oil. Either way, the engine had less than ten seconds left to live. I pulled the mixture to full lean and shut it down.

Remembering the adage, "Aviate, navigate, communicate," that was beaten into my head at The Ranch when I learned to fly, I gripped the controls and began trimming the elevator for best glide speed.

"I have the controls," I said. "You have the radios."

Clark didn't hesitate. He pressed the "nearest airport" button on the GPS and scrolled through our options. Spruce Creek, a private airport with a four-thousand-foot-long asphalt runway was less than three miles northeast, so I pointed my airplane in that direction.

Clark keyed his mic. "Orlando Approach, Cessna Six-Eight-Two-Charlie-Fox is declaring an emergency. We've had an engine failure, and we're turning for Spruce Creek." The calm tone in Clark's voice sounded as if he were ordering cheeseburgers at a drive-through window.

The controller's tone came back just as smooth. "Cessna Two-Charlie-Fox, roger. Say souls on board and fuel remaining in time."

Clark scanned the fuel gauges. "Two souls on board and four hours of fuel."

"Roger, Two-Charlie-Fox. The runway at Spruce Creek is closed for construction, and I don't know the actual conditions, but New Smyrna Beach is at one o'clock and six miles. Say intentions."

Clark brought New Smyrna Beach Airport up on the GPS and pressed the "direct" button. I wordlessly nodded and began a gentle turn to the east. The airplane was gliding perfectly, and I mentally calculated our glide ratio. We'd easily make the airport if nothing else went wrong.

Clark spoke into his mic. "Approach, Two-Charlie-Fox is going to New Smyrna, but we don't have it in sight. There's a cloud layer below. Can you give us the current conditions?"

The controller said, "Roger. At EVB, wind two-six-zero at zero-niner, visibility one-zero, ceiling two-thousand-two-hundred broken, altimeter three-zero-zero-two, landing and departing runway two-niner."

"Thanks, Approach. We're proceeding direct to the field, unable to maintain altitude, and we'll be looking for the visual approach as soon as we get below the clouds."

"Roger, Two-Charlie-Fox, cleared direct Echo-Victor-Bravo. Report the field in sight for the visual approach. We're rolling the trucks."

Clark turned to me. "Are you okay, College Boy?"

Although I trained for inflight emergencies, I'd never actually lost an engine before that day. "I'm fine. Let's get the emergency checklist going."

He flipped through the spiral-bound checklist to the engine failure list and started down the page. He called each item on the checklist, and I answered.

"Airspeed?"

"Seventy-two knots indicated, best glide."

"Flaps?

"Up."

"Carburetor heat?"

"Off."

"Fuel selector?"

"Off."

"Mixture?"

"Lean."

"Primer?"

"Locked."

"Gear?"

"Up for now. Recheck on final."

"Seatbelts?"

"Secure."

"Cabin doors?"

"Secure for now. Recheck on final."

"Master?"

"On for now. Recheck on final."

My airplane had a glide ration of just over ten to one, meaning for every foot of altitude we lost, we would travel ten feet across the ground. When we lost our engine, we were over two miles high, so we could glide for over twenty miles before reaching the earth on Florida's east coast.

The controller's calm voice filled my headset again. "Cessna Two-Charlie-Fox, the airport is twelve o'clock and three miles."

Clark answered, "Approach, we're still above the clouds. We'll stay as high as possible until we're directly over the field."

"Roger."

I watched the mileage tick off the GPS until we were directly over the airport.

"And Approach, Two-Charlie-Fox is directly over the field, and we're going to start a slow spiral to the left. We'll call you when we're VMC below the clouds."

I silently hoped we wouldn't be in the clouds for more than a few seconds. I had the skill to manage the airplane, but without the engine, it would be a partial-panel spiraling descent. That made an already complicated situation even more demanding.

We entered the cloud tops at forty-seven hundred feet in a slow, gentle turn to the left. It was my goal to pop out of the bottom of the clouds with the airport just under my left wing. I kept my instrument scan precise and slow as our altitude bled off, and the earth got closer with every passing second. When the blue of the Atlantic Ocean spread out in front of us, and we were no longer imprisoned inside the confines of the cloud layer, I breathed a sigh of relief.

"Airport in sight for Two-Charlie-Fox."

"Cessna Two-Charlie-Fox, cleared visual approach to the runway of your choice. Contact New Smyrna Tower on one-one-niner-point-six-seven-five if able. If unable, I'll get a landing clearance for you."

Clark said, "Two-Charlie-Fox is cleared for the visual. We'll take runway two-niner, and we're off to the tower on nineteen-sixty-seven. Thank you, Approach."

"Godspeed, Two-Charlie-Fox."

Clark looked at me. "Do you have any idea what *Godspeed* means? I don't have a clue, but it sure sounds fast."

He had the strangest sense of comic timing, but his sense of what to do in the cockpit was flawless. He'd already tuned the tower frequency into the standby side of the radio, so he pressed the button, bringing it into the active window. "Tower, Cessna Two-Charlie-Fox, emergency aircraft, on the left downwind for the visual to two-niner."

The tower controller wasn't quite as calm as the approach controller had been. Perhaps it was because he'd actually have to watch the crash since he wasn't confined to a dark radar room somewhere outside of Orlando.

"Uh, Cessna Six-Eight-Two, uh, Charlie-Fox, check wheels down. Uh, wind two-six-zero at eight, cleared to land runway two-niner."

Clark glanced at me and smiled that crooked smile of his. I didn't know if he was happy we'd made it through the clouds without incident or if the tower controller's nervousness amused him. Either way, I shared his feeling and smiled along with him.

He keyed the mic. "Two-Charlie-Fox is cleared to land runway two-niner, and stand by for the gear."

I turned onto the final approach leg. "Flaps ten and gear down."

Clark lowered the flap handle first and watched the indicator glide smoothly down the scale until it pointed to the ten-degree mark. I felt the airplane pitch up slightly, so I retrimmed for final approach speed. Clark lowered the landing gear lever, and I heard the electric hydraulic pump whir, sending the landing gear down until three green lights appeared.

Clark said, "Gear down and locked. Cleared to land."

I reached for the master switches and flipped off both the alternator and battery, eliminating any source of electricity that could start a fire. With the master switches off, our headsets were useless, so I slid mine off and laid it on the floor of the cabin. Clark did the same. In addition to the headsets falling silent without electrical power, all red warning lights on the panel, which had previously warned of the various aircraft systems not functioning without the engine running, immediately vanished. The warning lights going out was soothing, but the eerie absence of engine noise while gliding through the air at seventy knots was a bit disconcerting. Even though flying an airplane without the engine producing power is a bizarre feeling, everything was relatively under control. I unlatched and opened my door a few inches and stuck the pilot's operating handbook in the hinge. Clark did the same using the checklist binder. If my landing turned into a crash, neither of us wanted to be locked inside an aluminum coffin.

That's when I remembered the approach controller saying he was rolling the trucks. I wasn't certain what he meant at the time, but the six fire trucks, two ambulances, and two police cars lining the sides of runway two-nine cleared up any lingering confusion I had.

We crossed the landing threshold at sixty-five knots, and I started slowly pulling the nose up to bleed off the airspeed. The main landing gear touched down with a reassuring chirp, and I held the yoke in my lap as the airspeed fell through forty knots and the nose gear settled gently to the runway. We rolled to a stop, pursued by the firetrucks and other emergency vehicles. I kept both feet firmly on the rudder pedals, my left hand on the yoke, and my right hand on the useless throttle—mostly out of habit, I suppose—consciously remembering to fly the airplane until every piece stopped moving—just as I'd been taught.

Clark turned toward me and stuck out his hand. "Not bad, College Boy. Not bad."

I grabbed his hand and shook it as if we'd just won the World Series. "Thanks for not killing me when you were supposed to."

He laughed. "Thanks for not killing me today."

We stepped from the plane, and I was both pleased and proud to discover that my knees weren't shaking too badly to support my weight. A bevy of heavily suited firefighters approached at a gallop but soon realized the emergency was over. The only remaining problem was getting my crippled airplane off the runway. An airport tug soon arrived with a tow bar, solving that issue.

Clark and I declined an offer to ride with the firefighters and instead chose to ride on the tug across the airport and onto the tarmac. When we came to a stop, I was surprised that the belly of my airplane was completely covered with oil. Something that hadn't been apparent during Clark's preflight inspection had caused a catastrophic failure, sending the contents of the oil pan spraying down the underside of the once spotless airplane.

I pointed toward the belly of the plane. "Do you see that?"

Clark knelt on one knee and peered beneath the Skylane. "Yeah, I saw it after we touched down, but I don't know what could've caused it yet."

I looked up at Clark and squinted against the sun. "Do you remember the cracking or snapping sound right before we lost oil pressure?"

He nodded. "Yeah, I heard that, too, but I don't know what it was. I've never heard anything like that before."

"Neither have I, but I'd sure like to know what it was."

He looked up at the tug operator. "Hey, do you have a toolbox we can borrow? I'd like to get that cowling off and take a look."

The tug operator pulled a canvas bag from behind his seat. "Sure. Here you go. Just make sure you get 'em back to me before you run off." He looked at my plane and chuckled. "Well, on second thought, I guess you won't be runnin' off anytime soon, will you?"

"No, probably not," Clark said. "Thanks. We'll get these back to you in a few minutes."

Ten minutes later, we had the top and bottom cowling off the nose of my airplane and made a discovery neither of us had expected.

Clark pointed to the bottom of the engine. "What the hell could've caused that?"

I peered into the hole in the bottom of the oil pan. "I don't know, but it's blown inward. If we'd thrown a rod or something inside the engine, wouldn't the hole be forced outward?"

"It sure would," Clark said. "This was a shaped charge, just like the ones we use to breach a door. Somebody sabotaged this airplane, and they did it well enough that I didn't catch it during the preflight."

Chapter 10
Cotton Coincidence

I stuck my hands on my hips in utter disgust. "Well, this day keeps getting better and better. First, we learn the D'Angelo family is mobbed up, then we discover their lawyer also represents the pornography ring that was holding Skipper, and now, somebody tries to blow up my airplane with us in it."

Clark was still lying on the tarmac, beneath what was left of the airplane engine. He looked up at me and squinted against the sun. "Whoever did this knew quite a bit about explosives, but I don't believe they were trying to kill us."

"What makes you say that?"

He pointed at the hole in the bottom of the engine. "Whoever set this device had to know that an engine failure at altitude in this airplane isn't a death sentence. We proved that a few minutes ago. If they were trying to kill us, they'd have set the bomb in the fuel tank, or somewhere in the flight controls—something we couldn't survive. But this...this feels more like a message."

I grimaced. "What kind of message?"

"I don't know yet, but we'd better figure it out."

A gravelly voice came from behind me. "Humph, that don't look good."

I turned to see a middle-aged bearded man in a pair of coveralls and a Cessna hat. I surveyed the man and made him for an airframe and power plant mechanic. At least that's what I hoped he was.

"Are you an A and P?"

He nodded but didn't take his eyes off my engine. Grunting, and joining Clark, he lowered himself to the ground. "Well, would you look at that? I ain't never seen one do that. Usually, they blow out, not in. Are the mags off?"

I stuck my head inside the cockpit to make sure the magnetos were turned off, then showed the mechanic the key.

He reached up and pulled the propeller through a full revolution. "Hmm, she didn't come apart. What the hell happened?"

Clark looked my way, silently asking permission to tell our story. I held my thumb and index finger slightly apart, indicating it was okay to tell him a little.

Clark nodded his understanding. "We were at eleven thousand when we heard a sharp crack, and the oil pressure went to zero almost instantly. We shut it down and glided into here."

Seeming to ignore Clark's description of events, the mechanic stuck his finger through the baseball-sized hole in the bottom of my oil pan and withdrew an oily finger. Holding it up to the sunlight, he rubbed the oil between his fingers for several seconds and then smelled the results. "Have you got a plan?"

I wasn't sure if he was talking to Clark or me, but I said, "Right now, you're my plan. Can you fix it?"

"Sure I can, but there ain't no way I can tell you how much it'll be 'til I get the engine torn down. Even if you got her shut down right away, you'll still want me to take a good look inside. Might as well rebuild it while I've got it down. There ain't no tellin' what kind of shrapnel went flying around in there. How many hours is on it?"

"Around three hundred," I said.

He made a painful sound deep in his throat. "Boy, that's a shame. If she was run out, then rebuildin' her wouldn't hurt so bad, but a new engine like that with only three hundred hours…. Man oh man, that sucks."

I sighed. "Yeah, it sure does. How long would it take to get a new engine from Lycoming?"

He wiped his oily fingers on the leg of his coveralls and clambered back to his feet. The man scratched his head and looked skyward. "A factory remanufactured motor will be around forty grand, and a new one'll run you 'bout sixty-five."

"My question was how long?"

"Oh, I figured you'd wanna know the prices, too. I can get a remanufactured—"

I shook my head. "I want a new one."

"A new one? Hell, boy, if you've got the cash, I can have a new one here in two days and have this thing flying again by the weekend."

I didn't like the prospect of sinking another sixty-five thousand dollars into my airplane, but it was worthless without an engine. "Based on the hat you're wearing, I assume you're a Cessna Authorized Service Facility."

The man stuck his hand toward me. "You betcha. I'm Cotton Jackson. I don't run the shop, but the boss is gone to lunch. He'll be back directly, though. I'll have the lineman tow her over to the shop while we're waitin' for him."

I shook his hand. "Chase Fulton. It's nice to meet you, Cotton. You look familiar for some reason. Have we met?"

He raised his chin. "No, I don't reckon we have. I don't never go nowhere 'cept here to work and home, and a time or two a year, I go up and see my big sister up in Saint Augustine. She's a mechanic like me, 'cept she don't work on airplanes. She's a boat mechanic mostly, but really, she can work on anything with a diesel in it."

I shook my head and laughed almost out of control. "By any chance, is your sister's name Earline?"

He looked at me with confused suspicion. "How'd you know that?"

"I keep my boat at the municipal marina a few slips down from Earl. I don't let anybody but her touch my engines. She'd kill me if I did."

Cotton lunged forward and wrapped me in a most unexpected bearhug. "I'll be damned. You ain't Stud Muffin, are you?"

I couldn't stop laughing. "I'm one of them. I suspect I'm not the only one, though."

"Ha! That Earline told me all about you. How you're always a-comin' and a-goin', and how you always got some good-lookin' young girl with you. You've got that great big fancy catamaran boat up there. Ain't that right?"

"Well, I have one of the cats up there."

"It's a small world, ain't it? Hell, boy, you're practically family. I'll make sure the boss knows who you are. He's been sweet on Earline for thirty years, and he'll give you a helluva deal on a new motor. And on top of that, I'll make sure nobody but me touches that airplane of yours." He wiped his brow with a filthy rag. "We might as well go ahead and do the annual inspection while we've got it. You know you can trust us Jacksons when it comes to motors, don'tcha?"

"I do, indeed." I couldn't stop smiling. "I can't tell you how glad I am this happened at your airport. The mechanic gods must have been smiling on me today."

"Ha! You can say that again, Chase. Get on in here, and we'll write this up and get you boys something to eat and drink. I reckon your bellies could use a little settlin' down. I sure am glad you made it. That's too pretty a plane to pick up out of the trees somewhere."

I glanced at Clark. "Yeah, I guess that would be a shame, not to mention what might've happened to Clark and me."

"Oh, yeah. I didn't mean to leave you two out of it. I just meant .... Ah, hell, you know what I meant."

We ate stale peanut butter crackers from the vending machine and drank room-temperature Cokes from Styrofoam cups while Cotton searched for the necessary paperwork.

Finally, he threw up his hands. "Ah, to the devil with it. Here, just write down some way I can get ahold of you on this paper. The boss'll know where the paperwork is when he gets back."

I wrote my name and number on the torn piece of paper and handed it back to him. "Cotton, we need a way to get to Miami. Is there something we can rent while you're putting my plane back together?"

"No, there ain't no way I'm gonna let you rent nothin'. You can take my old truck. Norma can run me back and forth to work 'til I get your engine in. That's my wife, Norma. She ain't much to look at, but she makes the best chicken 'n dumplings you ever put in your mouth, and that's a rare find these days, boys—a good woman who'll cook. It don't matter if she's uglier than a bowlin' shoe. Them looks fade in time, but them dumplin's just keep gettin' better every year."

Clark raised his hands above his head. "Preach on, brother. That's what I've been telling Chase for years, but he's hung up on those cheerleader-looking girls."

Cotton pointed his finger at me. "You oughta listen to your buddy Clark, there. He's got it figured out."

I chuckled. "Yeah, I know. He tells me that almost every day."

Just then, a man who could've been Danny Devito's twin came waddling through the door of the shop. Cotton opened up with his "you're never gonna believe who these boys are" story. When he got to the part about Earl, the man's eyes lit up, and Cotton had his full attention. Twenty minutes later, we paid for a new Lycoming engine at twenty percent off and shop labor at half the standard rate...in return for putting in a good word for the boss the next time we saw Earl.

"Here you go!" Cotton yelled from fifty feet away. I turned to see what he was shouting about and caught a glimpse of keys flying toward me. I instinctively snatched them from the air.

"Whoa!" Clark said. "Nice catch, catcher."

"It's what I do."

"No, it's what you *used* to do. Now you kill people who throw metal objects at you...sometimes."

"Touché."

I walked across the shop and handed the keys back to Cotton. "I wasn't clear earlier when I said we needed to rent something to get to Miami. I meant an airplane, but I greatly appreciate your willingness to lend me your truck."

Cotton took the keys from my hand and wiped at his brow. "Hell, why didn't you say so? I've got one of them, too. It ain't as nice as yours, but it'll do something yours won't."

"What's that?" I asked.

"It'll land in the water more than once."

I rubbed my chin, more than a little confused.

Cotton laughed. "Don't hurt your brain, boy. It's a Lake Amphibian Renegade. It's built to land in the water or on land. I don't recommend tryin' that with what's left of your Skylane out there."

"You've got a point, Cotton. How much would you charge us for using your Renegade for a few days—maybe up to a couple of weeks?"

"Ah, hell, boys. Just bring her back full of gas and don't wreck 'er. If Earl trusts you, I reckon I can, too. Have either of you boys got a seaplane ticket?"

Clark said, "I do. In fact, we just flew a PBY Catalina from east of Moscow to Kiev a couple weeks ago."

"Moscow?" Cotton tilted his head. "Ain't that in Russia or China or somewhere over there?"

Clark nodded. "Yep, that's exactly right, Cotton."

"Thought so. Well, the keys is in the airplane. Consider her yours for as long as you need. I've got too much work to do 'round here to be flying anyhow. I'll call you when your motor's in. Do you mind if I test-fly it, or would you rather do that yourself?"

"I'd love for you to fly my airplane, Cotton. In fact, I'd love for you to do the break-in if you have time."

"All right, but I'll need to do it off the clock." He glanced over his shoulder at Danny Devito's twin. "Otherwise, *he'll* make me charge you the regular shop rate for my time."

"No problem, Cotton. Just fly it when you have time through the break-in period, and I'll pay you off the clock."

He nodded. "That's good enough for me. Now you two go on, and don't worry about a thing. Ol' Cotton'll take care of everything."

Chapter 11
Boring

We looked into the setting sun as we landed in Miami, more than three hours behind schedule. The time we'd lost gliding into New Smyrna Beach and dealing with the aftermath had added at least two hours to the trip. I blamed the remaining time on the difference in the one-hundred-forty-knot cruise speed of the Renegade versus the one-hundred-sixty knots we could've gotten out of my Skylane. My perfectly terrible day got exponentially better when I saw Dominic's new Porsche 911 convertible waiting by the FBO. Clark had been hoping for the Range Rover because of its utility, but I'd been silently praying for the Porsche.

Miami's South Beach is a haven for the young, rich, and beautiful. By most people's standards, I qualified as meeting at least two of those qualifications. Perhaps Penny may have thought I hit all three, but she was somewhere offshore making twelve knots down the coast aboard *Aegis*. Last time I'd been to South Beach was just before leaving for Eastern Europe to rescue Anya. On the surface, Penny had taken that front-page news relatively well, but I never planned to make such a revelation to her again, on South Beach, or anywhere else on the planet. If I survived the mission I was on, I had every intention of simplifying my life and spending a lot more time with the woman who was way too good for me, but who loved me anyway.

We checked into the hotel on A1A overlooking the famous South Beach strip. The suite was nice enough, but the view across the beach to the Atlantic Ocean was spectacular. I watched bikini-clad beauties skating, bicycling, and strutting their way up and down Beachfront Avenue and couldn't help wondering if one of the sleazy-looking dirtbags drooling over them could be the attorney, Mario Righetti. I would find him, rattle him, and get to the bottom of the long string of assholes who were trying their best to make my life a living hell. They had no idea how bad their decision to mess with me had been. The wise-guys and wannabe hitters thought they were deadly and scary enough to make the devil quiver in his boots, but when it came to pouring fear and regret into the hearts of an enemy, Clark Johnson and I were world-class. And we were only days away from introducing our own brand of terror into the lives of the D'Angelos—and everyone in their world.

We had dinner at a sidewalk café only feet off the main drag. The later the evening grew, the wilder the life on the street became. Duval Street in Key West was insane when the sun went down, but South Beach had its own brand of crazy. Where Key West was laid back and full of people who had far more interest in having another toke from their buddy's joint than hurting anyone, South Beach had a different vibe. It was somehow more sinister, with more attitude and grittiness. Margaritas and ganja fueled Duvall, while cocaine and Courvoisier drove Beachfront Avenue.

Just as our goldfish bowl margaritas arrived, a gaudy, purple Lamborghini pulled to a stop in the traffic lane, less than a dozen feet away. The driver ignored the valet lane, stepped from his quarter-million-dollar car, and tossed his key nonchalantly into the air. A valet, clad in a black leather vest and bedazzled white shorts, caught the key before it hit the pavement, then disappeared behind the wheel of the mega-sportscar. South Beach was quite a spectacle. I looked forward to leisure time in Miami someday, but leisure was not in the plan for the coming days. We had work to do.

We watched the human zoo for an hour while we ate fresh seafood of every description and discussed what the next day would bring.

"I say we start at Righetti's office tomorrow morning."

Clark nodded. "That's as good a plan as any other. It's going to get ugly as soon as they know we're poking around, so we might as well announce our presence in style."

"Sort of like Lamborghini Boy?" I asked.

Clark chuckled. "Yeah, something like that."

We hit the sack and were both snoring before the party on the street below had begun in earnest. When we awoke the next morning, the scene outside our window was a study in contrasts to the night before. Families of tourists sparsely populated the beach, sidewalks, and streets. Fitness freaks sprinkled in against the backdrop of delivery trucks replenishing the depleted stores of liquor and seafood. There were no gaudy cars or flashy uber-wealthy.

We drove our borrowed, not-too-flashy Porsche to the business district and parked on the street one block away from the offices of Righetti, Capriati & Associates, P.C. The elevator sent us fifteen stories into the sky, and we strolled into the offices wearing our blue jeans, tactical boots, and untucked button-downs that hid the holstered pistols behind each of our right hip bones. Clark had chosen a Sig Sauer P226 in nine millimeter, but I had opted for something a little more subtle, and perhaps even a bit sinister. My weapon of choice was the Walther PPK three-eighty with a suppressor fitted nicely on the threaded barrel. It occurred to me that our selection of weaponry mirrored our operational styles perfectly. Clark's would make a lot of noise and leave a bloody mess in its wake, while mine would quietly dispense a carefully measured dose of necessary evil while drawing nothing more than a passing, curious glance from anyone in the vicinity. Righetti was going to see at least one of our styles this morning. He would get to decide which.

"Good morning, gentlemen. Welcome to Righetti, Capriati, and Associates. Do you have an appointment?"

The voice was laced with enough Cuban tone to be at least one generation away from immigration, while still solidly American enough to belong to anyone from L.A.

I looked through the olive-skinned, dark-eyed beauty behind the obscenely opulent marble reception island. "We're here to see Mario Righetti."

"Do you have an appointment?"

I leaned over the counter and glared at the young woman. "Tell him Salvatore D'Angelo sent us. That'll be appointment enough."

The previously painted and mysterious eyes of the woman turned to saucers as she stared up at me, wholly unsure of what to say next.

I pulled a pen from a gold-embossed stand and tapped it against the switchboard in front of the woman. "This is the part where you call Mario's secretary and let her know we're on our way up. He's on sixteen, right?"

Instead of speaking, she hastily nodded in staccato motions of her head.

I pointed toward the private elevator twenty feet across the cavernous office. "You'll be opening those doors now. Oh, and go ahead and make that call to Mario's secretary. I'm sure she wouldn't like to be surprised by the two of us when we step off that elevator, now would she?"

The woman slid her hand beneath a mahogany panel, and the doors of the private elevator silently separated. We rode up one floor, not sure about the quality of welcome we'd be receiving when the doors opened, but we were prepared for whatever might appear.

It turned out to be far more cordial than I'd expected. An older version of the receptionist on the floor below appeared behind a nearly identical mountain of marble. "I understand you gentlemen are here to see Mr. Righetti on behalf of Mr. D'Angelo. Is that right?"

"Yeah, something like that. Is Mr. Righetti in and receiving guests this morning?"

The lady swallowed visibly. "I'm afraid you'll have to take a seat. Mr. Righetti is extremely—"

I didn't let her finish whatever ridiculous declaration she was about to make. "No, we're not the kind of guys who wait to see self-important people. We'll just start kicking down doors until we find good ol' Mario's office."

I wanted her to believe I was a mere thug who lacked the intellect to communicate with any degree of courtesy, but my speech had, in fact, been carefully crafted to garner a specific response: The woman's instinct to protect her boss would send her eyes flashing almost imperceptibly in the direction of Righetti's door. It would be instinctual and impossible for her to suppress. Although I'd admitted I didn't know which door led to Righetti's office, her reaction immediately gave me all the directions I needed.

"We'll start with this one right over here." I took an accelerating stride toward the door, and the woman burst out, "No! Stop!"

I smiled. "Just as I thought."

The door, as it turned out, didn't need to be kicked down. The gold knob turned easily, and the ornate paneled door swung into a second sitting area.

Clark stepped behind the marble counter and within two feet of the woman. "Now would be a great time for you to go take a powder or have a smoke. Whatever you do."

Instead of scampering away, she pressed a pair of buttons on the panel in front of her. "I'm calling security."

Clark placed the toe of his left boot on the base of the woman's chair and calmly rolled both the chair and the woman several feet across the floor. "You call whoever you feel you should, but we're going in to see Mario. It would be best if you disappeared for ten minutes."

She leapt from her seat and bounded through a side door that appeared to lead to a stairwell. It didn't matter where she was going, but I did wonder if her call to security had been successful.

The second set of doors into Righetti's office was even more ornate than the first. I gave the handle a tug, but they didn't budge. I prepared to send the sole of my boot through the door, when Clark said, "Wait! Allow me."

He stepped back into the area vacated by the frightened woman, and pressed a small, poorly disguised button that dislodged the magnetic lock on the French doors. I pulled again, and open they came.

Sitting behind a two-acre desk was a sixtyish man with glistening black hair slicked straight back across his scalp, wearing a suit that probably cost nearly as much as the Porsche we were driving. Across the desk from him sat a slightly younger man with a two-hundred-dollar spray tan and an open-collared shirt that exposed far too much unruly chest hair. Spray Tan started to stand up as we moved into the room, but Clark stuck a knuckle into his collar bone, sending him back into the leather chair. Righetti reached beneath his desk, but before he could claim whatever he was grasping for, I landed a palm in the center of his chest and wheeled him backward until the back of his obnoxious office chair careened into the glass of the sixteenth-story power office.

Righetti chose bravado rather than submission. "Security is on their way up here right now. If the two of you ever leave this building, it'll be in handcuffs with blood dripping from your faces. You have no idea how badly you've fucked up by coming in here like this."

Clark reached across the back of Spray Tan's chair and grabbed the man by the chin. He tilted the chair backward and dragged it, and the man, across the carpet of the opulent office until they were positioned near the French doors.

I playfully slapped Righetti across the right cheek several times. "Keep talking, Lawyer Boy. I suspect that's your coping mechanism for high-stress situations like this. Oh, and we're counting on security being on their way. I hope there's at least eight of them. Any fewer than that would be boring for us...and we hate getting bored. When we get bored, we hurt people like you, Mario. I repeated my degrading slaps to the face until he violently shook his head and jerked away.

"Let's make ourselves comfortable and presentable while we wait for those hotshot security guys of yours. Shall we?"

I tightened Righetti's necktie until it cut into the flabby flesh of his bulging neck. His face turned bright red, then pale. He tried to swallow and worked his chin in a wasted effort to loosen the knot.

"Oh, come on now, Mario. Don't you want to look good for the security guards? How many do you think they'll send?" I waited a beat. "Don't get quiet on me now. That's rude. Giovanni Minelli was rude to us, and I'm sure you remember what happened to him."

I'd originally shunned Clark's desire to bring up the pornographer's name to Righetti, but under the circumstances, I came around to Clark's way of thinking. The lawyer's eyes bloomed into terror-filled orbs, and he croaked against the knot of the necktie. "What do you want?"

I smiled. "Oh, something tells me you've already figured that out. Now it's a matter of time—and maybe a touch of pain—to convince you to give it to us. But we always get what we want in the end. You see, we just keep killing people until we find one who's willing to give it to us. It's really quite simple."

Clark let out a smooching sound and glanced toward the elevator.

I turned back to Righetti. "Oh, goody. Your rent-a-cops are here. Let's hope they're more competent than the typical minimum-wage badge bearer."

The four uniformed security guards came through the door in the worst possible formation—trotting forward, two men side by side, and two more directly behind them. Clark shoved Spray Tan's chair forward toward the guards, sending the man who was so proud of his chest hair flying through the air and landing at the feet of the first two heroes. The lead echelon of guards descended on Spray Tan as if he were their attacker and pinned him mercilessly to the floor, twisting his arms behind his back. While those two were occupied with their perceived aggressor, Clark grabbed one of the rear guards by the nape of the neck and yanked him forward, driving his chin into the skull of the guard kneeling in front of him. Both men collapsed atop Spray Tan in a heap of uniformed blubber. The guard who remained standing reached clumsily for the can of pepper spray on his Batman utility belt. Clark captured the man's wrist and forced the hand holding the pepper spray to the guard's face. Reaching across his body with his other hand, Clark depressed the trigger of the canister, sending a three-second blast of spray directly up the man's nose. The guard yelled in agony and spun away, as if trying to drill himself through the carpet. With blinding speed, Clark grabbed him by the neck and bent him backward, slamming his head into the remaining guard's skull. Less than a second later, all four guards lay motionless on the floor.

I smacked my palm on top of Righetti's head, sending stars dancing in his eyes. "That was boring, Mario. You should be ashamed, sending four idiots like that up here to take on the two of us. Well, actually, just the one of us. My partner made short work of your team of crackpot crime busters." I looked at Clark to make sure he was okay.

He licked the tips of his fingers. "I love the taste of pepper spray in the morning."

"All right, back to business," I said. "It's time for you to do what you do best, legal eagle. Talk."

Righetti was still struggling against the bite of the necktie depleting his ability to breathe.

"Oh, I'm sorry. How rude of me. Here, let me fix that tie for you." I grabbed the end of his tie and quickly wrapped it once more around his neck, and then across the back of his chair, using it like a garrote.

The man's body rose upward, and his feet bicycled in panic as he tried to catch the breath that wouldn't come.

I continued the assault and pulled even harder. "There, Mario. Is that better?"

In choking, gasping heaves, he said, "Who the hell are you guys?"

I released the tie, allowing him to slide back down into his chair, and I tugged at the knot, loosening the tie around his neck. "I'm sorry, Mario. We didn't introduce ourselves. Forgive me. My name is Chase Fulton, and this is my partner—"

Clark bounded forward to Righetti's desk and leapt it like an Olympic hurdler, landing with his right knee in Righetti's crotch and the barrel of his nine millimeter pressed against the bridge of the lawyer's nose. "I like to make my own introductions. My name is Dude Who's Going To Put A Bullet Through Your Brain If You Don't Tell Us What We Want To Know. It's nice to meet you."

I liked Clark's style, but Righetti obviously did not. "You're not going to shoot me. That thing will make so much noise that you'll never make it out the door before every cop in Miami is crawling up your ass."

"You make an excellent point," Clark said. "So, I yield back the balance of my time to the gentleman from the great state of Georgia."

I stuck the muzzle of my suppressor up Righetti's nose. "You see, Mario, this one hardly makes any noise at all. Tell me. Did you see Giovani Minelli's body after his unfortunate accident? Did you see the bullet hole in the back of his hand and the one in his knee? Huh? Did you? Those were nonfatal wounds, but they had to hurt the poor guy. The one between the eyes—that one didn't hurt a bit. But those starter holes...well, those were a bitch. You're not going to make me drill a couple starter holes in you before you start talking, are you, Mario?"

Clark stood and withdrew his knee from between Righetti's legs. "I'll be over here playing with my new friends. Let me know if you need me."

"Oh, okay. Have fun. I'll be fine without you, but I'll let you know if our friend, Mario, decides he isn't interested in chatting."

Clark headed back for the pile of security guards. Soon, he had all four of them handcuffed to each other around a bronze statue of something that probably qualified as art in Miami. Then he helped Spray Tan back into his chair and began fastening the man's shirt. "It looks like a couple of your buttons came undone. Let me help you with that."

I turned my attention back to Righetti. "Let's hear it."

"What? What do you want to know?"

"That's good, counselor. I like that you want to make sure you understand what I want so you can deliver. I want to know why you think the good congresswoman, Barbara D'Angelo, would send a pair of"—I made air quotes with my fingers—"'cops' to arrest me."

Righetti closed his eyes for several seconds. "You don't have any idea what you're up against, do you?"

"Why don't you tell me? What am I up against?"

"You're so far out of your league. You can beat up my security guards. You can throw my associate around like a ragdoll. You can burst into my office. And you can even kill me if you want, but none of that's going to change a thing. This is so much bigger than the two of you. You're just a minor inconvenience—a bump in the road. Ha! You're not even that. Nothing you do will change anything."

It was time to make him understand that he was going to talk or die, so I slid my hand inside the waistband of my jeans and drew out my most prized possession—the machete that Diablo de Agua, the South American assassin, had used to slaughter my parents' murderers.

I laid the razor-sharp blade beneath Righetti's right ear. "Killing you would be easy, but torturing you would be far more productive…and a lot more fun. I can cut off your ear, and you'll bleed for hours before you pass out. Every second will be a new foray into your own private Hell. I don't have to kill you. I can simply hurt you for as long as I want, and all you can do is endure it, but it doesn't have to come to that. You have the option of telling me everything I want to know, and if you do, you get to live. Well, you get to live for a while. I suspect you have a few clients who wouldn't enjoy letting you remain among the living after talking to me, but there is a slim chance I could keep you alive. A slight possibility I could protect you, even from those clients of yours, but it's up to you. You can either talk, bleed and talk, or you can die. You make the decision."

Chapter 12
Undue Credit

"The two of you killed Minelli?"

I began to believe I'd gotten my point across and Righetti was ready to talk.

"Well, which one of us *actually* pulled the trigger isn't necessarily important—"

Clark threw his hand in the air. "I did it!"

I smiled. "Fine, my partner wants the credit, so I'll concede. It was him, but I drilled the starter holes."

The lawyer was instinctually trying to move away from my machete, but the more he pressed his head into the chair, the harder I pushed the metal against his neck. A tiny trickle of blood trailed across my blade, and I rotated my hand slightly to avoid cutting his throat.

One of the handcuffed guards started to stir, and Clark struck him on the mastoid gland at the base of his skull. The man melted back to the floor, and Clark looked up apologetically. "I'm sorry. I didn't mean to let him interrupt your sharing moment. Go on."

I pulled my machete from beneath the lawyer's ear and pressed the tip into the flesh beneath his nose. "Do you know what this indention right below your nose is called, Mario?"

His eyes crossed as he looked down at the thirty-inch-long glistening blade and tried not to flinch.

"It's called a philtrum, Mario. It's sometimes referred to as a ves-tigial medial depression. Do you know what that means? Come on, now. Don't be shy. Speak up. Surely you took Latin in law school."

I twisted the blade just enough to drill a pinprick hole in his quivering lip. "Biology clearly isn't your thing, so I'll help you out. Basically, it's a meaningless, leftover part that has no real value...just like you, Mario. Now, let's try to focus. Who sent the fake cops to arrest me?"

He drew a long full breath, which I took as a sign of submission. Still staring at my machete, and obviously terrified, he said, "Look. I'll tell you what I know, but I've got to get some kind of immunity."

I lowered my eyebrow. "Immunity? What do you think we are, Mario? Cops? There's no immunity deal for you or anyone else. We don't give immunity. You tell me who sent those goons to arrest me, and in return, you get immunity from me cutting your brain out of your skull through your nose hole."

He pressed his eyelids closed as if he were trying to ward off the worst headache of his life. Perhaps he was. Maybe Clark and I quali-fied as exactly that—the worst headache of Mario Righetti's life.

When he reopened his eyes, they bore the look of acceptance, perhaps of finally being forced to face up to the costs of living the life of a mob lawyer—recognition of the day he always knew would eventually come.

"Look, you're going to kill me for not talking, or they'll kill me for talking. Either way, I'm a dead man, and I have to decide if that happens now or later. Take that knife out of my face, will you? I'll tell you what you want to know, but I can't do it with you sticking me with that thing."

I backed the machete an inch from his nose and stared into his eyes. "Listen closely to me, Righetti. I know a lot more than you think, so if you try to feed me a line of BS, I'll be the one who de-cides just how quickly you get to meet your maker. Have you got that?"

He swallowed the bitter taste that must've been lingering on the back of his tongue. "It's all over now, and there's nothing I can do about it. Can I, at least, have a drink? There's a bottle in that bottom drawer."

I extended my right foot and pulled at the corner of the drawer he'd indicated. It slid open, revealing a bottle of scotch and a single tumbler. Righetti was staring into the drawer as if it held the last meal of a condemned man. Perhaps it did.

Not taking my eyes from him, I lifted the glass and bottle from the drawer, placed them on the desk, and uncorked the scotch. Righetti licked his lips as I poured the amber-colored liquor into the crystal tumbler.

I took my eyes off of him only long enough to see how much I'd poured, and Clark yelled, "Gun!"

I dropped the bottle and immediately shot my gaze back to the lawyer. In the briefest moment when I'd looked away, he'd secretly retrieved a small semi-automatic pistol, but he wasn't pointing it at either Clark or me. The muzzle was pressed deeply into the bulbous flesh beneath his meaty chin. His thick finger was pressing the trigger, and the hammer was receding.

Clark accelerated toward the lawyer, but I knew he'd never get to him before the hammer of the pistol reached its zenith and fell on the firing pin. I was less than three feet from the man whose head was on the verge of exploding; the head that held volumes of information I so desperately needed. I couldn't let a bullet leave the barrel of the gun.

As quickly as I could command my hand and arm, I swung my machete and watched the glistening blade race through the distance between me and the lawyer.

The hammer cracked and began its instantaneous descent toward the firing pin, but the microsecond before it made contact, my blade slid between the hammer and the frame of the pistol, absorbing the blow before it could ignite the deadly explosion that would've painted Righetti's ceiling bright red.

With one more blindingly swift motion, I yanked the pistol from his grip and tossed it toward Clark. He caught and pocketed the weapon in one smooth arc.

"Mario, look at me. What the hell is so bad that you'd rather eat a bullet than tell me the truth?"

The man was trembling and had lost all natural color from his face. The horror within him was pouring from his flesh. I almost let myself pity him, but finding compassion for a man who'd built a life and career protecting the vilest of society was not something I'd be doing. In my book, he deserved everything he was going to endure in the days and weeks to come. Letting him off the hook at the muzzle of his own gun would not be happening.

"All right. Nice try, but it's not going to be that easy for you, Righetti. It's time to confess your sins, and I'm your priest. Let's get you into the confessional."

I turned to Clark. "I'll bet that private elevator goes all the way down to the parking garage. I'll meet you at the exit. You get this scumbag down there alive."

"Done." Clark nodded and moved toward Righetti.

I sprinted through the double doors of the office and hit the call button for the private elevator. Ignoring the main elevator, which would've taken four times as long, I opted for the stairs. I could descend the sixteen stories back to the street in less than a minute, and the chances of encountering anyone else in the stairwell were slim.

One of the features of the Porsche 911 Carrera was a perfectly useless back seat. With my thirty-eight-inch inseam behind the wheel, the back of the driver's seat touched the front of the rear seat, leaving no room for man nor beast behind me. For the first time since we landed, I found myself wishing Dominic had left us the Range Rover.

The turbo engine roared to life, and the agile sports car leapt from the curbside parking spot like a pouncing leopard. I was reminded of how Anya had driven the rented Porsche on Jekyll Island as if she'd spent a few years on the IndyCar circuit.

When I braked to a stop at the exit of the private parking garage, I saw a black Mercedes sedan racing toward the ramp. The driver's window of the blacked-out luxury car lowered, revealing Clark's left arm wind-milling in a follow-me motion. I trusted him more than any man on Earth, so I waited for him to clear the exit, and I accelerated behind him, easily keeping pace with the far heavier and less nimble Mercedes.

Clark and I had been through the same tactical driver training at The Ranch, so anticipating what he was going to do next was second nature. He avoided use of the turn signals and ignored most traffic lights and signs, unless a collision was imminent, in which case, he hesitated only long enough to avoid a crash. I stayed within fifty feet of him as we maneuvered through the busy streets of downtown Miami. When we turned east and accelerated through eighty, I knew where we were heading.

I dialed Dominic. "Get the southern gates open, and get everyone out of the yard. We'll be there in four minutes with your Porsche behind one black Mercedes sedan."

Just like Clark, "Done," was all he said.

I pressed the end button and quickly dialed my partner. "Your dad is opening the south gates and emptying the yard."

"Copy. I've got Righetti and Spray Tan."

How he was able to get both men down the elevator and into a "borrowed" Mercedes was beyond me, but Clark's operational mindset and execution were second to none. Righetti was the important preliminary target, but we needed to know who Spray Tan was and what connection, if any, he had to the D'Angelo family.

Dominic's shipyard was a two-acre piece of gravel-covered, hard-packed sand on the waterfront. Had there been a pair of high-rise buildings on the property, it would've been valued in the billions, but the fact that such a massive piece of real estate still existed with the apparent sole purpose of restoring, servicing, and maintaining yachts of every size was a marvel in modern Miami.

Gravel flew from the rear tires of the Mercedes as Clark slid between massive, multi-million-dollar yachts on stands and wound his way toward the northeast corner of the yard. I followed closely behind, barely able to see the silhouette of the sedan through the dust and debris he was kicking up.

As the red glow of the brake lights exploded through the cloud of dust in front of me and the rear bumper of the Mercedes got closer by the second, I pressed the brake pedal to its limit, barely stopping before plowing into the car.

I leapt from the Porsche and coughed through the dust. Clark was already out and pulling Righetti from the back seat. He was handcuffed and seemed to offer no sign of struggle or resistance.

"Get the other one from that side," Clark yelled as he led the lawyer toward a monstrous motor yacht tied alongside the dock.

I opened the passenger side rear door to find Spray Tan sitting on the opulent leather seat and laughing.

"What's so funny?"

The man shook his head and grinned up at me. "I hope you enjoyed the sunset yesterday, asshole, because it's the last one you're ever going to see. You and your buddy up there just pissed in a den of rattlesnakes, and I know which part of your body they're going to strike first."

I delivered a left jab to the man's jaw hard enough to blur his vision, but not solidly enough to turn out his lights. "From this point on, you speak only when I ask you a question. Otherwise, keep your mouth shut. Got it?"

He spat a long stream of red blood from his mouth, directing the spittle toward my feet. I shot my right hand past his head and grabbed the collar of his shirt. With one forceful yank, I dragged him from the seat and sent him sprawling face-first to the gravel of the shipyard, right on top of the bloody puddle of spit he'd made.

I took a knee beside his head. "That wasn't very nice of you. I don't like when people spit at me. Now repeat after me. I'm sorry, sir. I won't do it again."

He spat gravel and sand from his lips. "Fu—"

My knee to the back of his head stopped his verbal assault before he could say something I would find particularly hurtful. "I'm sensitive and easily offended, so let's keep our tone civil. What do you say?"

He grunted, and I took that as a verbal contract between us that I wouldn't hit him again, and he wouldn't misbehave anymore.

I won't claim to have been particularly careful helping him to his feet. In fact, if memory serves, he may have fallen a time or two on his way to a vertical position. When he was upright and somewhat stable, I dusted him off and encouraged him to walk with me. I can be quite encouraging, and even influential at times.

We boarded the floating yacht and followed the trail of open doors toward a luxurious salon where I found Clark, Righetti, and Dominic. A little more encouragement from me landed Spray Tan on a sofa probably made from rare Peruvian goatskin and cost a thousand dollars per yard.

Dominic approached and grabbed Spray Tan's arm. "I'll take this one. You two let me know when you're finished with the lawyer."

Dominic turned out to be even more encouraging than me, and Spray Tan offered almost no resistance, even though Dom was nearly three times my age and eighty pounds lighter.

Righetti never took his eyes off his compadre as Dominic led him from the salon. "Taking me is one thing, but you should've never messed with him."

I watched Dominic and Spray Tan disappear through the stern of the yacht. "Why? Who is he?"

"That's Antonio D'Angelo."

Chapter 13
Pennies from Heaven

Clark leapt to his feet. "I've got it. You stay with Righetti."

"I'd rather be lucky than good" is a phrase that's tossed around without much thought. In my experience, luck is the direct result of being good at what one does. Having Antonio D'Angelo fall into our laps wasn't something we'd expected. Perhaps we could chalk that one up to luck, or maybe he was just an example of pennies from Heaven.

I turned to Mario Righetti. "Obviously, the game has changed. You're clearly way over your head in this thing and were ready to punch out. Aside from knowing my name, you have no idea who or what I am. I'm going to answer a few questions you may not realize you have, and then we're going to shoot straight with each other. Capiche?"

He nodded but couldn't keep his eyes off the door through which Antonio and Dominic had gone.

I snapped my fingers in front of his face. "Hey. Focus! Look at me. Quit worrying about him. He has a few debts to pay, and we're here to collect."

Righetti closed his eyes and slowly shook his head. "You have no idea what you're doing. You, the guy you're calling Clark, and the old guy—you three are out of your league here, kid."

I smiled. "Let me tell you a story about the Black Dolphin Prison. Have you ever heard of it?"

He shook his head.

"It's a nice, quaint bed-and-breakfast joint in Sol-Iletsk, a south-central Russian town near the Kazakh border. That's where Clark and I were a week ago. We were breaking a political prisoner out of one of the highest-security prisons in the world, and we were successful. Before that, we put a bullet in the face of a Russian mafioso and burned his house to the ground on the Moscow River less than a mile from the Kremlin. So, Antonio D'Angelo doesn't scare me. A hundred Antonio D'Angelos wouldn't scare me. You see, I eat people like him for breakfast and pick my teeth with people like you. I'm not your run-of-the-mill street thug. When somebody wants you dead, you better pray to God they don't send me to do the job, because I don't miss. And more importantly, if someone is trying to kill you and I want you to stay alive, you can make all the long-term plans you want because people on my watch don't get dead. That's especially important for you to remember."

There was a nicely stocked bar on the port side of the main salon, so I poured Righetti four fingers of Laphroig, one of Scotland's finest exports. I removed his handcuffs and offered him the glass. He rubbed at his wrists and took the drink from my hand. "Thank you."

I sat on the settee across from him. "Now, talk to me. First, I need to know who the two goons were that came to arrest me."

He swallowed half the contents of the tumbler and licked his lips. "They were hired muscle. The family uses them for collections and when situations might get rough. They aren't the kinds of guys who negotiate, if you know what I mean."

"Well, one of them isn't the kind of guy who does anything now —he's roasting marshmallows with the devil. And the other one is being arraigned in Saint John's County for a whole bevy of charges, not the least of which is impersonating a police officer. Oh yeah, there are a few weapons charges and that whole attempted murder thing he's going to have to plead to as well. I guess legal trouble like that falls into your lap most of the time, huh?"

He nodded. "It used to, but I don't do that sort of thing anymore. Associates handle that now."

"That's a good start. Now, let's get down to business. I thought Antonio went down on a capital murder wrap in the seventies."

Righetti took another sip. "Yeah, he did, but we beat it on appeal. He's done a couple of stretches since then for some petty things—racketeering, embezzlement. You know, stuff like that."

"So what was he doing in your office this morning when I showed up?"

For the first time, Righetti laughed. "You wouldn't believe it, but we were talking about you."

"Oh, really? Specifically what about me?"

"We were discussing how you weren't as easy to get to as we thought you'd be. We underestimated you. The family's not going to let you get away with what you did to Salvatore."

I grinned. "Good ol' Sal is lucky to be alive. He made some bad decisions, and I gave him a second chance to get his life back on track. I should've killed him, but I showed some mercy. I don't do that very often, and now I see I shouldn't have done it for Sal. I should've put a bullet through his eye and saved myself and the whole world a lot of trouble."

He stared at the floor. "Yeah, well, the family wishes you'd done just that."

"What?"

Righetti sighed. "Yeah, that toad has been a thorn in everybody's side for a dozen years. He's nothing but trouble, but he's blood, so what can you do?"

"So, let me get this straight. The D'Angelo family wants Salvatore dead, but they're going to come after me because I kicked his ass and shook him up a little?"

He nodded. "That's how it works. He may be a bastard, but he's our bastard, and we don't let anyone kick us around.... None of us."

"Well, Mario, I have a feeling that what you and the D'Angelo family allow and don't allow is about to change quite dramatically."

He smiled. "You have no idea what you're doing. You and your friends out there aren't going to change anything. No matter how much of a badass you think you are, a year from now, nobody will

remember your name, and things will be just like they were yesterday before you showed up. You can kill me, or even Antonio, but in
the long run, you'll never stop this train."

I glared at him. "We'll see about that. Let's get back to sharing
means caring. I've got plenty more questions."

He peered through the door again, and I'd had enough of him
wondering when Antonio was going to come back to save him. It
was time to get his attention—and keep it. I pulled out my Secret
Service credential pack and a microcassette recorder. Holding the
badge and ID up for Righetti to see, I pressed the record button.
"Mario Righetti, thank you for the information on the D'Angelo
family."

He scowled. "I don't know what you're talking about. I haven't
told you anything."

I held the recorder up in front of my mouth. "You've been very
helpful with the information you've provided, especially with how
forthcoming you've been about Salvatore, Antonio, and the others.
You can rest assured the government of the United States will see
that you are well protected. You're free to go now."

I clicked off the recorder and stared at the lawyer as his face grew
tighter and angrier with every breath. My phone chirped. "Hold
that thought, Mario. I'd better take this."

Two minutes later, I hung up and turned to Righetti. "That was
a call you'll find interesting, Mario. That was one of my team members, and she's been doing some research on you. It looks like your
lovely wife, daughter, and granddaughter are at your exquisite house
on Bimini. At least that's what our surveillance team on a boat fifty
yards off your dock is reporting."

The anger in his face turned to something else—perhaps fear,
dread, or acceptance. I couldn't be sure.

He narrowed his eyes. "If you hurt my family...."

I patted his head—an act meant to completely demean him.
"Oh, come now, Mario. An hour ago, you were ready to make your
beautiful wife a widow and leave those two precious girls—Paulina
and Marissa—without a father and grandfather. Those are their

names, right? Paulina, your daughter, and Marissa, her three-year-old daughter? How about you guess which dress Marissa is wearing today. The yellow or blue one?"

Rage overtook him, and he leapt from the seat. I struck him hard in the center of his chest, knocking the wind from his lungs and sending him back onto the chair. He clawed at his chest.

"You sit down and pay attention."

He gasped, trying to reclaim his breath, and I stood over him like a lion, daring him to resist.

"If your family gets hurt, that's your fault. It will be one hundred percent your responsibility, and I won't lose a minute's sleep over it."

Slowly, his breathing turned from desperate gasps to shuttering, shallow jerks, and finally to deep, anxious inhalations.

I knelt in front of him. "Now that I have your attention—and your taped confession, sort of—it's time for you to resign yourself to doing whatever I say. Is that clear enough for you?"

With submission overcoming his rage, he nodded, and his shoulders slumped several inches.

"Good. Now, let's get started. Let's go back a couple decades and work our way from there. Who killed Mildred Huntsinger in nineteen seventy-eight?"

Utter confusion poured over him. "Who?"

"Mildred Huntsinger, Judge Barnard Henry Huntsinger's wife in Saint Marys, Georgia. Who killed her?"

The look on his face made it clear that Righetti had no idea why I'd be asking about a twenty-three-year-old murder that had nothing to do with me.

He took a long, full breath. "It was a hitter by the name of Loui Giordano."

"Is Giordano still alive?"

He almost laughed. "Yeah, he's still alive."

"Where can I find him?"

"Who the hell knows? When you need Loui, you page him. If he wants to call you back, he will. If he don't, he won't. It's that simple."

I pulled the pad and pen from my pocket and wrote Loui Giordano's name at the top of a page. "Page him."

Righetti stared blankly at me as if I'd asked him to call the Pope. I lifted the phone to my ear, locked eyes with the lawyer, and whispered, "Blue dress…yellow dress."

"Okay, okay. I'll page him."

"That's more like it. Now, make the call. When he calls you back, you're going to hire him to kill me. Do you understand?"

He blinked in a rapid-fire pattern. "But we've already—"

"You've already what?" I demanded.

"We've already done that."

"You've already done what?"

"We've already hired him to kill you."

A thousand bells went off in my head. I love when things start to make sense. Obviously, Giordano had planted the explosive on the engine of my airplane.

I grinned. "It would appear that he failed. Wouldn't you say so?"

Righetti was speechless, so I gave him an out. "When he calls back, let me answer. Page him."

The man pushed a speed dial key.

"Turn on the speaker."

He did as I said, and soon the electronic voice came on the line. "Please enter your number after the tone."

Righetti typed the ten digits into the keypad and hung up. I snatched the phone from his hand and tucked it beneath my leg on the settee.

"While we're waiting for Mr. Giordano to call back, we have time for a few more questions. Care for another drink?"

Righetti sighed. "I'm going to need it."

I poured another and placed it in his hand, then returned to my place on the settee. "So, who is Salvatore's father?" I flipped to the second page of my pad.

"Big Sal," Righetti said, "but he's been dead for twenty years."

I made a note. "How did he die?"

"A sailor out at Mayport beat him to death in a bar fight in nineteen eighty-two, when Sal was just a boy."

"And he was married to Gail, the congresswoman?"

Righetti actually laughed out loud. "Yeah, but that bitch wasn't a congresswoman back then. She was a second-rate divorce lawyer scratching out a living representing battered wives all over North Florida."

I didn't let him lead me astray. "And she never remarried after Big Sal's death?"

He shook his head, "No. She sued the Navy, the owner of the bar where the fight happened, the bartender, the bouncers, the off-duty cops in the joint, and everybody else she could name in the lawsuit. She won and got a big check—well, several big checks, actually—and cashed them in on political campaigns until she finally made it to Washington."

I was feverishly taking notes as he continued his narrative, but my pen froze in place when I felt the vibration of Righetti's phone beneath my leg. My prey had just taken his first nibble at the bait I'd dangled in front of him.

Chapter 14
The Caravan Plan

I only half expected Giordano to call back, and I wasn't fully pre-pared for the conversation. "Hey, Loui. How's it hangin'?"

"Who the fuck is this?"

"Loui, watch the language. I'm delicate and easily offended. And trust me, you don't want to offend me. Your friends Mario Righetti and Antonio D'Angelo are learning that lesson right now, so listen closely. You don't strike me as the sharpest arrow in the quiver, so I'm going to speak slowly. My name is Chase Fulton. I'm the guy you were supposed to kill. I don't know how much they paid you, but it looks like you owe them a refund."

I could hear him breathing like an angry bull. "Is this some kind of fu—"

"Loui! Again with the language. I told you once about that. Don't make me tell you again."

I punched the speaker button. "Go ahead, Mario. Tell your buddy about me."

Righetti swallowed hard. "Look, Loui. This guy is some kind of whacko fed or something, and he's got me and Tony-Two-Rocks."

Tony-Two-Rocks, I thought. *That's an interesting nickname for An-tonio D'Angelo.*

I punched off the speaker and stuck the phone back to my ear. "There you have it, Loui. I'm some kind of whacko fed or some-thing, just like your lawyer friend said. So, here's the deal. You're not getting the other half of your money even if you do find me and kill me. There won't be anyone left to pay you. The ones I leave alive will be going to prison, so unless you want to join one of those two groups, the dead or the incarcerated, I recommend that you disappear and stop answering your phone."

I could still hear his exaggerated breaths on the other end.

"You may have the piece-of-shit lawyer, but you ain't got Tony-Two-Rocks."

I pressed the speed dial number for Clark. "Bring Antonio back in here. There's someone who wants to talk to him."

Thirty seconds later, Clark came through the door to the salon, frog-marching Antonio Tony-Two-Rocks D'Angelo, who was still handcuffed but looked like he'd been standing in the shower with his clothes on.

I punched the speaker button. "Loui, say hello to your old friend, Tony-Two-Rocks."

"Is that you, Tony. Is this guy for real?"

Antonio closed his eyes. "These guys ain't no cops, Loui. I don't know what they are, but they—"

Clark apparently decided Antonio had said enough. He wedged a thigh behind Antonio's knees and threw a haymaker to his throat, sending the big man collapsing to the deck of the salon, unconscious.

With the speaker of the phone off, I said, "Ooh, that really looked like it hurt. Are you convinced we have both Righetti and Antonio now?"

"What do you want?"

I smiled, confident my expression showed in my tone. "Oh, nothing, really. I just thought you'd like to know what's going on down here. There's nothing you can do to stop me—it's too late for that. At least one of these guys already flipped on you, Loui. Your days are numbered, but we'll get to you when we've gotten our pound of flesh from who we're really after."

I hung up before he could start cussing again and immediately called Skipper from Righetti's phone.

"Hello?"

"Skipper, it's Chase. I need you to trace the last call that was received by the number I'm calling you on. Can you do that?"

"Sure, no problem. Give me just a second. I can do it right now. Hey, I heard something on the news about a plane like yours losing an engine. Is everything okay?"

"Yeah, that was us. Everything's fine. The plane will have a new engine in a few days. How are you coming on that trace?"

I heard her pouty sigh. "All right, I've got it. It was from a payphone in Panama City."

I frowned. "Panama?"

"No, silly. Panama City, Florida, from the Buccaneer Beach Motel on West Beach Drive."

"That's amazing. I don't know how you do that, but I'm glad you do. I need to get eyes on the guy who made that call. His name is Loui Giordano. See what you can do to get him under surveillance."

She started to ask a flurry of questions, but I hung up and stared at Antonio lying on the deck. "Why is he soaking wet? Have you been water-boarding again? I thought I told you no more water-boarding."

Clark shrugged. "I can't help it. It's my thing. Besides, I don't like you calling it *water-boarding*. I prefer the term *tactical baptism*."

"So, now you're Clark the Baptist?"

"No, but I do get a lot of confessions this way."

Righetti's eyes were the size of saucers. I took a knee in front of him. "So, this is the defining moment of your life. You get to pick which side you're on. The gig is up, and the D'Angelo family is going down. Two hours ago, you were ready to pull the plug on your drain and disappear with the bathwater. If you want to stay alive and keep your family alive, I can protect you. If you want to stay curled up in bed with the vermin you've spent your whole life protecting, I can't do anything to save you or your family. So, what's it going to be, Mario? Am I keeping you and your family alive, or am I turning you loose back into the wild? The choice is yours."

The lawyer's chest swelled with one long breath, and his chin fell. "You'll protect my family if I do what you ask?"

I stuck my thumb under his chin and lifted his face. "Look at me, Mario. Do I look like the kind of man who doesn't keep his promises?"

He squeezed his eyes shut and swallowed audibly.

"If I tell you I'll keep your family alive, that's what I'll do, no matter the cost. Now, pick a side."

He whispered, "Protect my family, and I'll do whatever you want."

I held his cell phone toward him. "Call your wife and tell her to pack a bag for herself, your daughter, and granddaughter. Make it a big bag. The four of you are going on a vacation."

He dialed the number. "Listen closely. Pack your bags—yours and the girls'. We're going away for a while, the four of us. I'll explain later."

He paused, listening intently, and then turned to me. "Warm or cold?"

"Definitely warm," I said.

Righetti passed the word and closed his phone. I quickly took it from his hand, tucked it into my pocket, and turned to Dominic, who had followed Clark and Antonio back aboard. "Do you have someplace you can keep old Tony-Two-Rocks for a few days?"

"Sure. I've got just the spot. It's not all that comfortable, but it's better than living under a bridge."

Unable to stand the suspense any longer, I turned to Righetti. "Why did Loui call Antonio 'Tony-Two-Rocks'?"

The lawyer almost smiled. "It goes way back to when we were kids in the neighborhood. Antonio caught another kid shoving his kid sister around on the playground, and Tony picked up two rocks the size of soup cans, one in each hand, and cracked the kid's head right between two rocks. He's been Tony-Two-Rocks ever since."

Clark nodded his approval. "That's a good story, but ol' Tony-Two-Rocks can't take a punch and stay on his feet these days. Maybe he's lost his touch."

I called Skipper again. "I need the surveillance team to pick up Righetti's wife, daughter, and granddaughter from Bimini and bring them to Key West."

"Are you in Key West now?"

"No, we're still in Miami, but we'll be in Key West by the time they get there. Any luck finding Giordano?"

"I've got a team en route. Do you want to snatch him up or just watch him? Snatching is cheap. Watching is five hundred a day, plus expenses."

I considered her question but couldn't come up with anything to do with the man if we snatched him. "Just watch him for now, but make sure they know if they lose him, they're not getting paid."

"I will, but seriously, is the plane okay?"

I liked how much she cared about my airplane. Skipper had demonstrated a natural talent in the cockpit, and with Clark as her instructor, she was quickly becoming an amazing pilot. She'd soon outgrow the 182, but she'd never forget the plane that taught her to fly. No one ever does.

"She'll be fine in a few days. I promise to fill you in as soon as I can. I'll call you from Key West."

I turned to Clark and Dominic just as Antonio was waking up. "Let's get Two-Rocks tucked away, then Clark and I have to get Righetti to the airport."

Dominic pressed his fingertip between Antonio's eyes. "I've got him. Did you say you're having a surveillance team bring Righetti's family to Key West?"

"Yeah. The team is watching them from a go-fast boat at Righetti's house on Bimini. They'll pick them up and run them across the Straits and then down to the Keys."

Dominic turned his wrist and checked the time. "I've got a Caravan on floats. It'll be a much nicer ride if you want to hop across and grab them instead of pounding through the six-foot seas in the Gulf Stream."

I didn't have to look at my partner to know he was grinning from ear to ear.

"Definitely the Caravan," Clark said.

Dominic fished in his pockets and tossed us a set of keys. "Take the Range Rover. The Caravan is at the Miami Seaplane Base on the MacArthur Causeway. I'll call and let them know you're coming."

I caught the keys, motioned for Righetti to get up, and headed for the stern of the yacht.

"Whose boat is this?" I asked.

Dominic smiled but didn't answer. He'd been in the covert ops game longer than I'd been alive. His knowledge and connections in the intelligence community were unrivaled. He may not have known whose yacht we were on, or whose seaplane we were about to borrow, but he certainly knew the game well enough to know what hardware was and wasn't available. The yacht and the Caravan were both, obviously, in the negotiable category.

Righetti offered no resistance on the ride to the Miami Seaplane Base. He sat in silence with his hands folded on his lap. I tried to imagine the torrent of emotion spinning out of control inside his head. He'd spent a lifetime working for the D'Angelo family and had amassed a fortune doing so. That fortune had to come with an unimaginable psychological price. If he had a conscious at all, he had to fear this day of reckoning would come. I'd become that reckoning, and I had, most definitely, come in grand style. I believed he was ready to walk away from the life he'd allowed to consume him. I believed he wanted a way out but never imagined there would be an avenue of escape that didn't include a bullet in his brain. I knew he didn't trust me, but I also knew he saw me as his only option to keep his family safe. As much as I disliked using his family as a tool to gain Righetti's cooperation, I didn't see any other options.

We taxied the Cessna 208 Caravan from the tarmac at the Miami Seaplane Base, and down the concrete ramp into the main channel, between the MacArthur Causeway and the cruise ship terminal. A collection of massive cruise ships lined the waterway to our right. Carnival, Celebrity, and Royal Caribbean all had their floating resorts securely moored alongside, taking on a new batch of thousands of tourists hoping to forget about real life for six days and seven nights while they stopped at tropical paradisiacal ports that represented almost nothing of the truth about life on most Caribbean islands.

Merchants by the hundreds would line the ports, begging for those almighty American dollars, while the tourists willingly opened the floodgates of their wallets to pay for an excursion—as the cruise lines love to call them—to a beach and a picnic lunch. Seventy-nine dollars American, plus a twenty-percent automatic gratuity for each traveler, would cover the stinky van ride and local-flavor meal on the beach. Penny and I could sail up to any one of those beaches, catch and cook our own fish, and make ourselves right at home without standing in line or forking over the gratuity-laden fees. I'm sure life aboard the cruise ships was luxurious and relaxing, but when I wasn't chasing Russians, the Chinese, or a Florida mob family, my life on my boat, *Aegis*, certainly qualified as luxurious and relaxing, especially with Penny Thomas aboard. I looked forward to the day when we could spend more of our time exploring paradise, cooking our own fish, and enjoying each other. The time would come, but duty places demands on the young, of which I still qualified at the time, and those demands must be met.

Clark ran through the pre-takeoff checklist and soon had the Pratt and Whitney PT-6 turbine engine driving the propeller through its whirring arc and pulling us through the gray water of the main channel.

Mario Righetti was staring out the window as the pontoons began to plane and our Caravan transitioned from a floating machine to a flying machine. I wondered what must be going through his mind. Life as he knew it was over. The practice of law on behalf of the D'Angelo family was vanishing behind him as quickly as the MacArthur Causeway was disappearing beneath the tail of our airplane.

Suddenly remembering the instructions I'd given Skipper, I dialed her number. "Slight change of plans. Have the surveillance boys sit on Righetti's family instead of bringing them across to Key West.

We'll be taxiing up to Righetti's dock in a blue and white Cessna Caravan seaplane in less than thirty minutes to pick them up."

I expected Skipper to have a dozen questions, but she surprised me by simply saying, "Done," and hanging up.

She was learning quickly, and I was thankful to have her on my team.

The cabin of the airplane was relatively quiet compared to other similar-sized seaplanes, but we were wearing Bose noise-canceling headsets, making conversation even easier.

I turned to Righetti. "Here's the gig. You can tell your daughter and granddaughter this is some grand adventure. They'll buy it for a while, especially your granddaughter, but your wife is another story. You'll have to come clean with her. When you do that is up to you, but she is getting on this airplane, no matter what you have to tell her. Do you understand? I can protect them, and I will, but they'll have to do what I say, and it's up to you to make her understand that."

He pulled the microphone to his lips. "My daughter, Paulina, and of course my granddaughter have no idea what the truth is behind what I do. They believe I'm a successful Miami attorney. Gloria, my wife, is a different story. She's too sharp to miss the truth. She's known for a long time that sooner or later we'd have to pay the piper. I guess that makes you the piper, huh?"

I grimaced. "No, I'm not here to make you pay. We've moved past that. If you're truly willing to cooperate and help me bring down the D'Angelo family, I'm here to keep you and your family alive."

The submission in his eyes gave him the look of a condemned man who had just made a deal with the devil.

Chapter 15
Common Scars

I don't know what Skipper told the surveillance team, but when we splashed down in front of Righetti's ocean-front palace, Gloria, Paulina, and Marissa were sitting in deck chairs at the end of the dock with luggage strewn around them. One man, who I assumed to be a member of the surveillance team, was stationed where the dock met the sandy shore of Righetti's property, and two more were visible at the front of the house as we flew over on our approach. Whoever the team members were, they were protecting the family and the scene just as Clark and I would've done. I was reassured by that fact.

The portside pontoon kissed the side of the floating dock as if Clark had practiced the arrival a thousand times. He stepped from the cockpit, landed on the dock, and constantly scanned the environment for threats. Apparently seeing none, he tied the plane to the dock with a quick cleat hitch and opened the door behind Righetti's seat. The lawyer descended the ladder and joined Clark while I stayed in my seat, ready to restart the engine for a hasty retreat should things turn sour. Clark left his door open so I could hear and see what was happening on the dock.

Righetti hugged his granddaughter as she leapt into his arms. "Poppa, I didn't expect to see you until the weekend. I love it here. Why do we have to leave?"

Setting the girl on the dock, Righetti said, "We have to go away for a while, mi piccola principessa, but you're going to love where we're going just as much as this place."

The girl beamed up at Righetti. "I like being your little princess, Poppa."

He ruffled her hair and said something I couldn't understand as his daughter approached. "What's going on, Dad? What's this all about? Mom's not telling me anything. Who are these men?"

Paulina was the classic Italian beauty with long dark hair and a flawless olive complexion. Her dark eyes radiated intensity and a knowing suspicion that could, in situations like this, only lead to trouble.

Righetti kissed her cheek. "Don't worry, my child. We need to get away for a few days. I'm having some trouble with a client, and I'm just being cautious. It'll all blow over soon. It's best not to take any chances."

"Is he dangerous?" Marissa asked.

"He has the potential to be dangerous in the right circumstances, but nothing's going to happen to you. I've hired these men to protect you."

That's not the lie I'd expected him to tell. Clark and I weren't on his payroll, but the first part about having trouble with a client couldn't have been truer.

The surveillance man from the end of the dock moved toward the plane and helped Clark load the baggage onto the Caravan.

Clark asked Righetti, "Do you need anything from inside the house? When they realize you're gone, they're going to search your place. Now's your only opportunity."

"I'll need some clothes and a few things."

Clark climbed up the ladder and leaned into the cockpit. "Righetti needs a few things from inside the house. Do you want to go with him, or should I?"

I unbuckled my shoulder harness and lap belt. "I'll go."

As I climbed down from the plane, I had a sense of dread that nothing was as it appeared. "Hey, Clark. Something's not right. I don't like the way this feels."

Clark looked up at the palatial home and then back at me. "I don't know. It seems all right to me, but never ignore your instinct. What do you think it is?"

I scanned the area, and my sight fell on the surveillance team member who'd helped Clark load the bags. "Do you know that guy?"

Clark looked the man over. "I have no idea who he is. I assumed Skipper set up the surveillance."

"Yeah, she did, and I'm sure everything's fine. I'm just being paranoid."

"Hey, mister," Marissa said. "Where's your doggy?"

I turned to the girl, but she wasn't asking me the question. She was talking to the surveillance man, who was ignoring her, but she persisted. "Hey, where's your doggy?"

The man turned toward the child. "Are you talking to me?"

"Yeah, you had a doggy, a big black-and-white one, when you came up in your boat. What's his name, and where is he?"

Children don't always perceive the world as it is, but they always notice a dog. Marissa had seen one, and the man clearly didn't know what she was talking about.

The surveillance man lifted his shirt with his left hand and reached for something inside his waistband.

I yelled, "Gun!" and instinctually grabbed Marissa by the collar of her blue dress, then threw her into the cabin of the airplane. We were less than a second away from being in the middle of a gun-fight, in the middle of the day, on Bimini, and the last thing I wanted was a little girl caught in the crossfire.

Continuing the turn my momentum from throwing the girl had created, I spun into a kneeling position on the portside pontoon of the Caravan with my weapon drawn and rising to meet my target. Before I could put a pair of rounds into his chest, I heard the tell-tale spitting of the nine-millimeter rounds exiting the suppressor of

Clark's Sig. The man fell where he stood with a Glock pistol clenched tightly in his right hand.

Righetti had dived onto his daughter, knocking her to the wooden planks of the dock.

Clark grabbed his arm and yanked him to his feet. "Get in the airplane, and get everyone strapped in. We'll be back in two minutes or less!"

The lawyer went to work herding his family into the Caravan as Clark and I sprinted toward the house, pistols drawn.

"You go right. I'll go left," I said as we picked up speed.

Remembering where I'd seen the men posted at the front corners of the house when we'd flown our approach, I came to a stop at a section of the house that jutted outward about ten feet. I used the corner as cover as I quick-peeked to determine the man's location. He was right where I'd seen him from the plane, and he had his back to me. That gave me the element of surprise, but nothing more. I didn't want to kill him until I'd learned the extent of what was actually happening, and I was still confused about what was actually happening. Unless it was absolutely necessary, more dead bodies to explain was not something I wanted.

I crept from my cover as quietly as possible, hoping to get to the man before he heard me coming. The ground was sandy, but seashells were scattered, making it impossible to move silently. I abandoned my attempt at a stealthy approach and opted, instead, for speed. Springing from my right foot into a bounding sprint, I covered the twenty feet between me and the man in less than six full strides. I hit him low across the back with my right shoulder, driving him to the ground, face-first. He grunted from the unexpected attack but immediately tried to roll himself onto his back to face me. My superior size and training made his efforts nothing more than flailing expenditures of energy. With my knee in the small of his back, I forced an elbow into the base of his skull, pinning his head to the sandy ground. That left the man powerless and with no choice but to cooperate.

Barely above a whisper, I said, "What was the name of the dog you brought with you?"

Through a mouthful of sand and pain, he moaned, "Cutter. Why do you care about the dog's name?"

"I'm going to let you up now, but if you get aggressive, I'll put you back down permanently. Got it?"

"Yeah, I got it. Who the hell are you?"

I removed my elbow from his neck and slowly moved backward toward his feet. He rolled to his left, watching me cautiously, but making no effort to attack.

We locked eyes. "I'm Chase. I'm here to exfiltrate the Righettis. The guy on the dock didn't know you had a dog."

He frowned. "What are you talking about? He's the dog's handler. Of course he knows we have a dog. It's his dog, for God's sake."

I shook my head. "He wasn't your guy. I believe he took out your man and took his place on the dock. He didn't know about the dog, and he drew a Glock on me."

"A Glock?"

"Yeah, a Glock."

He squinted. "We don't carry Glocks."

"We need to get to your buddy on the other side of the house before my partner does." I started a sprint across the front of the house. As I passed the front door, I yelled, "Stand down, Clark!" But I was too late.

The other surveillance man's body came crashing forward around the corner with Clark plowing into his back. My partner had chosen the same method to take down his prey.

"Let him up, Clark. These two are our guys. The one on the dock was the plant. He must've taken out the dog handler."

Clark climbed back to his feet and helped the other man up. "Sorry about that, but the guy on the dock turned out to be less than friendly, so I wasn't taking any chances with you."

The guy stood and dusted himself off. "I'm Tuck, and he's Clay. We'd better take a look at the dude you two took out on the dock."

The four of us ran toward the water, arriving at the dock just as a man came lumbering from the neighboring beach, rubbing his neck.

Clark drew his pistol, but Clay motioned for him to put it away. "That's Kurt. He's our third, the dog handler."

Tuck sprinted toward Kurt while the rest of us continued out to the dock.

Clay pressed the toe of his boot against the corpse. "He's definitely not one of ours. Did you put the holes in him?"

Clark nodded as they stared at the corpse with two nine-millimeter holes in the center of his chest.

Kurt arrived only a few steps behind Tuck and began his story. "I didn't see him. He hit me with a dart to the neck, and I went down a few seconds later. I woke up over there." He pointed toward a secluded section of beach. "I can't find Cutter. If that son of a bitch hurt Cutter, I'll cut him off at the knees."

"You're late," Clay said. "These two beat you to it, I'm afraid."

As Clay's eyes met mine for the first time, a look of recognition came across his face, but nothing about him registered in my memory. He was taller than average, maybe five feet eleven and two hundred twenty pounds. He was muscular, not ripped, but thick, as if he'd lifted heavy iron for a decade. His close-cropped haircut made him look like a highway patrolman, but he carried himself like well-trained private security.

He held my gaze for several seconds. "You're Chase Fulton." It was a statement, not a question. "You played ball at Georgia."

I nodded and held up my scarred wrist and hand. "That was a lifetime and a bunch of broken bones ago."

Clay pulled up the right leg of his pants, revealing a pair of long surgical scars and one the size of a half dollar that was unmistakably an entry wound. "I graduated UGA the year before you and joined the Georgia Department of Revenue as an agent. I took a forty-five round to that ankle. Four surgeries and two years later, I was a twenty-eight-year-old retired cop, bored, looking for work, and ran across an old psych professor from school. Dr. Richter. Do you remember him?"

I laughed. "Yeah, you could say that."

"Anyway, Dr. Richter hooked me up with these folks and put me to work doing surveillance and general sneaky stuff. The hours suck, but the pay ain't bad. Looks like you got the same deal as me."

I nodded. "Well, not exactly. I don't do much surveillance, but the sneaky stuff seems to be my gig. I'm sorry, Clay, I can't say I re-member you from school. But it is a big school."

He stuck out his hand. "Ah, there's no reason you'd remember me. I wasn't exactly in your clique. Mark Clayton is the name, but everybody calls me Clay now."

I shook his hand and took a moment to savor the irony of two UGA graduates meeting on a Bahamian island after a gunfight, all because of the best psych professor on Earth. The world is, indeed, a much smaller place than any of us is willing to admit.

Chapter 16
Hail Mary

Just as Clay and I were wrapping up our stroll down the University of Georgia memory lane, a black-and-white dog of nearly a hundred pounds came waddling up the beach, staggering in a clumsy, crooked course, making him look as if he'd been drinking from the still instead of his water bowl. Kurt, the dog handler, started toward the dog in a similar wavering track. It was impossible to tell who was happier to see whom. Kurt performed a cursory examination of the dog, looking into his eyes and mouth before plucking a tranquilizer dart from Cutter's neck.

The two made their way back to the dock, and introductions were made. Cutter wasn't the typical tactical dog I'd expected. He was friendly, curious, and playful, in spite of the remnants of the tranquilizer coursing through his veins.

I rubbed his ears and looked up at Kurt. "He doesn't behave like a police dog."

Kurt laughed. "He's not. In fact, he's an idiot. The dummy flunked out of every school they sent him to. He started out as a drug sniffer, but he couldn't tell the difference between cocaine and candy corn. Then they gave him a shot at being an attack dog. The only thing he'd attack was lunch, so that didn't work out. Somebody thought he might make a decent seeing-eye dog, but he found a way to twist his head around far enough to chew his way out of the harness so he could sleep without interruption. I ended up with him because nobody else wanted him. He's turned out to be the best all-around dog you could ask for. He doesn't do anything perfectly, but he does everything well enough."

Smiling down at Cutter, I said, "Well, boy, it looks like you've screwed up just enough to make a pretty good life for yourself...except for occasionally getting tranquilized."

I assumed the Righettis were getting a bit anxious on the plane, so I climbed aboard to reassure them. "Everything's fine now. We had an issue with the surveillance team, but we've got it all sorted out."

"Is that man dead?" Marissa asked.

I looked back out the door of the Caravan at the body on the dock. The girl was too sharp to fool, so I gave her the truth. "Yes, I'm afraid he is, but he was a very bad man. He tried to hurt the doggy. Would you like to meet the doggy?"

She grinned and nodded enthusiastically. "Yeah, yeah, please! Can I, Mommy?"

Before Paulina could answer, I yelled out the door, "Hey Kurt. Can you send Cutter up here? There's somebody who'd love to meet him."

Giving a command I couldn't understand, Kurt pointed toward the door of the airplane, and Cutter lazily climbed the ladder.

Marissa plopped down on the floor in front of the dog and put her arms around his neck. "What's his name?"

I said, "Marissa, this is Cutter, and he's very happy to meet you."

Cutter endured the affection of the girl and seemed to revel in the attention.

"I love you, Cutter. I'm sorry that bad man was mean to you, but my friends killed him, and now he can't hurt you anymore."

I hadn't expected that, but I was thankful Cutter couldn't understand what the girl was saying.

"It's time to go." I stood to help the dog from the plane.

"Wait," Marissa cried. "Why can't Cutter come with us?"

Paulina took Marissa's hand, encouraging her to return to the seat. "Cutter may come to see us later, but he has work to do right now. He's a dog with a job—just like a person. Isn't that cool?"

The girl ran her hand down the dog's back, then giggled. "That's silly."

I smiled. "Yes, it's silly, but it's true. He does have a job. How about you give him one more hug, and then we have to go?"

She knelt in front of him, whispering something in his ear, and he let her wrap her arms around his neck and hug him. It looked like Cutter was trying to smile, and he licked at Marissa's face.

Kurt, Clay, and Tuck were moving the body of the imposter aboard their boat. I didn't want to know what they planned to do with the dead guy, but I had more pressing issues to deal with.

The wind blowing in off the water made powering away from the dock more challenging than I'd expected, but Clark made it look relatively easy.

"I want to learn to do this."

"Do what?" Clark asked.

"I want to get my seaplane rating."

He looked at me across the rim of his sunglasses. "You mean you don't have it already?"

"No, I've never been in a seaplane except with you."

"Well, it's not hard, but I can't teach you. I'm not a seaplane instructor, though I know a good one. Maybe when all this is over, we'll get you out on the water with him for a couple of days and get that knocked out."

I watched carefully as Clark ran through the checklists and started our takeoff run. With the addition of two more adults, Marissa, and seven suitcases, the plane was heavier than she'd been on the flight to Bimini. The extra weight didn't seem to faze the Caravan other than slightly lengthening our takeoff run.

As the pontoons left the chop of the water, the ride became smooth and quiet. Flying the seaplane, once it had left the water, was no different than piloting a conventional airplane, but her ability to land on a runway or any suitable body of water made the airplane more valuable in operations, like the one we'd found ourselves in.

Clark flipped the switch to isolate the headsets in the cockpit from the rest of the cabin. "Where are we going?"

I glanced over my shoulder at the Righettis and then back at my partner. "Ultimately, I want to get them to the Caymans, but I want to do that aboard *Aegis*. I think they're safer at sea than in a hotel in Georgetown. Don't you?"

He grimaced and stroked his beard, obviously considering my idea. "I don't know. Maybe. But we've got a lot of work to do. Spending a week on a boat isn't the best idea for the two of us."

"I agree," I admitted, "but do you have a better suggestion?"

"Maybe. What do you think about the surveillance team?"

"Uh, they seem all right. Other than one of them letting himself get tranquilized."

Clark shrugged. "It happens."

"Yeah, I guess. But what difference does it make what I think of them?"

"What if we put them on the boat with our guests back there while you and I go hunting?"

I inhaled through my clenched teeth. "I don't know. I mean, we don't even know if they can sail."

"It doesn't matter if they can sail. Penny and Skipper can sail. All we need from those guys is to have at least one of them awake at all times and for them to keep an eye on the lawyer."

I considered his suggestion, but I had my concerns. "I don't know how I feel about putting Penny in that position. She's not trained for anything like this."

"Did she shy away from the thing with Salvatore?"

He was right. She enjoyed the excitement, and maybe even the danger, of working with me when we kidnapped and scared a million bucks out of the D'Angelos' problem child in St. Augustine.

He held up his hands. "I'm not saying it's the only option, but it's worth considering."

"I don't like putting her in harm's way, but she is the best sailor I know. I just don't want something to go wrong and blow up in her face."

When those words escaped my lips, I felt my heart pound in my chest, and my mouth instantly felt like the Sahara Desert. I yanked the shoulder harness and lap belt off and climbed from the cockpit as if my seat were on fire.

Gloria's eyes met mine in horror when she saw me bounding into the passenger compartment. I didn't need her panicking, but I was having trouble keeping myself under control.

"Look at me, Gloria. How many bags did you bring on board?"

Without hesitation, she said, "Six. Two for each of us. Why?"

I grabbed her right shoulder and pulled her forward. "Get your head down and stay down!"

Mario's face instantly turned powder white as he met my gaze. I yanked him forward just as I'd done with his wife, and continued toward the rear of the plane. Paulina didn't have to be told. She pressed her shoulders to her knees and began praying aloud. I was thankful someone was talking to God. If my suspicion was correct, we were only seconds away from meeting Him face-to-face.

I unbuckled Marissa's seatbelt, then drew her tightly to my chest while retreating toward the cockpit. A bit more roughly than I'd wanted, I placed her in the copilot's seat and buckled her in securely.

Clark calmly asked, "What's going on?"

"There's an extra suitcase."

"Oh, shit!"

"Yeah, exactly. Get us slowed down as much as possible, and start a slip to the right. I have to open the door."

Clark's hand went instantly to the throttle, pulling the power well back from the cruise setting. Next, he shoved the propeller control full forward, flattening the pitch of the blades until they acted almost like air brakes. The big airplane responded and began bleeding off speed.

I thundered back through the seats. "No matter what you hear or feel, keep your heads down until I say otherwise! It's about to get loud in here! Paulina, which of these bags isn't yours?"

She pulled her head from between her knees and scanned the stack of luggage strapped to the rear bulkhead. "That blue one! I've never seen it before. It's definitely not ours."

I pounded my fist against the cabin overhead and yelled to Clark, "Slip to the right! Door coming open!"

The Caravan was fitted with a two-piece door, the top half of which opened upward while the lower half hinged forward. Because of the one-hundred-mile-per-hour wind and propeller wash blowing over the fuselage, it wouldn't be possible to push the bottom half open, so I prayed I could push the top half far enough to get the extra bag outside.

The plane twisted in the air and slipped sideways as the nose pointed ten degrees left of our actual course. The aerodynamic advantage of having the long, bulky fuselage blocking some of the wind from the door would hopefully make it possible to get the luggage out.

I simultaneously yanked the blue bag from the straps and unlatched the upper half of the door. As one final check, I yelled, "Gloria! Is this your bag?"

She raised her head and peered around the seat, immediately shaking her head. "No! That's definitely not ours!"

I drove my shoulder into the door hard enough to force it open about eighteen inches, but as soon as it met the slipstream across the top of the airplane, the door was driven back downward with more force than I could overcome.

Determined to get the bag anywhere other than inside my airplane, I shoved it against the upper door with all my strength. Digging my heels into the carpeting of the Caravan, I powered against it like a defensive lineman hitting a tackling sled, but the harder I pushed, the more the door pushed back. My plan was quickly falling apart.

Remembering what Dr. Richter had taught me about how the human mind tends to narrow its thoughts during moments of extreme stress, I forced myself to slow my breathing and think outside the box. There had to be a way to get the bag outside the airplane.

That's when it hit me. The bag was no threat. The contents were.

I yanked my knife from my pocket and threw open the blade. The faux leather of the bag surrendered to the steel in seconds, revealing a half-pound block of plastic explosive and three blasting caps. The first cap was attached to an altimeter and another to a timer. Eighteen seconds remained on the timer, and a bright-red LED was flashing on the altimeter. Leading through a plastic tray on which the bomb was mounted, was a third blasting cap connected to a pair of wires. The tray was glued inside the case, and I pried at it in a desperate attempt to separate it from the lining, but it didn't budge.

Thirteen seconds.

I considered yanking the blasting caps from the explosive, but I had no idea what kind of trigger was embedded beneath the tray. One wrong move could set off the bomb, and that much C4 plastic explosive would pulverize the Caravan and every human aboard.

Seven seconds.

I plunged the tip of my knife through the material of the case and began sawing around the plastic tray. My heart thundered, beating in time with the flashing timer.

Five...Four...Three...

The shredded case tore apart, and the bomb-laden tray fell into my hands. I forced the upper half of the door as far away from the fuselage as I could manage, and the bomb, now devoid of its suitcase, fell through the opening and into the bright afternoon sky.

I closed my eyes and turned my head away from the imminent blast. The concussion and resultant shockwave from the explosion only feet below the Caravan lifted the tail of the plane violently, sending the nose pointing down at the vast blue nothingness of the North Atlantic Ocean. Instantly deafened, I felt like I'd been inside cathedral bells when the priest pulled the rope.

I forced my head and shoulders back inside the airplane and landed with a thud. Feeling the unusual attitude of the airplane, I peered over my shoulder. Clark was wrestling with the controls in a desperate attempt to return the plane to straight and level flight. I crawled back to my knees and pulled on the upper half of the door, surprised to discover that it was still intact and latching perfectly.

I exhaled just before I collapsed into the seat beside Paulina. "Everyone can sit up now."

Tears streamed down her face, and she was unable, or unwilling, to open her eyes. She continually crossed herself as her trembling lips whispered, "Hail Mary full of grace, the Lord is with thee. Blessed are thou among women, and blessed is the fruit of thy womb Jesus. Holy Mary, mother of God, pray for us sinners, now, and at the hour of our death. Amen."

Chapter 17
Statistically Speaking

I placed my hand on Paulina's shoulder. "It's okay now. Everything's all right."

With eyes the size of saucers, she gripped my shirt in two white-knuckle fists. "What is going on? You've got to tell me the truth." Her trembling voice cracked on every other word, and veins visible beneath the skin of her neck throbbed with every beat of her pounding heart.

I took her hands in mine, primarily to keep her from ripping my shirt from my chest. "There are some people who aren't particularly happy with your father at the moment. It's going to be up to him to tell you the details when he feels the time is right, but for now, I'm going to keep you and your family safe."

"People? What people? What do they want? What do you mean *safe*? We almost got blown up, and you think you can keep us safe? Who are you anyway?"

I squeezed her hands. "*Almost* is the keyword. We didn't get blown up, and we're still alive. That's what's important. My name is Chase, but beyond that, all you need to know about me is that I promise to keep you, your mother and father, and especially Marissa alive and safe."

I placed her hands on her lap and stood, making my way back toward the cockpit. As I passed Mario's seat, I bore holes through him with my gaze. "You need to tell your daughter the truth."

Marissa was kneeling on the sheepskin-covered copilot seat with both hands on the yoke and Clark grinning at her. Her dark, Italian eyes beamed up at me. "Look at me! I'm driving the airplane."

I couldn't suppress my grin. "You certainly are, but it's my turn to drive, so let's get you back to your mommy."

She stuck out her bottom lip at a well-practiced attempt at pouting, but she couldn't suppress her giggle. "Okay, if you say so. But it's my turn next." She squirmed out of her seatbelt without unbuckling it and reached up for me. I hefted her from the seat and tried to set her down so she could walk to the back of the plane, but she clung to me like a baby chimpanzee. The Caravan wasn't tall enough for me to stand up, but I did my best to waddle back to Paulina's seat with Marissa hanging on for the ride. She finally let go when we made it back to her mother.

"Mommy, I was driving the airplane!" Her excitement was contagious for me, but her mother was still trembling. "Mommy, what's wrong? Why are you crying?"

Paulina brushed her fingers through Marissa's dark hair and wiped at her eyes. "It's okay, baby, I was just scared. Everything is fine now."

She pulled her daughter onto her lap and hugged the child as if she feared she'd never see her again.

Back in the cockpit, I repositioned my seat and connected my harness.

Clark had that look of mischief twinkling in his eye. "Where've you been? You missed all the excitement."

"Oh, I was getting some fresh air. You know…going for a stroll."

He laughed. "Well, how about strolling your way into putting our destination in the GPS? Even though we've got pontoons out there, I'm not crazy about wandering over the open ocean any longer than necessary. You know me…I'm afraid of sharks."

"The only thing you're afraid of is missing a nap." I began programming our flight plan into the GPS and discovered we were east of the Ocean Reef Club in North Key Largo, so I programmed the TWNNS intersection southeast of Lower Matecumbe Key and then Key West International. We'd make a decision about where to land when we got closer, but our destination would definitely be Key West.

I chose the route because I knew Penny would be sailing a similar course called the Hawk Channel, along the southeast side of the Florida Keys, as long as the current and wind didn't force her behind the island chain into Florida Bay. As long as the weather permitted, Hawk Channel was a much faster and safer route. Florida Bay was riddled with tiny islands, shoals, and water twenty feet deep in one spot and six inches deep only a few feet away. Unless they'd already made Key West, I hoped to catch a glimpse of *Aegis* and Penny.

"There you go, Shark Whisperer. There's your flight plan. We'll fly Hawk Channel to Key West."

Clark smirked. "Thanks, Navigation Boy. You come in quite handy sometimes."

As the miles ticked off and the anxiety of the explosion waned, we settled into the serenity of flying over some of the most beautiful seascapes on the planet. Watching the string of seemingly endless Florida Keys drift beneath our right wing made it easy to forget the severity of our situation.

As my mind toiled, trying to piece together what to do with the Righettis while I went after Loui Giordano—the hitman who'd now tried to kill me with explosives *twice* on an airplane—I flashed back to the memory of jumping into Kazakhstan with Singer, Smoke, Snake, and Mongo, the four commandos who fought by our sides on our last mission in Russia.

I pulled the microphone to my lips and double-checked the isolation switch, ensuring only Clark could hear me. "What are the chances are of getting the guys from Brinkwater Security down here to babysit Righetti and his family on the way to the Caymans?"

"I don't know, but that would be expensive. Those guys are seven or eight hundred bucks a day each. Three grand a day for babysitters is pretty steep."

I raised my eyebrows. "How much is it worth to keep Righetti alive long enough to testify against the D'Angelo family?"

Clark pressed his lips into a thin horizontal line. "Who's paying for all this?"

I swallowed hard. "Right now, I am, but I'm hoping to get reimbursed from the feds when we hand them the D'Angelos wrapped up with a nice Righetti bow on top."

"Is that your plan?" he asked. "To convince the lawyer to testify against the D'Angelos and then hand him over to the Marshals Service?"

"No, only half of that. He's going to testify, but I'm not letting him go into witness protection. He's got plenty of money tucked away somewhere nice and safe. Probably in the Caymans, like me. He can afford to hide anywhere on Earth he wants to go, and I plan to help him get there. I don't trust the Marshals to keep him alive for a long weekend, let alone the rest of his life in WITSEC. There are so many holes in that program it might as well be a sieve."

I caught a glimpse of a big white catamaran a couple of miles ahead. "Is that *Aegis*?"

Clark looked over the panel. "Could be, but I can't tell from here. We'll know in a minute."

He pulled off just enough power to let the big airplane begin a slow, lumbering descent toward the Straits of Florida below. The closer we got, the more the boat looked like mine, until we passed five hundred feet overhead and all doubt vanished. It was definitely my boat, and the woman I wanted to spend every day of the rest of my life with was lying on the trampoline at the bow, soaking up the subtropical sun.

Clark rocked the wings in the universal aeronautical wave and circled back around for another pass. When we flew across *Aegis's* bow, I saw Penny sitting and peering upward through a pair of binoculars. When she realized it was my face looking back, she began waving her arms wildly above her head. Another wing waggle and one more circuit around the boat punctuated our nautical-meets-aeronautical rendezvous, and we continued southwestwardly at fifteen times the speed of the big cruising catamaran.

I smiled unconsciously. "Well, what do you think the chances of that are?"

Clark rolled his eyes. "One hundred percent today, College Boy. Didn't they make you take statistics at that fancy school of yours?"

I showed him a finger. "Statistically, you're number one."

"Yeah, whatever. Now, let's get back to hiring a babysitter. If they're not off on another job, the boys from Brinkwater will do it. I'm sure of that, and they'd do it well, but that's a hefty price tag. I think the surveillance team from Bimini might be good enough, and I'm sure they'd be a lot cheaper."

"Sometimes you get what you pay for," I said, still unconvinced.

"Yeah, you're right, but let's decide where we're going to land and then we'll make the big decisions."

I zoomed in on the GPS screen, looking for a seaplane base in Key West, but was surprised to discover there wasn't one. "I guess it's international since there's no proper seaplane base in Key West."

He nodded slowly. "It's just as well. We'll need to top off the tanks anyway. Tune up the ATIS, and I'll teach you how to land this thing on the concrete."

The Automatic Terminal Information Service is a recorded message usually prepared hourly by an air traffic controller in a tower, detailing weather conditions, active runway, notice to airmen information, and other tidbits of useful information a pilot will want and need to know before arriving at an airport. I tuned the frequency and listened as the recording played in my headset.

"Key West International Airport ATIS information Foxtrot, time two-two-five-three Zulu, wind two-six-zero at zero-niner, visibility one-zero, sky clear, altimeter three-zero-zero-seven. Expect the visual approach, landing and departing runway two-seven. Advise on initial contact you have information Foxtrot."

I let the recording play through its loop three times before tuning the tower frequency at NAS Key West. Naval Air Station Key West is situated on Boca Chica, four and a half miles northeast of

Key West International Airport. The Navy's airspace extends from the surface up to twenty-five hundred feet, so we'd want to give the sailors a shout before blasting through their chunk of sky in our extremely civilian Cessna 208.

The Navy controller cleared us through her airspace and handed us off to Key West tower for a landing clearance. I watched carefully as Clark flew the visual approach, holding the big Caravan level as he let the airspeed bleed off, and allowing all four of the amphibious landing gear to kiss the runway simultaneously.

"There's no flair," Clark said. "You just hold her dead level and let her settle in. Got it?"

"I think so."

We rolled off the runway and onto the taxiway leading to the parking apron. A lineman directed us to a parking spot, and we shut down the engine.

I popped open my door and looked back at Clark. "I'll be right back. I'll have the lineman top off the tanks, and I'll see what's available for lodging."

He glanced back at our passengers. "I'll keep an eye on these guys. We'll be right here when you get back."

The not-so-young lady behind the terminal desk perked up when I explained that I needed to find a place for at least ten people for a few nights.

"Oh, you may be in luck. My sister is a leasing agent, and she just had a big group who left early. Hang on a sec, and I'll get her for you."

Before I realized she'd made the call, the woman was handing the phone across the counter.

"Hello. This is Chase."

"Hey, Chase. I'm Charlotte. My sister tells me you need a big place for ten people for a few days. Is that right?"

I cleared my throat. "Yes, that's right, but I don't know exactly how long—probably no more than three nights."

"You're in luck. I've got just the place. It's out on Sunset Key, though. The only way out there is by boat. Is that going to be a problem?"

I couldn't suppress my smile. "That's perfect."

I could almost feel Charlotte's excitement. "Oh, good. I had a group of fourteen who had to leave this morning, four days early. It was some medical thing. I don't know, but anyway, it's a six-bedroom guesthouse on the western beach with amazing sunsets. It's eighteen hundred a night plus a cleaning fee."

"So, if we don't stay the full three nights, you'll refund the excess, right?"

"No," she said, "unfortunately, we don't offer any refunds for early departure."

That's the answer I was hoping to hear. "Excellent, then you kept the full fee from the guests who left this morning. That means you can discount the rental for me because you've already been paid for the next four nights. I'm sure eight hundred a night is more than fair. Don't you agree?"

She did not agree, but she couldn't put together a very good defense, and we finally settled on a thousand bucks a night with no cleaning fee. I didn't know if I'd ever get a penny back from the feds when I finally turned Righetti over to the U.S. Attorney, so every penny mattered.

I thanked Charlotte for her flexibility and gave her my card number for the guesthouse.

"Thank you, Mr. Fulton. I'll send the limo to pick you up and take you to meet the Sunset Key Ferry."

For the first time since I'd set foot back on American soil after my adventure in Eastern Europe, something was finally going right.

Chapter 18
Once in a Lifetime

The limo, as Charlotte had called it, turned out to be a high-top van capable of carrying at least twenty people. The six of us were barely noticeable in the cavernous space…except for Marissa. She turned every experience into an adventure and told the driver all about "driving the airplane." Her story was replete with sound effects and exaggerated demonstration as her arms stretched outward in a perfect imitation of Cessna Caravan wings.

The driver, a Rastafarian with dreadlocks longer than Marissa was tall, listened intently to her story and responded with the animated reaction the girl's story deserved. Paulina finally rescued the driver from Marissa's onslaught and buckled her into the second seat from the front.

Before stepping aboard, I made sure we had precisely the correct number of suitcases. "Do you only drive between the airport and ferry dock?"

The driver's brilliant-white teeth shone in absolute contrast to his ebony skin. "Oh, no, mon. I dribe you anyplace you wan go, mon."

His sing-song patois made me long for the simplicity of the islands. My life had become so complicated and entangled, with forces beyond the comprehension of most people, that nothing about my existence qualified as simple. Every day I fell deeper into the web of deceit, murder, and evil that seems to line the depths of human existence. It's easy, and preferable, for most people to live

their lives far above and blind to that web, pretending evil is somehow never going to touch them and their families. I'd come to live
my life well beneath that belief, surrounded by the very people who
would, given the opportunity, elevate that web and enslave those
who sleep soundly at night, blissfully ignorant of even the existence
of such forces at work. The necessity of people like Clark and me
would never go away. We'd never destroy the web. We served only
to keep it beaten back so disbelief in its existence could remain possible for most of society. Regardless of the architect of the web—be
it Russian oligarchs, Chinese spies, or Miami mobsters—it never
varied. It has always been woven with the threads of fear, intimidation, and greed. To hack at the web requires, for me, walking an
ever-changing tightrope. I had no choice but to implement the tac-
tics of intimidation with the hope of driving daggers forged of fear
into the souls of my enemy, but I could never, without exception,
allow myself to be drawn into the third and most truly evil element
of the web: greed. What I do must be done of loyalty to humanity
and faith in a power greater than the evil that seems to grow
stronger day by day. Dr. Robert Richter taught me the meaning of
loyalty and devotion to protecting the truly innocent of society, who
rely on people like him and Clark and me to tuck them in safely every night and serve as a shield they'll never see—but should always
feel—against the swords and arrows wielded and fired from within
the web. It was my father who gave me my faith in a higher power.
That power has many names—God, the Universe, the Almighty—
but regardless of its name, I must believe. I am bound by my belief
to trust that a goodness, a purity, a light exists, and must, when everything else crumbles into dust, remain steadfastly unshaken.

"Where'd you go, mon?"

"What?"

His smile was gone. "You go someplace deep inside youself,
mon. Me Rasta, and Rasta be about knowledge and understanding.
Me see in dem eyes of you dat you fighting on da inside—and too
on da outside. You young, mon, but you responsible for all dese

peoples, and dat be more heavier weight dan you shoulders may can maybe bear."

His insight was both terrifying and brilliant. How could a Jamaican bus driver look into my eyes for the briefest of moments and see directly into my soul?

"I was j-just thinking. We need to get our bags to our guesthouse on Sunset Key and then get something to eat. I thought maybe I could hire you to wait for us at the ferry dock and take us to dinner."

His gleaming grin returned. "Yeah, mon. I do dat for you. I know juss da place. We feed you belly *and* you spirit, mon. Me tinks you be hungry for both."

I slid three hundred-dollar bills into his weathered black hand. He took one of the bills and shoved the other two back into the top of my pocket. "No, no. Dis be too much, mon. You gib res to udda peoples who need it more. I have good job and good home and good family wit plenty food to eat. You see soon enough."

I stuck out my hand to shake his, but he grabbed my fist in the classic thumb-wrestling grip and bounced the pad of his thumb against mine. "Peace and love, mon. Me tinks you have da love, but it be da peace you be needin'. It will come, bruddah. It will come. You dus have to believe."

I took a seat, and we pulled from the international airport onto A1A. As we did, I gazed out over Smathers Beach, where Anya had promised to tell me everything she knew about my family. Reliving that moment made me think she, somehow, knew our time together was almost over. Like my new Rastafarian friend, she may have had some insight into my soul. I've never been a believer in the old concept of everything happens for a reason, but Anya may have been dropped into my life to teach me a thousand lessons about the reality of the world. On the surface, she was delicate and breath-takingly beautiful, but behind those smoky blue-gray eyes that hypnotized me every time I looked into them, was a weapon tempered in the fires of Moscow and honed to such an edge that she could mindlessly tear the immortal soul from any enemy she faced, leaving a bloody, empty corpse where a formidable foe had stood only seconds before. Perhaps I was to learn from her that deception comes in the form of what we most desire. I was powerless to resist her. She cast a spell over me that words could never define, and my desire for her would have been my undoing had fate, or the universe, or God not driven ten thousand miles and an unimaginable world between us. She would have cost me everything, perhaps even my very soul, had that power not intervened.

My greatest fear will always be that I have not learned all the lessons that have been placed in front of me. "Rasta be about knowledge and understanding," he had said. Maybe that's what life is about. I could only pray I'd acquire both if I could just stay alive long enough to do so.

We arrived at the ferry dock, and the driver unloaded our bags. "Desomond be right here when you get back from the island, and me take you someplace you nebber been before."

We climbed aboard the ferry and motored out of the protected harbor and into the channel between Mallory Square and Sunset Key. There were boats of every imaginable size and shape coming and going in a beautiful, seemingly choreographed ballet. Sailboats lumbered silently along on the never-ending breeze, while cigarette boats roared and cut through the waves. A cruise ship was tied alongside the pier, and I wondered if her occupants would wake up the next morning in Miami, where I had been only a few hours before.

The guesthouse turned out to be an astonishing piece of architecture. Every bedroom opened to a balcony facing the worshipped western sky. Sunsets in Key West are practically a religious experience. Every night of the year, providing the clouds haven't consumed the sky, thousands of tourists flock to Mallory Square to watch the closest star to our world melt into the welcoming waters of the Gulf of Mexico.

Perhaps one in a thousand sunsets, or maybe fewer, offer a phenomenon known as the "green flash." A brief flash of green appears to emanate from the top edge of the sun just as it's sinking below the horizon. The green flash is so rare that it's said to be a once-in-a-lifetime experience, even for people who spend their lives on or near the ocean.

After everyone had chosen a bedroom and deposited their luggage, the six of us stood on the balcony, peering hypnotically westward. I pulled out my phone, pressed a speed dial button, and waited to hear Penny's voice.

"Hey, Fly Boy. What was that all about today, and where did you get that sexy airplane?"

Her voice and subtle North Texas drawl made everything else melt away. "It's a long story, but we're on Sunset Key in a really nice guesthouse. Come out here when you arrive instead of heading for the bight."

"Okay, but who is we? I thought I saw more faces than just you and Clark in the windows of that seaplane. What is that thing, anyway?"

I chuckled. "It's an amphibious Cessna Two-Oh-Eight Caravan. It belongs to Clark's dad, Dominic. He's letting us use it for a few days. The other faces you saw were the Righetti family. It's a long story, but I'll fill you in when you get here."

"Okay. I'm exhausted, so I'm going to anchor for the night and sail the rest of the way in the morning."

An idea popped into my head. "Hey, I could have someone drive me up the Keys, and I could join you for the rest of the trip if you'd like."

The excitement in her voice was unmistakable. "I'd love that! I'll be in Boot Key Harbor tonight. I just motored in. I didn't want to try it after dark, so I had to hustle."

"You get anchored, and I'll call you in an hour."

A collective gasp rose from the balcony, and I looked up to see five faces locked in awe. Even Marissa was speechless.

A tear clung to Gloria's eye as she gazed at her husband and ran her fingers through his dark hair. "It's a sign, Mario. The green flash means good things are on the horizon for us."

The man whose face I'd watched tumble through almost every human emotion over the past twelve hours revealed a new sentiment. Perhaps the look was hope. That's an emotion I suspect Mario Righetti hadn't experienced in decades. He exhaled, smiled, and kissed his wife's forehead.

We filed back down to the dock to meet the ferry just in time. Desomond was where he said he'd be. Something told me he was a man of impeccable character, whose word was as good as any contract.

"Ah, welcome back. Did you see da green flash? I have been on dis ol' Earth for almost twenty-tousan' of dem sunsets, and dis one be da firs' one ever make da green flash for me. Me tinks it means good omen you…for all of you. You come to da island, and da bery nex' sunset be da deliverer of da green flash. It don't be no accident, dat's for sure. Now, let's go to feed dem hungry bellies of yours."

Each time Desomond opened his mouth, I liked him more. I couldn't say that about many people, but he was far from typical.

As we headed down Whitehead Street toward Jamaican Village, I knew instantly where Desomond was taking us. We were headed for Blue Heaven, one of the best restaurants on the island. The food was always unforgettable, and the atmosphere, perfectly Key West. I was excited that our driver had made such an impeccable choice, but my excitement sank when we drove right past Pretonia Street and kept heading south.

We finally turned on Julia, and Desomond stopped the van in front of a hundred-year-old house that looked like it hadn't seen a paintbrush in decades.

"Ah, here we are. Eberybody out. Dis be our destination."

I hoped Clark knew what was going on, but he was looking around, just as confused.

"Dis be our destination, mon."

We stepped out of the van, and Desomond led us down a long crushed-conch-shell alley between the unpainted house and one next door that appeared to be in worse shape than the first. As we rounded the corner at the back of the house, we were greeted by a huge plume of white smoke rising from a concrete block pit. A shoeless woman, dressed in a man's white T-shirt and a multi-colored wraparound skirt, stood amid the smoke with a pair of wooden sticks, turning pieces of chicken on a metal grate. Fire lapped at the grill from below, and the woman expertly repositioned each piece of chicken to avoid being scorched. Perhaps that's what Desomond was doing for me—helping me avoid being scorched from the flames below.

Our Rastafarian driver-turned-philosopher motioned toward the woman. "Dis be my beautiful wife, Virginia. She be da best jerk chicken cook in all da world."

Virginia smiled, revealing a mouthful of pearly-white teeth that matched her husband's. He waved his hand across the yard, presenting at least half a dozen children, from toddlers to teenagers. "And dis be my family. Welcome to our home."

Marissa's eyes lit up as if she'd been dropped into Disney World. "Mommy, can I go play?"

Paulina smiled and nodded, and Marissa galloped across the yard, immediately joining the group of frolicking children. Such blindness to differences and celebration of life together should be a lesson to those of us who've allowed ourselves to grow bitter and jaded. Innocence and acceptance of happiness in its purest form is what makes children capable of so much joy.

The jerk chicken was, by far, the best I'd ever tasted. We drank Red Stripe Jamaican beer and ate fried plantains and rice until we couldn't cram another bite into our mouths. The children ate sporadically between sessions of hopscotch, tag, hide-and-seek, and other games that had been passed on through generations.

Gloria watched her granddaughter dance, giggle, and tumble with the other children, and she smiled as if she hadn't smiled in decades. From the adjacent yard, a wave of music wafted through the banyan trees. Bob Marley and the Wailers belted out "Stir It Up" to the beat of bongos, steel drums, and island guitars.

Desomond took his wife's hand. "Come, come. Dance, dance."

Gloria's smile grew broader, and she shouldered her husband. "Come on, old man. Dance with your wife. It's been too long."

Mario offered no resistance, and the two were soon swaying and twirling in time with the reggae beat. The seemingly oldest of Desomond and Virginia's children, a girl of perhaps thirteen, looked up at Clark from beneath a mane of ebony hair. He took her hand, and she led him to a sandy spot in the yard where she set about teaching the rhythmless, former Green Beret how to dance island style.

Paulina met my gaze and tried to smile, then motioned toward the yard. "Come on. We don't want to miss out on all the fun."

We danced through four or five songs, all with the same island reggae feel as Bob Marley. The music penetrated our skin, leaving us all believing—if only for an evening—that inside, we were all islanders.

I glanced at my watch and immediately grabbed my phone. "Penny, I'm so sorry. I told you I'd call in an hour, but I got—"

"Relax," she said, "it's fine. It sounds like you may have your hands full anyway, and I'm getting ready for bed. There's no need for you to drive up here tonight. I'll call you tomorrow when I spy Cayo Hueso off the starboard bow."

"Thanks. I love you, Penny. Get some rest."

I had a feeling things were going to get interesting over the next couple of days, and she was going to end up right in the middle of it all.

Chapter 19
No Promises

I was standing on the Sunset Key dock when *Aegis* came into view from the southwest. Aloft were the bright white genoa and mainsail as well as the red, white, and blue stars and stripes. Although I've never worn a uniform, I feel a deep sense of devotion to that flag, and especially to the beliefs that first sent Betsy Ross's thirteen-star spangled banner up a pole over two hundred years ago.

The flag wasn't the only thing aboard that vessel I held dear. At the helm was the beautiful, feisty, and capable Penny Thomas. As the boat drew nearer, I could see her hair playing wildly on the midday breeze. It'd been less than four days since I'd last seen her, but the two weeks prior to our last reunion saw me thousands of miles away in Eastern Europe. To say the least, we were due for some time together. I doubted the coming days would grant us our due, but that didn't keep me from wanting it or from being overjoyed to see her.

Five hundred feet from the dock, the mainsail came down, landing gently atop the boom with the lazyjacks catching and flaking it into position. Seconds later, the diesels drew their first breath, and the genoa furled slowly around the forestay as Penny hauled in on the roller furling line. She laid the thirty-five-thousand-pound boat alongside the dock as if it were a dinghy.

I had taught her nothing about boats. She came to me already better versed in seamanship and possessing more skill at the helm than I'd ever learn. To say I was proud and thankful to have her in my life, and especially aboard my boat, would be an understatement of the highest magnitude.

I secured the mooring lines, and the engines fell silent. Penny climbed down from the helm station and leapt from the starboard hull and into my arms. We embraced and kissed as if one of us, or perhaps both, was a soldier home from war. Perhaps we were.

That's when the high-pitched yelp came crackling from the boat. Charlie, the puppy I'd bought for Penny on my way home from Russia, was squirming about and waiting impatiently for one of us to help him down from the boat. I reached up for the black ball of fur, and he leapt into my hands almost as enthusiastically as Penny had. He licked at the air and squirmed like a Tasmanian devil until I set him on the dock, where he sniffed at everything before finally coming to rest at Penny's feet.

She slid her hand into mine as we strolled toward the guest-house. "So, now that the reunion ceremony is over, let's hear it. What's up with the Righetti family?"

"I'm afraid that's a long story, but here are the highlights. Righetti is, as you know, the attorney for the D'Angelo family. When Clark and I found him yesterday morning, he was ready to put a bullet in his mouth. In fact, he tried to do just that, but we got him calmed down and unloaded. After some encouragement from us, he agreed to cooperate with us and the U.S. attorney to put an end to the D'Angelo crime family. But there's more. He also represents a guy named Loui Giordano."

Her eyebrows were drawn down tightly. "Who's he?"

"Believe it or not, he may be more important than the D'Ange-los. Good ol' Loui, as it turns out, is a contract killer who tried—unsuccessfully so far—to snuff out Clark and me. He's quite the fan of plastic explosives. He took out my airplane engine with a nicely placed shaped charge on the oil pan. Fortunately, we survived that one, and the plane is getting a new engine as we speak. Although, he probably wasn't directly responsible for the second explosion—"

Penny held up her hand. "Second explosion? How many were there?"

"Just two…so far."

"So far? Are you expecting more?"

"I don't really know what to expect next, but the good news is that Skipper has a surveillance team on Giordano now. Last time I spoke with her, he was in Panama City."

Penny was shaking her head. "And all of this is the result of us scaring the crap out of Salvatore?"

"Well, it started with Salvatore, but it keeps getting deeper."

"So how does that end up with you flying the whole Righetti family to Key West in a borrowed seaplane?"

"I made a gentleman's agreement with Mario."

"Who's Mario?"

"Mario Righetti. I agreed to keep him and his family safe if he'd agree to help me bring down the D'Angelo family."

She raised her eyebrows. "And he agreed to that?"

"Not at first," I said, "but after some convincing, he came around. Honestly, I think he's afraid for his family. His wife is Gloria, the daughter is Paulina, and the granddaughter is Marissa. She reminds me of a three-year-old version of you."

She laughed. "I hope that's a good thing."

"It's a very good thing."

"So, now that I'm up to speed on how everyone got here, what's next?"

I sighed. "That's the tricky part. I want to take the whole family to the Caymans."

"It should be simple on that seaplane. It looks like it could easily make that flight, even if you have to go around Cuba."

"Yeah, the Caravan could make the trip in a few hours, but that's the problem."

"Why is that a problem?"

"Because I need to buy some time before putting the Righetti family back on dry land."

Her eyes lit up. "Oh, so that's it. You want to take them to the Caymans aboard *Aegis* so nobody can get to them."

I bit at my lip, unsure how to proceed. "That's not exactly what I have in mind, but close. I actually want *you* to take them to the Caymans aboard *Aegis* while I go after Loui Giordano."

"That's a long cruise if I'm the only sailor on board."

I looked up at the guesthouse and then back at Penny. "I don't know if any of them can sail, but I thought I'd bring Skipper down to go with you, and I also plan to put a security team on board. It would be at least three well-trained, well-armed men."

"Are you sure that's safe for them?"

"What do you mean?"

She grinned. "Are you sure it's safe for three Clark-and-Chase wannabes to be subjected to a couple of hotties like Skipper and me for a week? They may kill each other fighting over us."

I gave her a playful shove. "Oh, you're funny. You think you're irresistible, huh?"

She flipped her hair and flirtatiously crossed her legs. "Whatever I am seems to work on you, and you're quite the catch."

Remembering what Cotton had said about his boss back in New Smyrna Beach, I said, "Speaking of irresistible, I found out Earl from the End has an admirer. I'll tell you all about it later, but for now, come on. I'll introduce you to the Righettis."

Before introductions were complete, Marissa had already climbed onto Penny's lap and begun telling her all about the party and playing with Desomond's children and how Clark had danced with a girl and how I had danced with her mother.

That earned me a hairy eyeball stare from Penny, to which I offered turned-up palms. "What can I say? I'm a catch."

Charlie saved me when he made his entrance, causing Marissa to forget about everything else in the world. Thankfully, it looked like Penny let the dancing comment go, but something told me she only tucked it away for future use.

I left Penny alone with Clark and the Righettis while I excused myself to make a call. "Hey, Skipper. It's Chase."

Her voice bearing none of the usual playfulness, she got straight to business. "I was about to call you. A lot is happening that you need to know about."

I sat in an Adirondack chair and listened as she laid out what she'd learned.

"First, Loui Giordano is on the move. He was in Tampa last night, and he's on his way to Miami now. The word on the street is that Antonio D'Angelo is missing and presumed to be cutting a deal with the FBI. The feds have no idea why the D'Angelos believe that, but they aren't doing anything to quiet the rumors. Antonio has vanished. I mean, dropped off the radar."

I interrupted her. "Dominic has Antonio in Miami. At least he was in Miami yesterday, but I doubt he's still there now. Dominic is too smart for that. I can't say for sure where he is today, but the point is, we have him."

"Geez, Chase. You've got to tell me these things. I've been hacking and racking my brain trying to find him, and you've got him in a box somewhere. You're not making this easy, you know."

"It all happened so fast. I should've told you. So, let me tell you what else I've done before you continue."

She scoffed. "Yeah. That's a pretty good idea."

"So, I have Mario Righetti, his wife, daughter, and granddaughter in Key West—well, Sunset Key to be precise. We're in Dominic's amphibious Caravan. I plan to have Penny take them to the Caymans with a security team...and you."

"Me? Why me?"

"Because you know how to sail, and with the satellite uplink on the boat, you can do anything from the water you can do from land."

"What satellite uplink?"

"The one you're going to buy and install when you come down."

"Whatever, but who is this security team you want to use?"

"I want you to arrange that, too. I'd like to use the same guys you put on surveillance in Bimini, if you can get them. If so, have them here as soon as possible, and I'd like you to be hot on their trail. By the way, where are you?"

"I'm on my way to Saint Marys, Georgia, to see Judge Hunt-singer's law clerks, Ben and Jeff. I need some face-to-face information from them, and then I'll be on my way to the Keys with your —I mean *my*—shiny new satellite uplink. You know, this would all be a lot easier if Clark would hurry up and finish teaching me to fly so I wouldn't have to rely on other people."

"Yeah, you're right. We'll make that a priority as soon as all of this is over."

"Is that all you have to tell me?"

I thought for a moment. "Yeah, that sums it up for now."

I heard her rustling some papers. "All right, so here's the deal. The D'Angelos are nervous, and they're already circling the wagons. They're gonna start running pretty soon if Righetti and Antonio don't turn up."

"You're right. I didn't think of that. See what you can do to get an assistant U.S. attorney to come with you."

She made a guttural sound. "Are you serious? You think I can get an assistant U.S. attorney on a sailboat with me and sail to the Cay-mans just to talk to Righetti?"

"Yeah, that's what I think. They'll jump at the chance. They'll need to make some arrests before the rats start fleeing the sinking ship."

"I'll try," she said. "But no promises."

"I suggest bringing it up to Judge Huntsinger and his clerks. They have connections. And it wouldn't hurt to bat your eyelashes and smile if the U.S. attorney happens to be a guy."

"Now, that's a good idea. I'll do that—the asking part, not the flirting part. So, to recap, you want the surveillance team from Bi-mini in Key West ASAP, and you want me and a U.S. attorney right behind them."

"Yes, that's right. And keep me posted on Loui Giordano's where-abouts. I'll see you here by tomorrow night."

"Ha! Tomorrow night, my ass. Maybe the day after tomorrow, but no promises."

Chapter 20
Better Than Sex

I briefed Clark on the plan, and he liked all of it except the part about bringing in a U. S. attorney.

"I don't know, man. What we're doing isn't exactly by the book. I'd rather not have the Justice Department aboard your boat and poking around in our business."

"We have to get them involved sooner or later," I argued.

He cocked his head and chewed on his cheek. "What if Righetti tells him about us yanking him and Antonio out of his office and threatening him and his family?"

I waggled my finger in the air. "We never actually threatened. We just asked Righetti to guess what color dress his granddaughter was wearing. That's not a threat. That's a playful game of pick a color any color."

"I don't know. It's slippery. This isn't the kind of thing we're supposed to be doing."

I locked eyes with him. "Then what are we supposed to be doing? We're stopping a dangerous and deadly enterprise that threatens the lives and welfare of many Americans. Isn't that what we do? Isn't that why we exist?"

He huffed. "Life's about perspective, I guess."

"You'd better believe it is. And I can prove it."

He furrowed his brow, obviously challenging me to prove it.

"There was a terrible head-on collision between two turtles. When the police officer showed up and questioned the snail who saw the whole thing, all the snail could say was, 'I can't really explain it. It all happened so fast.'"

"There's something deeply wrong with you, Chase. I'm pretty sure you need a vacation."

"I'm on vacation! Look around."

He shook his head. "Speaking of vacation, why don't you and Penny go to Key Wasted and have dinner and a few drinks? She'd like it, and it'd be good for you."

I started to look over his shoulder at the Righettis, but he took me by the shoulders and turned me around. "Don't worry about them. I'm a good babysitter. Just take your wife-to-be on a date."

"I never finished asking, and she never answered, so technically, she isn't my wife-to-be just yet."

"Oh, come on, man. Asking and answering are formalities. Even *I* am smart enough to know the two of you are joined at the hip, whether you asked or she answered. Now go have some fun. I'll hold down the fort."

Penny was on the floor playing with Marissa and Charlie when I walked through the family room of the guesthouse.

I plopped down beside Marissa and playfully pulled at her long curly hair. "Hey, I have a really big favor to ask. Can you do me a favor?"

She giggled, and her dark eyes went wide. "Sure, what is it?"

Miss Penny and I need to go somewhere for a little while. Can you look after Charlie while we're gone? He needs a lot of love and attention, and it's a very big job. Can you do it?"

Her already bright expression turned into pure glee. "Yeah! I can do that! He'll be safe with me." She leaned in close to my ear and whispered, "And if he poopies, I'll tell Mr. Clark."

I couldn't contain my laughter. "Yes, you do that, Marissa."

Penny rubbed Charlie's belly and looked up at me. "Where are we going?"

I held my nose. "First, you're going to shower. You smell like a sailor. And then we're going on a date."

She stood and placed her hands on her hips. "I happen to know you like girls who smell like sailors, and if that's your way of asking me on a date, then this is my way of saying yes." She tipped a pretend sailor hat and ran off down the hall.

Marissa curled her finger at me, motioning for me to come closer. Again, she whispered in my ear, "I think she likes you."

My jaw dropped open, and I stuck my hand to my chest. "You really think so?"

"Uh-huh. Do you like her, too?"

I nodded excitedly. "I really do."

The girl twirled around, incapable of containing her excitement. "Are you going to get married and have babies?"

Bashfully, I answered, "Maybe."

Penny was back in no time, looking as if she'd taken two hours. "I love how you do that."

She twirled about, much like Marissa. "Do what?"

"Look so amazing in fifteen minutes."

She curtsied. "Thank you, but I looked amazing before I showered. Now I happen to look clean *and* amazing." She leaned down to pet Charlie. "You be a good boy for Marissa, and we'll be back soon." She turned to the girl. "Thank you so much for babysitting Charlie. I'll bring you back something really special."

Her eyes lit up again. "Really?"

Penny hugged her. "Yeah, really."

* * *

I lowered *Aegis's* dinghy from the davits mounted on the stern and watched it settle into the water. We climbed aboard and started the engine before disconnecting the rigid hull inflatable boat from the davit lines. Just as Earl promised, the engine started at the first touch of the key, and we were headed away from Sunset Key and toward Key West.

Approaching the Key West Bight was like Christmas morning. I loved almost everything about the island, from the music and food to the just-don't-hurt-anybody way of life. As long as you didn't intentionally do anything to harm anyone else, there were almost no rules.

Tourism is the only real industry on the southernmost outpost of the continental U.S., but there was a well-defined divide between the tourists and the locals. The inhabitants of the island call themselves Conchs, and refer to the island as the Conch Republic. In fact, on April 23, 1982, the City of Key West seceded from the United States after the Border Patrol set up a roadblock at the northern end of the chain of islands, terribly disrupting traffic flow for both tourists and locals. Immediately following the secession, the Conch Republic declared war on the United States and symbolically broke a loaf of stale Cuban bread over the head of a man dressed in a U.S. Naval uniform. One minute later, the officials of the island surrendered to the man in uniform and demanded one billion dollars in foreign aid. The money never showed up, but the legend remains, and the publicity sent a tourist boom to the Keys that more than made up for the failure of the U.S. government to write that check.

We motored up to the dock near Schooner Wharf Bar and tied our painter into the mess of lines from other small boats practically piled on top of each other. Cruisers and full-time live-aboard boaters used their dinghies to transport everything from laundry to liquor, to and from the island and their boats. There's an unwritten and wildly obeyed rule about never messing with another boater's dinghy. My RHIB was one of the nicer boats in the nest of tenders, but I knew that even the rattiest, barely floating vessel would receive the same respect as my shiny new craft.

We climbed onto the dock, then headed for a plastic table and chair beneath a colorful beach umbrella in the gravel-covered main dining area of the bar. Michael McCloud was playing guitar and singing the Key West national anthem, "Conch Republic Song," with his trusty—and lazy—dog sound asleep only a few feet away. It wasn't long before margaritas and seared tuna nachos landed on our table. We sang along with Michael, a Key West musical icon, as he picked and belted out the words to "Chasing the Wind," a song about a sailor who'd rather be sailing to nowhere than doing anything else on land. Two margaritas later, we tipped Michael, a self-professed alcohol-powered jukebox, and strolled off toward Duval Street.

The last time I was in Key West, I was holding a very different hand. Anya and I had cut a swath through the city, leaving a trail of bodies in our wake, as we did whatever was necessary to find and rescue Skipper. But I didn't want to think about that. I wanted to enjoy being with Penny, the woman who was so much more than the Russian, and also so much less: less spy, less double agent, less assassin, and less deadly to me and everyone around her. I don't know if I loved her more for what she was than what she wasn't, but I knew without a doubt that hers was the hand I wanted to hold every time I was in Key West—or any other place on Earth.

We watched an artist in the window of a gallery painting a giant yellow and green pineapple on a canvas as large as a door. The artist was young, beautiful, and covered head-to-toe in thick globs of dried oil paint from years of honing her craft. It was fascinating to watch her work and see her creation come to life. A part of me envied her. The work she did produced a tangible result of significant value. My work was nothing like that. It was my job to keep my work hidden from everyone, regardless of its value to humanity. Maybe life as a painter in a window on Duval Street is the pinnacle of human evolution, or maybe I was too much philosopher and not enough spy. Only time would tell.

The hordes of people walking, crawling, and cycling their way up and down Duvall made the city look like an indescribable parade of characters. Missionaries and drag queens walked the same sidewalk, neither condemning the other, and both knowing they were welcome in the country's southernmost collection of freaks.

I decided to take Penny to Blue Heaven for dinner, the restaurant I'd thought Desomond had selected the night before. I'd been wrong about the Rastafarian's selection, but Penny made certain I knew I'd made the perfect choice this time. There was a three-piece band playing behind a girl of perhaps twenty-five, who looked like Joan Jett but sounded like Carol King. A family of chickens strutted in front of the stage, pecking at the ground, oblivious to the action around them. The band was spectacular, almost studio quality, and the lead singer was three decades and a half too late. She would've fit right in at Woodstock and San Francisco in the sixties.

We ate, drank, laughed, and even danced for two hours under the shade of the banyan trees and oaks. While we were slow dancing to "Big Yellow Taxi," Penny said, "So, I hear I'm not the first pretty girl you've danced with on this trip."

I hoped she was busting my chops, but I couldn't be sure. My terrified male instinct kicked in, and I began my defense. "It was just a dance at a yard party with jerk chicken and two dozen people. I wasn't—"

She pressed her fingers to my lips. "Relax, Secret Agent Man. I'm just busting your chops. If I'm so insecure that I can't handle you dancing with an Italian goddess while I'm toiling away at sea, then I'm not the girl for you."

I pulled her to me and kissed her with sincerity beyond words. "You're definitely the girl for me, Penny Thomas. I wouldn't trade you for Christie Brinkley. Well, that may be pushing it, but you know what I mean."

She stomped my toe. "Let's see Christie Brinkley bring *Aegis* all the way from Saint Augustine to Key West by herself."

I couldn't let it end. "You make an excellent point, my dear. Do you think Christie would let me watch her do that?"

"Keep it up, big boy, and you'll be looking for somebody who'll let you watch. I'm a commodity, baby. Chicks like me are hard to come by."

I took her face in my hands and stared into her eyes. "You are, indeed, one-of-a-kind, and I couldn't ask for anything more."

She pulled away and made a face I couldn't quite interpret. It was a cross between an awkward attempt at being sexy while trying to appear stern and demanding.

When she spoke, the mystery of the facial expression vanished. "*Spasibo, Amerikanets. YA lyublyu tebya.*"

I took her face in my hands. "Ah, your Russian is improving, but a beautiful Texas girl could never pull off the angry Russian look. It's in their DNA, and your Southern genes are a lot sexier anyway."

She twirled about, showing me her butt. "Well, thank you, Georgia Boy. My jeans are Levi's, and I'm glad you approve."

I took her hand and motioned toward the street. "Let's get out of here. I know a place you're going to love."

We strolled hand-in-hand down the sidewalk until we came to my destination.

Penny smirked at the sign. "Better Than Sex? Whoever named this place—whatever it is—has obviously never taken a ride on the Chase Fulton Express."

"Thank you, but you may change your mind once we get inside. I promise you've never experienced anything like this."

An hour later, we walked out of the finest dessert restaurant on Earth, bellies bulging, and still licking chocolate from our lips.

"Still disagree with the name?"

With her pinky, Penny wiped a smear of chocolate from the corner of my mouth, then seductively sucked the rich sauce from her finger. "I spoke too quickly. It's better than sex with *most* people."

Chapter 21
Duty Calls

As much as I wanted our evening in Key West never to end, duty called. More specifically, it was Skipper who called, and I had no choice except to answer.

"Hey, Skipper. What's up?"

"In case you didn't already know this, I'm the second-best operational analyst you know."

I laughed. "The only analysts I know are you and Ginger, so I'd have to say you're right."

"I've got some great news and some not-so-great news. The great news is I'm having dinner with Chris Kaminski in like ten minutes."

"Who's Chris Kaminski?"

She huffed. "If you'll shut up and listen, I'll tell you. And try to hold your questions until the end. I'll probably answer them in my briefing without you having to interrupt me."

I didn't say a word, and she apparently approved.

"Now, Chris Kaminski is the U.S. assistant district attorney from the Southern District of Florida, and based on Judge Huntsinger's call and a few teasers I dangled in front of him, I think he's all in. I'll know for sure after dinner, but I'm pretty positive he'll be coming with me to Key West tomorrow morning. The next news is that you were right about Judge Huntsinger. He's way cool, by the way, and Jeff and Ben are too easy. I had them eating out of my hand in minutes. They've been stuck out there in Saint Marys too long without anyone like me to entertain them."

I'd been silent as long as I could stand. "How's Tony going to feel about you 'entertaining' two bright, young lawyers when he's not around?"

Her tone became solemn. "That's another story for another day. Anyway, it turns out they had a lot more files than the one you got from them, and sweet-little-ol'-me talked them out of thirty pounds of documents. Well, copies of documents. They kept the originals, of course. Your buddy, the judge, was awesome, but I didn't know how much I was allowed to tell him, so I promised you'd call and fill him in as soon as you could. Is that okay?"

"That's perfect, Skipper. What about Giordano?"

"That's the not-so-great news."

I growled, "Don't tell me you lost him!"

"Oh, no! Nothing like that. We're still on him, and he's in Miami. The problem is that now there's a contract out on Antonio D'Angelo, the entire Righetti family, and you, Chase. Giordano plans to collect the bounty."

"That's not so bad. I knew Giordano was after me, and I figured he'd be dispatched to at least kidnap Righetti's family to use as bargaining chips. I expected this. What else have you got?"

She let out a sigh of relief. "That's it for now. I'll call you after my dinner with Chris, and I'll see you tomorrow. Oh, I almost forgot. The surveillance team is en route now and should be there in the morning. I gave them your cell number. I hope that's all right."

"That's more than all right, Skipper. You're the best. There's no need to call again tonight unless the attorney says he's not coming. Otherwise, get him down here ASAP."

"You got it."

Penny had been standing a few paces away, pretending not to listen to my conversation, but doing a poor job. "That was Skipper, right?"

"Yes, it was."

She raised her eyebrows in obvious expectation of more than a simple yes, so I gave in. "It's good news," I said. "She's having dinner with the U.S. attorney from the Southern District of Florida now, and she has a huge stack of files on the D'Angelos that she scored from Ben and Jeff, Judge Huntsinger's clerks out on Saint Marys."

"There's more you're not telling me."

How does she do that?

"Yeah, but I expected it, so it's nothing to worry about."

She cocked her head, and this time, her look was not an attempt at a Russian expression. "Chase, we've already been through too much together for you to be keeping the truth from me. Now let's hear it."

"It's Giordano," I said. "The D'Angelos have put out a hit on the Righettis—and on me—but that's not news. That's why I need to get the Righettis on a slow boat to anywhere. They're practically untouchable and unfindable at sea."

She sat on my lap and pinched my cheek. "See, that wasn't so hard now, was it?"

"I just have this instinct to protect you."

"Yes, and I appreciate that, but I'm right in the middle of this now, so I need to know what's going on. Don't you agree?"

I held her tightly against my chest. "Yes, of course I agree. I've just got a lot of mixed emotions about including you in stuff like this."

She took my hand, and we headed north, back toward Schooner Wharf and our RHIB. "You're not putting me in anything. I volunteered, remember? And besides, you're putting a team of well-trained, highly-armed security guards on the boat with us. It's not like I'm going to be shooting it out with the bad guys at the O.K. Corral."

"As always, you're right. When all of this is over, I promise—"

She stuck her fingers to my lips. "Don't make promises. When this is over, it'll be something else, and then after that, another mission will come up. I understand, and I'm okay with it."

I pulled her finger away from my lips. "No, that's not how it's going to be. I'm done, at least for a while, and when this is over, I'm taking some time for me...for us. I owe that to you and myself."

"You know that's not going to happen, Chase."

I shrugged. "We'll see."

* * *

Back on Sunset Key, I briefed Clark on the conversation with Skipper.

"That girl is something else, Chase. She's going to be a good one."

"Yeah, she's already a good one, and she keeps getting better. So how did it go here tonight?"

Clark looked around and then leaned in. "Honestly, I think Righetti is so relieved that all of the bullshit in Miami is about to be over, that he's enjoying himself for the first time in a long time."

I looked over my shoulder, concerned someone might be listening. "Are you sure it's not an act to get us to lower our guard?"

"No, I don't think so. I believe he's glad it's over and that he won't be going to prison."

"We can't make him that promise. I told him I could keep his family safe, and I will, but it'll be up to the Justice Department to cut him a deal that keeps him out of prison."

Clark ran his hand through his hair and exhaled. "You're right, but Righetti is counting on you to keep him out of prison, even though he's the lawyer. He knows how this stuff works." He paused and shook his watch down his wrist, checking the time. "Hey, I'm beat. I'm going to hit the sack. But how was date night?"

"I really needed that. Thanks, man. I owe you one."

"Hell, you owe me more than one. Good night, College Boy. I'll see you in the morning. Oh, I bribed the ferry captain to fake a mechanical failure and call one of us if the Righettis try to leave the island."

"Great call. Now, go get some beauty sleep. You could use it."

* * *

The Righetti women aren't as efficient as Penny when it comes to getting ready to go. It was almost nine o'clock before we left the guesthouse for breakfast at Latitudes, Sunset Key's only restaurant.

The seven of us sat at a pair of tables the hostess was kind enough to push together, and breakfast was a feast by any definition of the word. We were served a family-style buffet at our table, and everyone ate as if they hadn't seen a meal in days.

Twenty minutes into breakfast, a solid black cigarette boat of perhaps fifty feet pulled alongside the dock in front of *Aegis*, and the surveillance team that would be our bodyguards climbed onto the dock.

I folded my napkin, laid it beside my plate, and stood. "Excuse me for a minute. There are some people I need to talk with outside. I'll be right back."

Clark watched with the tactical curiosity he carries so well and smirked when he saw Clay, Kurt, and Tuck. Penny leaned toward Clark with inquisition in her eye, and Clark set her mind at ease.

"Gentlemen, it's good to see you again. How was the crossing?"

Clay stuck out his hand. "Not too bad, but this boat doesn't really qualify as a pleasure craft. It's a lot of work—even in good conditions."

I shook his offered hand. "That's because the mast is missing. Where do you put the sails?"

Tuck and Kurt laughed and stretched, both obviously glad to be off the boat.

I pointed at the restaurant. "Have you guys eaten?"

"We had a bite earlier," Clay said, "but I could go for a little something." He started toward the restaurant.

I placed my hand on his chest, stopping his progress toward the restaurant. "Let me give you guys a mission brief before we go in. Inside, you're going to meet Mario Righetti and Penny Thomas. You already know Mario's wife, Gloria, and his daughter and granddaughter, Paulina and Marissa."

I pointed toward *Aegis*. "That's my boat and your home for the next week or so. Penny is the captain, and a young operations analyst named Elizabeth will be the first mate. You'll be escorting the Righettis to the Caymans. I don't anticipate any issues since a sailboat in the middle of the ocean is a pretty good hiding place, but I want your team on board because we all know how quickly things can turn ugly when you start messing with people's money and freedom."

Clay was the first to speak up. "This sounds like easy money to me. What's the catch?"

"There's no catch, but the captain and first mate happen to be my fiancée and little sister."

Tuck interrupted. "You're marrying your sister? That's pretty weird, man. Even for a dude from Georgia."

"Oh, you're funny. Clay, shoot him as soon as you get a chance, please. There's an extra ten grand in it for you if he suffers."

Clay made a pistol with his fingers and pointed it at Tuck. "You got it, boss. One in the knee, and one in the gut. No problem."

I continued. "There's one more person who'll be coming along for the ride, hopefully. He's an assistant U.S. attorney out of Miami, and he'll be interviewing Righetti and building a case against the D'Angelo family."

Kurt slapped Clay on the shoulder and spoke up for the first time. "I knew it! I told you that's what this is about. You owe me twenty bucks."

Ignoring their banter, I asked, "Have any of you ever dealt with a guy named Loui Giordano?"

The three men looked skyward, searching their memories.

"I know that name for some reason," Kurt said, "but I can't place it."

I said, "He's a contract killer who's accepted a contract on the Righettis and me. I'm pretty sure he was behind the switcheroo in Bimini that ended up with a dead guy on the dock. That dead guy planted C4 in an extra suitcase that made its way aboard our Caravan. I got it outside the plane before the clock struck midnight and turned us all into pumpkins, but they might believe the bomb took out the plane, so that could buy us a couple of days before they start actively chasing us."

I could see Clay's wheels turning. "What's on your mind, Clay?"

He cleared his throat. "I'm just wondering.... What are you going to do while we're babysitting the lawyers and ladies on that big
fine boat of yours?"

"Clark and I are going after Giordano. We've got some scores to
settle. He tried to take us out once directly and then again by ordering the explosive suitcase plant. I'd like to have a chat with him
about those events."

The three men all nodded their understanding.

"All right. Let's go meet some new folks and have some proper
breakfast. When Skipper arrives with the attorney, we'll finalize the
plan and get you underway."

All three men turned to me with looks of confusion.

"Who's Skipper?" Tuck asked.

"She's my sister, but that's what I call her. Trust me—she'll like it
much better if you call her Elizabeth."

Chapter 22
Another Day at the Office

As we walked from the dock toward Latitudes Restaurant, the ferry was arriving from Key West. I hoped I'd see Skipper and U.S. Attorney Chris Kaminsky on board. I wasn't disappointed. Before the ferry came to a stop, Skipper had already leapt to the dock and began trotting toward me.

The security team, being the sharp-eyed professionals and red-blooded American men they were, noticed her as well. She was wearing khaki shorts with the cuffs rolled up, making her super-model legs look even longer, and a PFG button-up shirt with the lower half tied in a knot, exposing her sculpted stomach and new-found tan. She was no longer the gangly, awkward teenager I'd met years before in Athens, Georgia. She'd become not only a beautiful woman but also one of the best new operational and intelligence analysts in the business. But it wasn't her skill as an analyst that had the security team gawking over her. She skipped up the dock and threw her arms around me.

I returned the hug and began introductions. "Guys, this is the analyst—and my sister—Elizabeth. And this is Tuck, Clay, and Kurt. They're the security contingent for the op."

Hands were shaken, and the gawking continued.

She noticed and pulled a classic Skipper maneuver, turning to me and saying, "Oh, by the way, Chase. Thanks for what you did to get that weird guy off my back. He really creeped me out. They said he's going to—pretty much—be okay after he gets out of the hospital, but it's safe to say you made sure he won't be messing with me again."

I rolled my eyes. "Nobody messes with my baby sis. I'm glad I could help."

Her act seemed to throw a wet blanket over the security team's interest—at least temporarily. A week on a sailboat could result in short-term memory loss for the knuckle-draggers, but I was confident Skipper could hold her own, especially with Penny to back her up.

I peered over her shoulder toward the ferry. "Please tell me you brought the attorney."

She twirled around and pointed toward the boat. "Oh, yeah, he's coming. He gets nervous on boats, but we'll get him over that. He's also a bit strange, but definitely interested in what we're offering. This might be a pretty nice notch in his belt."

"I'm sure you're right. I need to talk with him alone before we meet the Righettis. Take these guys up to the restaurant for some breakfast. Clark's inside. He'll introduce you around. I'll chat with Kaminsky and be right behind you."

With the wave of her hand, Skipper urged the men to follow her. "Come on, guys. Let's eat."

There was no question who the assistant U.S. district attorney was. He was the only occupant of the ferry with a briefcase and a seasick look from the quarter-mile ferry ride. He had that Jersey-boy look, sort of like a modern-day Frankie Valli. I half expected him to break into a roaring version of "Sherry Baby."

I stuck out my hand. "You must be Mr. Kaminsky. I'm Chase Fulton."

The prosecutor looked down at his right hand and then stuck it in mine. "Hello, Mr. Fulton. Christopher Kaminsky with the U.S. Attorney's office from the Southern District of Florida. It's a pleasure to meet you."

"Likewise, but please call me Chase. We need to have a chat before we go inside." I took his elbow and led him toward a bench.

"Let's take a seat over here. Are you okay? Do you need some water or something?"

He wiped at his brow. "No, no. I'm fine. Thank you. It's just that I don't love boats."

"I'm sorry to hear that. That means the next week of your life is going to suck." I pointed toward *Aegis*. "That'll be your home for as long as it takes the wind to blow you to the Cayman Islands."

His Adam's apple rose and fell as he swallowed hard. "Oh, um, Ms. Woodley said we'd be cruising, but I thought she meant on a much bigger boat—like a cruise ship or something."

"Relax, Mr. Kaminsky. You'll do fine. She's a sturdy, well-equipped boat, and you're in very good hands. The captain is one of the best I've ever seen."

"Oh, well, that's good to hear. I guess I'm looking forward to meeting him."

"You'll meet *her* in just a few minutes, but first we have a few things to discuss."

"Oh, her, you say. Well, okay. I guess."

I laughed. "Relax. You'll be fine. So, here's the deal. Your boss wants the D'Angelo family, and you want your boss's job. I'm going to help both of you get what you want."

"Just inside those restaurant doors, I have Mario Righetti, the D'Angelo's attorney for over thirty years, and he's ready to spill his guts."

Kaminsky's face began to twitch involuntarily, and he ran his finger beneath his nose as if his upper lip were suddenly on fire. "I'm sure he wants immunity from prosecution, a new name, and a ticket into the Witness Protection Program."

"Nope. All he wants is the immunity part. I'll take care of the rest."

He eyed me suspiciously. "What do you mean, you'll take care of the rest? Exactly for whom do you work, Mr. Fulton?"

I smirked. "I work for the good citizens of the United States, just like you, Mr. Kaminsky. Just like you."

His suspicion wasn't quashed, but he was listening, so that was a start.

I started my pitch. "Here's what's going to happen. I'm going to put you on that boat with the entire Righetti family, a three-man security team, the best sailboat captain I know, and her first mate. You'll have several days to get Righetti's story out of him. If you threaten him, he'll clam up, and you'll get nothing. Strong-arming isn't going to work. He wants to talk. He's ready to put the bad old days behind him and spend what's left of his life somewhere nice and quiet with his family. That's his motivation."

He frowned. "I'm not sure what you think the U.S. Attorney's office is, Mr. Fulton, but we are not your puppets. You don't get to dictate how we conduct our investigations or what arrangements we make with witnesses and criminals. It doesn't matter who you work for, that's not how this works."

I looked at my watch and pointed toward the ferry. "That ferry is leaving in less than a minute. Get on it, or don't. I don't care. But we're done. I obviously misunderstood. I thought you were in the business of putting mobsters in prison, but you're clearly in the business of pissing on people who drop career-making gifts in your lap. I'm sorry you wasted my time. If you need bus fare back to Miami, you can sell that briefcase and those fancy shoes back on Key West."

I half-jogged up the ramp toward the restaurant, counting my strides as I went. I misjudged Kaminsky. I'd expected to get at least twelve strides away before he yelled at me to come back.

He passed me and grabbed my arm on the sixth stride. "Look, Mr. Fulton…Chase. I apologize. This is an extremely unorthodox situation, and I've never found myself in quite an ordeal as this. I want the D'Angelo family, and I'm willing to give Righetti immunity if his testimony is enough to bring down the family, but I can't blindly go off on some boat with—"

I punched the inside of his wrist, knocking his hand from my bicep. "I don't know what kind of men you deal with in Miami, but if you ever put your hands on me again—for any reason—I will crush you. Now get your ass on that ferry, and I'll find a prosecutor who wants this case. You clearly do not." I shoved my way past him, surprised at how solidly built he was beneath his sport coat and five-hundred-dollar haircut. Two steps away, I turned and locked eyes with him. "Righetti isn't the only big fish I caught. I have Antonio D'Angelo, too. Enjoy your trip back to Miami, Mr. Kaminsky."

The look on Christopher Kaminsky's face told me everything I needed to know about him.

"You have Antonio?"

"I do."

"Where?"

"I'll tell you in the Caymans. Now, on which boat are you leaving this island? Mine or the ferry?"

His shoulders slumped, and he exhaled every cubic inch of air he had in his lungs. "Fine. Righetti gets immunity, and I get Antonio."

I stuck out my hand. "Deal, but it happens in that order."

* * *

Introductions were made, and as I'd expected, Chris wasn't exactly the social butterfly. I wondered how much a thirty-something U.S. attorney and a sixty-something former mob lawyer would have in common. The psychologist in me would've loved to be a fly on *Aegis*'s bulkhead for the next week to listen and analyze the conversation.

When the breakfast spread had finally been depleted, it was time to set sail and establish a few more standards of behavior. Aboard *Aegis*, I stood silently while Captain Penny gave her briefing.

"I'm Penny Thomas, and as the lawyers already know, I am the law aboard this boat for the next several days until we disembark in the Caymans. I will make all decisions, and I'll be uniquely responsible for the results of those decisions. Welcome aboard *Aegis*. She's a magnificent boat and will be our home for approximately a week. Make yourselves at home. Enjoy the boat, and I'll be providing additional information about the boat and the journey as we go. With only a few exceptions, either Elizabeth or I will be at the controls throughout the trip. When she is at the helm, she has the same responsibility and authority as me, and I expect you to treat her appropriately. We're both well-qualified and experienced sailors, so you're in good hands. Leave us alone when we look busy, and feel free to interact with us when we don't. We're going to feed you well, and we expect some of you to do a few small tasks while aboard, but other than that, it should be an extremely relaxing cruise."

I took Penny below to our cabin. "Thank you for doing this. I know it isn't what you signed up for, but you have no idea what a difference you're making. I don't know what I'd do without you."

She smirked. "I know exactly what you'd do without me.... Blonde Russian girls."

"I've developed a taste for one particular Texas girl, and that's where I'll stay."

She placed her hands on her hips. "That's where you'd better stay, 'cause if you dump me, I'm taking the boat...and Skipper."

Hiding my smile was impossible. "I'll see you in Georgetown in a few days. You know where the satellite phone is. If you don't mind, check in at least once a day so I know how and where you are. If the weather permits, five or six days at sea would be perfect. That'll give me time to find and deal with Giordano."

"By deal with, do you mean kill him?"

"No, not necessarily. I have something more creative in mind."

She ran her fingers through my hair. "I love when you get creative. Promise you'll tell me all about it."

I kissed her passionately and held her perfect face in my hands. "I've never been one to make promises, but with you, all that's changing. If my plan works out, you'll be involved. And I'm sure you'll like this one."

She slapped me on the butt. "Get off my boat. I've got work to do."

I pulled Clay aside before stepping back to the dock. "Listen, I'd prefer you not shoot anybody if you can avoid it, but if it's necessary, keep each of these people alive by whatever means you deem appropriate."

He leaned in. "Do you anticipate any attempts at boarding?"

"I have no reason to think that'll happen, but you're trained to repel boarders if it does, right?"

"Yes, of course. No one will come aboard after we leave this dock unless the skipper or…Skipper says so. Oh, boy. That's going to get confusing."

"That's part of the reason you should call her Elizabeth, and Penny, the captain."

He offered his hand, and I shook it firmly. "Don't worry, Chase. We can take care of whatever comes up. I'll check in with you daily, and I'm sure you gave Captain Penny the same instructions."

His professionalism made me feel good about my choice, even though the Brinkwater team would've been a little more hard-core.

The mainsail started its slow ascent up the mast, followed immediately by the genoa unfurling and filling with the midday breeze. I envied the voyage, but not the minutia of the interaction of the attorneys. Soon, *Aegis*'s billowing white sails disappeared across the horizon, and Clark and I, like so many times before, were left to do the dirty work few had the stomach to endure. For us, it would be another day at the office.

Chapter 23
Take Me to Your Leader

Clark looked at his watch. "Well, look what time it is. It's let's-go-catch-a-hitman thirty. We're late."

Operating with Clark had become where I felt most at home. Each of us knew, without question, what the other would do in almost every situation. We'd fought side by side, back-to-back, and into and out of situations neither of us would've survived without the other. When the bullets started flying, we almost functioned as a single entity.

I checked my pretend watch. "You know how much I hate being late."

Ten minutes later, we'd secured our gear from the guesthouse and had the twenty-eight hundred horsepower of the cigarette boat breathing fire. In spite of the absolute necessity of finding Loui Giordano, the temptation of opening the throttles on the offshore race boat was too powerful to overcome. We pulled on helmets and plugged in the coms.

Clark's voice came alive inside my helmet. "I've got the throttles. You're on the steering."

The wheel felt as if it had been molded precisely for my grip. The raw power of the four V8 engines spooling up behind us doubled my heart rate. The bow of the boat rose like a rearing steed in an old Western movie but soon sank back into place as the enormous boat rose onto plane. The horizon became a vibrating blur in the distance, and the surface of the ocean seemed to vaporize into spray.

As if he sensed my burning desire to glance down at the speed-ometer, Clark said, "Passing ninety...one hundred...one ten...one thirteen."

Flying an airplane at twice that speed is typically quiet, comfort-able, and so docile I can take my hands completely off the controls with no fear of anything dramatic occurring. The thought of even loosening my death grip on the wheel of the cigarette boat was be-yond terrifying. At that speed, a gust of wind beneath the bow would send us tumbling like a gymnast across the surface of the ocean. We held the speed for several minutes until a blur of white came into view off the port bow. From my perspective, it looked like a snowball careening through the air toward me. We blasted by the object so fast it was impossible to determine what it was.

With my teeth rattling in my head, I called out, "Down... down...down," and Clark slowly reduced the throttles, decelerating the missile back to a manageable speed of thirty knots. The noise from the engines was still powerful, but the slightly choppy water was no longer pounding mercilessly against the hull.

I called for Clark to close the throttles, and he brought the boat to a drift.

"Let's trade seats," I said, disconnecting my helmet from the coms.

Clark offered no resistance. Situated, strapped in, and recon-nected to the coms, I peered through the windscreen to see *Aegis*, under full glorious sail, trekking toward us at a dozen knots, with Penny and Skipper waving and grinning as they passed. The blurry snowball was my boat. That was the second time in three days I'd flown past *Aegis*. The most recent flyby, however, was at a much lower altitude.

"All right, College Boy. Bring 'em up."

I slowly opened the throttles, once again feeling the massive en-gines a few feet behind us howl. Just as before, the bow came up but soon disappeared as I kept pushing the throttles forward. The bone-jarring vibration returned as the speed increased.

"Eighty…ninety…one hundred…one ten."

Although I trusted Clark more than any man on the planet, I felt helpless without a steering wheel in front of me. I watched the speed hit one hundred sixteen knots, and called out, "Steady at one twelve."

A green and brown mass appeared through the windscreen, and Clark called, "Down…down…down."

I backed off the throttles and slowed to forty knots as we motored through the main channel by Mallory Square and into Key West Bight. When we pulled into the slip near the harbor master's office, Clark tapped at the GPS, bringing up the navigation history.

When his speed of one hundred sixteen knots appeared at the top of the screen, he did that looking-over-the-sunglasses thing he loves to do. "That's what I thought, loser."

I held up four fingers. "I deducted the four-knot tailwind you had, so technically, you're the loser."

We paid in advance for a slip for three weeks, just in case things didn't go as planned, and things rarely go as planned in my line of work.

The Caravan was where we'd left her on the ramp at Key West International Airport. I paid the parking fees, and we were soon climbing out over the turquoise waters of the Atlantic…or perhaps the Caribbean. I've never been certain where one ends and the other begins.

Clark had surrendered the left seat to me, making me the pilot in command, at least until we made our splashdown. When we arrived off the coast of Miami, a pair of cruise ships were steaming away from the dock, so we had to do some offshore holding to allow them time to clear.

Clark pointed down the channel with his open hand. "Now that the ships are off our runway, fly your approach like we did in Key West. Hold the floats off the water, keeping the nose barely above the horizon."

I followed his instruction, and the Caravan obeyed flawlessly.

"That's it. Just keep letting the speed bleed off. Hold this attitude, and let her settle in."

I felt the floats kiss the water's surface, and we immediately began to decelerate.

"Keep the nose up...up...up as she settles in. Well done. Not bad for your first water landing. There may be hope for you, yet."

Clark took the controls and taxied us up the ramp to the parking apron at the Miami Seaplane Base. We tipped the attendant to wash off the salt water from the plane and refuel her.

"I wouldn't mind owning a seaplane," I said. "It might come in handy."

Clark motioned toward the Caravan. "Dad's is right there. I'm sure you're welcome to it anytime you need or want it. He doesn't fly enough these days to justify owning it. Of course, we'll have to get your seaplane ticket, but that should only take two or three days. You can knock that out in a weekend if nobody sends us off to save the world again."

"Would your dad consider selling this one to me?"

"It never hurts to ask, but you could always throw a set of floats on the One-Eighty-Two. It wouldn't have the range or useful load of this one, but it would be a lot less expensive to run and maintain."

"That's not a bad idea. We can talk about that later."

I dialed the guys who were tailing Giordano. I needed to know where he was and where he might've been headed.

A coarse voice came on the line. "Garret."

"This is Chase. I hear you're keeping an eye on a young man who has his sights on me."

"Hang on a minute. Let me step outside."

There was an audible click on the line and then silence for several seconds. I knew Garret wasn't stepping outside. He was calling Skipper to check me out, and I appreciated his caution.

"Okay, I can talk now," he said.

"So, I checked out, then?"

"Yeah, you did. Here's the skinny. Your boy is slippery, but we're not easy to shake. I first thought we'd been made, but I changed my mind. This guy is serious about not being watched. He runs SDRs every day."

Surveillance detection routes are old-school spy tradecraft designed to determine if an operator is being followed. The technique was perfected during the Cold War when Russian and American operatives played continual cat-and-mouse games with each other.

"Could he be agency trained?"

"No," Garret said. "He doesn't move like a spook. He's probably just read a few spy novels and figured out how to spot a tail. My team, on the other hand, has a nasty pedigree in counterespionage and countersurveillance. We don't get busted much."

"That's good to know," I said. "Now, down to brass tacks. Where's our target?"

"He's right here in Miami. The same place you are."

This guy is good.

"Where in Miami?"

"He's camped out in a big house in South Beach about seven blocks off the water. They shoot pornos and music videos there, so there's always a bunch of people coming and going. It's easy to hide out in a place like that. Everybody blends in, you know?"

A lump formed in my throat. "Yeah, I know what you mean, and I know the house. I have a history with it."

"Oh yeah? What kind of history do you have with a porn set?"

"It's a long story, but I know the place. Have you got an extra set of wheels you can send to pick us up?"

Garret paused for several seconds. "Who's *us*?"

"My partner and me."

"Hang on."

Another click on the line, and another long silence. "I'll be there in fifteen minutes. You're at the seaplane base, right?"

"That's right."

* * *

Garret's inconspicuous ride turned out to be practically invisible. It was a two-year-old Jeep Cherokee that looked like every other Jeep Cherokee manufactured by the hundreds of thousands over the past decade. It was a brown paper bag in a stack of brown paper bags.

We pulled to a stop a block and a half south of the house I'd rescued Skipper from two years before, and where Anya was shot in the back during the egress. I replayed the events a thousand times in my mind, my stomach growing sicker with every scene. The contents of my stomach rose into my mouth as I watched the film roll through my mind: blood flying from Anya's shoulder, and her limp form tumbling to the marble floor. I could smell her blood as I'd carried her from the house in a sprint, my ears ringing from the two dozen pistol shots that were fired in the upstairs bathroom and hallway. I could replay every gunfight of my life with flawless detail, but none was as vivid and agonizing as that one.

Fingers snapped in front of my face. "Hey, James Bond. Pay attention."

"I'm sorry. I was thinking about the last time I was here."

"Yeah? I'd like to hear that story sometime."

"No, you wouldn't."

"All right. So, here's what I think is going on. Giordano is looking for Antonio D'Angelo. Word on the street is that the feds have got him and the lawyer, Righetti, but I'm not so sure. My contacts at the bureau aren't saying a word, and that's rare. I think you've got 'em both."

Every time Garret opened his mouth, I was more impressed, but I wasn't going to show him my hand just yet. "What makes you think I'd have either of them?"

"Nothing else makes sense. The lawyer may have run off and taken his family with him, but that's not likely. Antonio wouldn't go to the feds for any amount of money or immunity. It's not in his blood. That leaves only one other option. Somebody's got both of 'em, and the most likely candidate is you, Mr. Bond."

"Stop calling me that," I said, hoping to change the subject.

"That's what I call all the spies I know. And before you say you're not a spy, just save it. So, have you got 'em?"

I held up my hands in mock surrender. "I've been on vacation doing some flying and boating. You know, the touristy stuff."

"Yeah, I bet," he mumbled. "What's your plan, double-oh-seven?"

I watched a young Latino lady scolding her boyfriend on the sidewalk for some transgression he'd apparently committed. "How much is the contract?"

Garret smirked. "The one on you, or the lawyer?"

"Both."

"Quarter million on you, and half on the lawyer, but that ain't all."

"I was hoping I'd be worth at least half a million."

Garret nodded. "Oh, you are.... Alive."

"So that's the game. They want to take me alive for a nice little meet and greet."

"You got it."

"Then that's the plan," I said. "I'll walk up to Giordano, stick out my hand, and say, 'Take me to your leader.'"

Chapter 24
On Second Thought

Some plans are better than others, and in my experience, sometimes no plan works out fine.

Clark immediately dismissed my idea. "I'm going to recommend against that plan—if it even qualifies as one. I'm pretty sure there's a better option. Hell, I'm sure there are a thousand better options."

"Yeah, but you've got to admit that does sound like fun. Can you imagine the look on Giordano's face?"

Clark chuckled. "Oh, I'm not saying you shouldn't walk up and shake his hand. I'm just not a fan of him taking you to his leader—or taking you anywhere for that matter. You know me. I'm all in favor of having some fun with him, but I'm not letting you out of my sight. I promised Penny I'd bring you to the Caymans in one piece...and still breathing."

I raised my eyebrows in appreciation and pointed at my partner. "That's one promise I want you to keep."

Obviously unamused by our banter, Garret sat behind the wheel of the Cherokee, cutting slices from an apple, and eating them from the blade of his pocketknife. "Do you want my advice?"

When a man who's been on the planet twice as long as me offers advice while eating an apple from the blade of a knife, that advice deserves some respect.

Clark must have shared my opinion because we both leaned in, waiting for the words of wisdom to come tumbling out of the man's juice-covered mouth.

"I'd let him fly into your web instead of you traipsing into his. There's a lot to be said for home-field advantage."

I was instantly intrigued. "What do you have in mind?"

The old PI shoved another wedge of apple into his mouth and chewed it slowly. "All I've got in mind is finishing this apple and getting paid for watching this Giordano character for you. That's what I do—find people, watch people, and get paid for doing it."

I glanced at Clark. "So, what if someone wanted to pay you to help spin a web instead of just watching? How much would that cost?"

He inspected the blade of his knife, dropped the remnants of the apple core into a plastic bag, and licked his fingers. "Hypothetically speaking, if somebody wanted my help spinning a web—and that somebody had deep enough pockets—I'd say I could spin the best damned web this side of Leningrad."

Clark rested his back against the jeep and folded his arms. "They call it Saint Petersburg now."

Garret eyed Clark. "No, I'm pretty sure the oblast around the city is still called Leningrad, and Saint Petersburg is a city over on the other coast of Florida, next door to Tampa. So, do you want my help or not?"

Witnessing Clark losing a battle of wits was a rare treat, but I tried not to let my amusement show. I turned to the PI. "You've not given us a price yet." It was my turn to catch Garret's experienced eye.

"The price, young Jedi, depends on how much fun it is for me. The more fun I have, the less you pay, and if it sucks for me, it's going to suck for your pocketbook."

In my best Yoda voice, I said, "Mmm, then fun we must have."

As stoic as the seasoned PI was, he couldn't suppress a brief chuckle. "That was terrible. I'm afraid the force wasn't with you on that one. Here's what I say we do…" He paused as if expecting some response from us, then held out his palms. "Aren't you guys going to take notes or something?"

Clark tapped at his temple. "Steel trap."

"Suit yourself, but try to keep up. I say we put the word out that we've got Antonio. You *do* have Antonio, right?"

"I don't have him," I said quickly, then turned to Clark. "Do you have him?"

Clark shook his head. "No, I don't have him. I have no idea where he is."

Garret sighed. "Lying to me isn't going to keep the price down, but ultimately, it doesn't really matter if you've got him or not, as long as we can make Giordano believe you do. Can we at least agree on that?"

Clark and I nodded.

"So, my guys and me, we're good enough on the street to plant some seeds and pray for rain. We can get somebody Giordano trusts to whisper what we want in his ear. What we can't do—well, what we *won't* do—is chop him up when he comes knocking. Capiche?"

"Yeah, we get that," I said, glancing back at my partner.

Clark grinned. "You might even say chopping them up is our favorite part."

Garret winked. "I thought that might be the case. We need a warehouse or a quiet, out-of-the-way spot where we can get this cat to come looking for you and his buddy, Antonio."

In what must have sounded like practiced stereo, Clark and I said, "How about a boat?"

Garret squinted with approval written all over his face. "You two should really take this act of yours on the road."

I chuckled. "We spend a lot of time together."

The PI threw up his hands. "Hey, it's the two thousands. I don't judge."

I wanted to have some fun with Garret, but I stuck to the business at hand. "We can get a boat in less than an hour. How quickly can you get your guys spreading the good news on the streets of South Beach?"

Garret checked his watch, closed one eye, and peered toward the sky. "As soon as you two get the boat setup, I'll put the word out that you've got Antonio and you're holding him on that boat. Giordano won't be dragging his feet. We'll have an hour after he gets the word before he comes knockin' at your door."

I followed suit and checked my watch. "Perfect. We'll be in touch as soon as we get settled."

We stepped from the Cherokee and flagged down a passing taxi. Twenty-five minutes later, we were walking into Dominic Fontana's office.

The stunning Cuban receptionist, with too much lipstick and hair the color of coal, locked eyes with my partner and immediately blushed. "Hola, Clark."

Clark winked. "Hey, Maria. I swear you're more beautiful every time I see you, girl."

The painted red smile broadened. "Gracias, mi amor."

"Is my dad here?"

"No, Papi. He's not been here in two days. I think he's on a little vacay or something. You know how he is."

"Yeah, I know, but I need to borrow a boat for a thing we're doing. Does he have something we could use for a couple of days? Something in the forty-foot range? Maybe a sportfisher."

"Yeah, sure, Papi. You can have anything you want, but if he gets mad at me, you have to tell him you made me give it to you."

Clark leaned in and kissed the Latin goddess on the cheek. "I'd lie for you any day, Maria. Every day."

"Do you mean tell a lie for me, or lie down for me, Papi?"

"Whichever you prefer, Chica."

She danced across the room in a salsa strut and pulled a set of keys from a lockbox. She slid them into Clark's hand and whispered something filthy in a language I knew far better than Clark. I blushed. He did not.

Emblazoned across the floating key chain in Clark's palm was the name "*C'est la Vie.*"

The boat was a forty-two-foot sportfisher with a modest interior. It was clearly owned and decorated by a bachelor, but a bachelor with reasonably good taste and more than a little spare change. There were no throw pillows or frilly curtains like every woman would insist on having aboard, but it had a nicely stocked bar, polished teak, and excellent electronics.

After a cursory inspection of the engine room, Clark declared the boat to be in shipshape, and the twin diesels purred to life in seconds. The lines were cast off, and Clark motored us away from the dock.

I unrolled a chart and began scanning for a place to set our trap. In no time, my finger landed on the perfect spot. "Here! Head for Key Biscayne, No Name Harbor."

As we passed Fisher Island, Clark buried the throttles. The bow rose for a few seconds before the hull made its way atop the waves and settled into a perfect cruising speed of thirty knots. The ride was smooth, comfortable, and impressive. In twenty-five minutes, we clocked off the eleven miles to No Name Harbor, and had *C'est la Vie* lying alongside the seawall.

"I don't know how you found this place from that paper chart, but I've got to hand it to you, man. It's perfect. There's only one way in by boat, and only one way in by land, so nobody's gonna sneak up on us."

Impressing Clark had never been easy, but when I actually pulled it off, I always had a private celebration in my head.

"It's not so much the sneaking in that worries me. I want to make sure there's no way out when Giordano shows up. If Garret's men can pull off the breadcrumb drop, Giordano isn't going to be subtle in his approach."

"I agree. I just hope he's not smart enough to realize he's walking into a trap."

"We have to assume he's no dummy. He's been in this game for thirty years or more, and staying alive this long, in his line of work, means he's smarter than the average bear."

No Name Harbor is a cut-out basin on the western side of Bill Baggs State Park, at the southern tip of Key Biscayne. The seawall can hold five or six big boats, and there's room for eight to ten more to anchor in the basin. Fortunately for us, the harbor was surprisingly empty, with only three boats at anchor and one cruiser along the seawall a hundred feet in front of us. I didn't know how ugly the encounter with Giordano would get, but I wanted to involve as few other people in the fireworks as possible. The relative emptiness of the harbor gave me a rare sense of things going well, and that made me nervous.

In what I'd come to know as true Green Beret form, Clark was already surveying the area to establish a perimeter defense. Defending a perimeter with only two humans isn't bulletproof, but my partner's situational awareness and tactical skill set more than made up for what we lacked in manpower.

Clark pointed southwest. "That stand of pines will make a nice observation point for one of us when Garret lets us know Giordano is coming, but the water is the only option in the other direction."

I surveyed the area and quickly agreed. "Are you thinking we need another boat?"

Clark bit at his bottom lip. "I don't want to involve any more hardware. I'd like to keep this as simple as possible. By the way, what are we going to do with Giordano when we catch him? It's not like we can just drop him off at the sheriff's office with a big red bow tied around his neck."

"Oh, I have a better plan than that, but it does involve a big red bow...of sorts."

Clark raised his eyebrows. "I think I'm going to like this. Do tell."

"All in good time," I said. "Let's catch our prey first, then we'll play with him."

"It's not nice keeping secrets."

I held my ground. "Let's just say there's an old friend of ours who'd love to have a chat with Mr. Giordano, and we should arrange that reunion."

Clark's sly grin was all the affirmation I needed.

Chapter 25
Shallow Water

Garret's team wasn't quite as good at cranking up the telegraph of the streets as he'd given them credit. It took over twenty-four hours to get the word out that I was holding Antonio D'Angelo aboard a sport-fishing boat in No Name Harbor.

The delay wasn't all bad news, though. It'd given Clark and me time to pick up Dominic's Range Rover, do some shopping, and arrange a reception party for the hitman who believed I'd be his next kill.

We bought a mannequin roughly the size and shape of Antonio D'Angelo, a wig to match his style and color, and set up the tableau in the main salon of the boat. A close inspection would reveal that we'd never be Hollywood set designers, but from a distance, it would be easy to believe Antonio D'Angelo's slumping, unconscious form was tied to a chair and just waiting to be rescued.

"I've got an idea how we can double our perimeter defense," Clark said, "but I need to call Tony."

Tony Johnson was Clark's younger brother and a Coast Guard rescue swimmer. He was also Skipper's boyfriend, or at least he had been. After her cryptic response when I asked her how he felt about Judge Huntsinger's law clerks flirting with her, I wasn't so sure anymore.

"Hey, Tony. It's Clark. How you doin', man?…I'm good, but listen—I need a favor. Do you know anyone in Miami who can get me a dry suit and a rebreather in the next hour or so?... Great. Thanks, man. I'll see you soon. Oh, hey, before I go. Is everything okay with you and Elizabeth?"

He listened intently, and his eyes met mine as he slowly shook his head. I didn't like the look of that. Skipper and Tony were hot and heavy, and I thought they were solid, but from the looks of things, I thought wrong.

Clark pocketed his phone. "He says it's a long story, but he screwed up, and he doesn't know if she'll get past it."

I rolled my eyes. "Well, that's theirs to deal with. What did he say about the rebreather?"

"He's got a Coast Guard buddy here who's going to hook us up. That'll put one of us in the tree line and the other in the water."

I liked Clark's way of thinking. "That's perfect. I'm sure Garret will let us know how Giordano will be approaching, but I like having both avenues covered. Do you want the trees or the water?"

He reached for his phone as it vibrated in his pocket. "It depends on how big the dry suit is."

I was over six inches taller than Clark and forty pounds heavier. Needless to say, I could never squeeze into a dry suit that fit him.

Two minutes later, he ended the call, and we were back in Dominic's Range Rover, en route to the Coast Guard station.

Just as I'd hoped, Tony's buddy was six foot three and two hundred ten pounds. I was going into the water.

Back at the boat, I gave Garret a call to check on what I hoped would be progress from his team.

"Hey, Chase. I was about to call you. It's on. Giordano took the bait, and he's headed your way. He's alone and in a black F-one-fifty pickup. I'm on him, but I'm playing it loose in case he decides to run a detection route. From the looks of it, though, he's coming straight to you, and he doesn't care if he has a tail."

"Thanks, Garret. We'll take it from here, and I hope it was fun for you."

"Oh, it was a blast," he said. "In fact, it was so much fun that this one's gratis. Do you want me to stay on him?"

I thought about his question and the possible ramifications of something going terribly wrong. "You've done enough, Garret. I don't want to put you at risk if this thing goes south. Just tail him long enough to make sure he's headed for Key Biscayne. If he is, there's nowhere else he'd be going except to give us a visit."

He grunted. "I've never been afraid of things going south, so I don't mind seeing this one through if you want, but it's up to you. You're the boss."

"All right, then. If you want to stay in this thing, tail him out to the Rickenbacker Causeway across the Bear Cut Bridge. There's a marina on the right as soon as you cross. If he keeps coming, he's definitely coming to us. Take up a position at the marina and watch for him to leave. There should be a good tree line for some cover. I'll be in the water, but Clark will have my phone. Got it?"

"Yeah, I got it."

The line went dead, and I briefed Clark. "Giordano's on his way, and Garret's going to tail him across the Bear Cut Bridge. Take my phone in case he calls. I need to get suited up."

I twisted my way into the dry suit and donned the rebreather. The closed loop of the Draeger rig would capture my exhaled breath, scrub it clean of carbon dioxide, add the oxygen I'd need, and redeliver the next breath. The science of the system is fascinating, but the real beauty is that it doesn't allow my exhaled breath to escape and send tell-tale bubbles to the surface. I could hover just beneath the water and occasionally sneak a peek. When Giordano climbed aboard, I could ditch the rebreather, climb the ladder, and have the hitman trapped inside the boat. Cornering an armed hitman is typically a deadly plan, but I had Clark Johnson.

I staged a forty-five auto in a locker near the boarding ladder on the stern of *C'est la Vie*, then tucked a second pistol inside my dry suit while Clark constructed a field-expedient lean-to as concealment about fifteen feet into the tree line, and armed himself with a 308 sniper rifle and a pair of nine-millimeter Glocks. I didn't want to shoot Giordano. I wanted him alive and well—or perhaps alive and not-so-well. We'd only shoot him if there was no other option.

I hoped I could get him in the water, which, even off the coast of South Florida, is chilly enough that time of year to sap the energy out of a middle-aged hitman not expecting to get wet.

"I'm splashing in. Are you good to go?"

Clark glanced over my gear to make sure everything looked the way it should, and then flinched as my phone in his pocket vibrated. He pressed it to his ear. A few seconds later, his one-word response of "Roger," told me Giordano had crossed the Bear Cut Bridge.

I slipped silently into the water of No Name Harbor and finned around the port side of the boat, keeping an eye on the road in hopes of seeing a black Ford pickup. I waited several minutes, but there was no sign of Giordano approaching, and I was starting to get uncomfortable. Something wasn't going as planned. Either he realized it was a trap and bugged out, or he stopped the truck before reaching the harbor and set out on foot. I hadn't considered that possibility, but given the circumstances, I probably would've done exactly that if the roles were reversed.

Swimming beneath the surface, I carefully counted twenty-five kick cycles. When I emerged, I was pleased to see that my kick count had placed me one hundred feet from the seawall, where I could clearly see Clark's improvised observation point. His head moved ever-so-slightly when I appeared on the surface, and I waited for any signal from him. None came, but his slow, methodical scan of the area told me he had yet to see our prey either.

I slipped back under the water and swam to the boat. When the outline of the hull appeared in front of my face, I placed my hand against the fiberglass and held myself in position while waiting to feel someone step aboard. According to the dive computer on my left wrist, twenty minutes had passed when I felt a subtle thud through the hull. It didn't feel like anyone climbing aboard. It felt more like something falling on deck.

I decided that whatever it had been was worth checking out, so I swam silently to the stern and slowly allowed my head to break the surface. The first thing I saw made my heart stand still. A bullet hole the size of my thumb was in the center of the glass window into the main salon. I grabbed the swim platform and pulled my chest and shoulders from the water to get a better look. The mannequin that was sitting mostly upright in the chair, was now piled on the cabin sole with the top of its head blown off.

Dammit! I should've expected that.

Giordano's contract was to kill Antonio D'Angelo, not rescue him. That's when I heard Clark break cover. I turned to see him sprinting across the road toward the Range Rover. He saw my head at the stern of the boat and yelled, "Get the boat around to the Bear Cut! He's on the run!"

I hefted myself aboard *C'est la Vie* and let the rebreather fall to the deck. Contorting my body, I hustled to free myself of the bulky dry suit and cast off the lines.

The twin diesels sprang to life, and I shoved the throttles to their stops, ignoring the no-wake rule inside the harbor. The heavy yacht responded with the agility of a boat half her size and came about on a dime as I accelerated toward the inlet to the harbor.

The inlet was less than two hundred feet wide, and I turned it into churning white water as I roared through at over twenty knots, still building speed. I pressed the switches to bring the chart plotter online, but the screens remained black. That's when I noticed the bullet hole in the console.

The bullet that had taken the mannequin's head off remained intact and burrowed in the electronics console, leaving me with no depth readings and no way to know where the dozens of sandbars between me and the Bear Cut Bridge actually were. Watching the color of the water as I raced across its surface, I hoped I'd see the shallows, but my speed made it impossible. Once clear of the inlet, I turned the boat to the west and prayed for deep water.

Glancing over my shoulder, a cloud of white dust poured from the rear tires of the Range Rover as Clark accelerated down the shell-covered drive.

Approaching Southwest Point, the color of the water turned dark green, and I aimed the boat toward an area that looked more like the color of the water I was in. The boat reached its maximum speed, and I kept my eyes trained ahead. The Bear Cut Bridge finally came into view off the starboard bow, and I quickly scanned the water, hoping to find something that looked deep. Every inch of the surface to my right looked as if the bottom was only inches beneath, so I kept racing westward.

A glimmer off the port bow caught my attention. To my left was a cigarette boat crossing my course at over twice my speed. Normally, I would be livid about someone ignoring the rules of the road and cutting me off from the left, but that day, I was happy to see him. He roared northward through a cut in the shallows that I hadn't seen, and I rolled the wheel to the right, following directly in the wake of the faster boat. I had no way to know how deep the draft was on the cigarette boat, but I hoped it was deeper than mine.

Although there was still no sign of the black pickup on the bridge ahead, I saw the Range Rover, with Clark at the wheel, careening westward at top speed.

There was nothing I could do to aid in the chase, and Clark made no effort to stop and pick me up, so I headed for the marina where I'd told Garret to pull off. I tied the boat to a bollard against the seawall and leapt ashore. If Garret hadn't seen Giordano race past, perhaps he was still parked in the marina parking lot. If so, he and I could join the chase, albeit several minutes behind.

As I crossed the parking lot, it became painfully evident that Garret hadn't seen the black pickup nor the Range Rover. The side window of his jeep was splattered with blood, and a bullet hole identical to the one left in the boat shone like a diamond in the opposite window.

My heart sank into my stomach. It had been a long time since I'd found myself at a loss for what to do next, but standing there in the crushed-shell parking lot, staring at the bloody Cherokee, left me without a clue.

The man who keeps his wits about him when the whole world is crumbling around him is the man who emerges the victor.

I couldn't remember where I'd read that, or who I'd heard say it, but those words kept pouring through my head.

I focused, slowed my breathing, and let my training take over. Before I consciously realized what I was doing, I had the passenger door of the Cherokee open and Garret's cell in my hand. My first thought was to dial 911, but there was nothing the cops could do for Garret. Instead, I pushed redial and waited to hear Clark's voice.

"I lost him, dammit! Where are you?"

I gritted my teeth. "I'm at the marina. Garret's dead. Giordano put one in his head, just like he did to our dummy."

I could hear the frustration in Clark's voice, but he remained calm. "Get the boat back to the yard. I'll meet you there, and we'll start cleaning up this mess."

I pocketed Garret's phone and headed back for the boat.

The ride to Dominic's boatyard was a study in psychological self-torture. I'd gotten Garret killed by not insisting that he break off and head back to Panama City, and I'd also blown my best chance at catching Giordano. Sending a bad guy to the grave never haunted me, but losing a good man because of my decision was a ghost that would haunt me without end. Having spooked Giordano, I knew he'd vanish, and I wouldn't be getting another shot at him anytime soon. The fear of leaving the hitman free in the world, even temporarily, made the sickening feeling in the pit of my stomach even more bitter.

Chapter 26
Not His Type

When I pulled into the boatyard, Clark was waiting for me on the dock. We tied up *C'est la Vie* and headed for the office.

"Why didn't we see that coming?" I asked.

"I don't know, man. We should have. I don't know what we were thinking."

I sighed. "There's no reason to beat ourselves up. We can't undo it, but we need a plan to deal with Garret's body."

Clark closed his eyes and groaned. "Give me his phone."

I handed it to Clark, and he gave me mine.

He scrolled through Garret's recent calls and pressed send. I met his gaze as he listened.

"No, this is Clark Johnson. Garret was working for me and Chase Fulton. You're part of his street team, right?" He licked his lips. "Giordano killed him. He's in front of the marina at the eastern end of the Bear Cut Bridge on Key Biscayne... Are you sure?... Okay. We'll get you paid. Just let us know what you need." He gave them my cell number and hung up. "They're going to take care of Garret and the Cherokee. We need to pay them more than they charge."

"I'll take care of that," I said. "As much as I hate to pawn it off on them, I'm glad they're taking care of Garret."

We handed the boat keys back to Maria, and her silence said she instinctively knew Clark was in no mood to be playful.

She locked the keys away. "Is there anything I can do?"

"I need to talk to my dad. If he checks in, or if you know how to reach him, would you tell him to call me?"

She pressed her red lips into a horizontal line. "Si, Papi."

Clark hugged her, and we climbed into the Range Rover. We sat in silence with the engine running until he finally spoke.

"Have you got any ideas?"

"Yeah, I do. I'm calling Skipper."

As I pressed my phone to my ear, Clark did the same. I briefed Skipper on the details of the past thirty hours. She seemed to be cataloging my account of events as if her mind had become a massive database of information. I expected an emotional response from the girl I'd known a decade before, but instead, I was faced with the analytical professional she'd become.

"There's nothing I can do about anything you've screwed up," she said, "but I can brief you on our situation here. Are you ready?"

I scrounged around for a pen and paper and found one in the console. "I am."

"Write this down. We're at twenty-three degrees, forty-four point two minutes north, eighty-four degrees, forty point eight minutes west, making nine knots. The security detail is solid. Mario is spilling his guts. His wife is somber and not saying much. The daughter, Paulina, is seasick, but we're keeping her hydrated, and she seems to be improving."

I interrupted. "How about Marissa?"

Skipper lost her intelligence briefer's tone. "Marissa is the best. She's in love with everything, especially Charlie. Those two are inseparable. She's the cutest thing ever."

For the first time in hours, I couldn't avoid smiling. "That's great. If all of this works out, she's going to have a wonderful life ahead of her. How about Kaminsky?"

The professional tone returned immediately. "I can't put my finger on it, Chase, but something's not right about him."

"What do you mean?"

She made a sound I couldn't identify. "Like I said, I can't put my finger on it, but something about him feels wrong. Sometimes he records the interviews with Mario, and other times he takes notes. I've tried getting him to talk to me, you know, kinda like flirting with him, but nothing. I get no reaction from him. I mean, I'm not like Miss America or anything, but on a sailboat in the middle of the ocean, I mean, I'm cute enough to get a geeky lawyer's attention. Don't you agree?"

"Maybe you're not his type."

"Not his type? What's wrong with me that I wouldn't be his type?"

I chuckled. "Maybe *I'm* more his type."

"Oh! I didn't think of that. Maybe you're right. Maybe I'm being overly analytical or whatever. I'm sure he's under a lot of stress. This is a pretty big deal for a young prosecutor, I guess."

"I'm sure that's it," I said. "How's Penny?"

"She's great. She's so good at the captain stuff. She's sleeping now, but I'm sure she'd love it if I woke her up to talk to you. Hang on a minute."

"No! No. Don't wake her. Just tell her I called, and she can call me when she wakes up."

"I'll tell her. By the way, Garret was in charge because he's the one writing the payroll checks. Those other guys who work for him, they're not just errand boys."

"Thanks, Skipper. I'll check in tomorrow." I turned to Clark. "I don't know why I didn't think of this, but Garret's team has been tracking Giordano for a week. Maybe they can pick up the scent again, even without the boss."

Clark waved his phone at me. "Way ahead of you, College Boy. They're on it, but it's not going to be cheap."

"I don't care what it costs as long as they find him. To hell with my plan. As soon as they find him, I'll put a bullet in his eye myself."

He held up his index finger as if he had a point to make. "Calm down, Kemosabe. I'm not sure I know what your plan was, but I have a pretty good guess, and I think it's worth sticking to. At least it is for our old friend."

I took a long, deep breath. "We've got dead bodies piling up from Bimini to Key Biscayne. We've kidnapped an old-school mafia guy, and your dad's holding him God knows where. Skipper and Penny are babysitting a U.S. attorney and the mafia's lawyer on a boat off the west coast of Cuba. And for what?"

He put his hand on my shoulder. "Relax. We've been in a lot worse fixes than this lately, and we came out of it just fine. This is just—"

I didn't let him finish. "I'll tell you for what. All of this is because I didn't listen to you when you told me to keep my nose out of the nun's business in Saint Augustine. If I'd listened to you, none of this would be happening."

"Look, man. You did what you thought was best, and it stirred up mess that no one could've predicted. We're on the verge of bringing down one of the biggest crime families on the East Coast, and that gets us a check mark in the 'good' column. We need all of those we can rack up. Hold it together for a few more days. We'll get through this, and then you and Penny can…hell, you and Penny can do anything in the world. You can afford it, and you deserve it. The time off will do you both some good. Sooner or later, we all get where you are. Grit your teeth and stay with me, and this'll all be behind us in a few days."

I placed my hand on top of his on my shoulder. "I'm sorry. It's all getting to me, you know? I just—"

"Papa! Papi! Your father, he is on the line inside."

Maria was running toward the Range Rover in her high heels, looking like a baby gazelle learning to walk.

Clark pointed at the Cuban goddess. "I'm pretty sure she likes me. What do you think?"

I followed him back inside and poured myself four fingers of whatever Dominic had in the decanter. It was bourbon of some quality, and it went down like spring water. I didn't like the episode I'd had in the truck with Clark. As a psychologist, I knew enough about the human mind to know when one was on the verge of burning out. I should've seen it coming. I ignored the warning signs, but Clark was right—I needed a break. I *deserved* a break, and Penny deserved a huge break simply for putting up with me.

By the time Clark was off the line with his father, I had calmed sufficiently to have a rational conversation. "What did he have to say? Where is he?"

Clark motioned toward my glass. "How many of those have you had?"

"Just the one," I said, "but I'm considering another. Join me?"

"Sure. Why not?"

I poured two more glasses and slid one across the desk to him. "Look, about earlier. I'm sorry about that."

He touched the rim of his glass to mine. "Don't be sorry. Be better. Let me tell you about my breakdown."

I couldn't imagine Clark Johnson, Green Beret, Airborne Ranger, ever having the slightest loss of composure.

He cleared his throat. "I'd been in the Ranger battalion about three years, just long enough for the new to wear off. We were supporting a convoy movement in Saudi during Desert Storm. It was a big supply convoy with all sorts of stuff: ammo, water, radios, food, gas, and who knows what all else. It was cake duty, man. We were basically pulling security for a bunch of National Guard pukes who didn't know which end of an M-Sixteen the bullets came out of, you know?"

I'd never seen a National Guard convoy, but I nodded as if I'd escorted a dozen of them through the desert.

"Anyway, I was bored out of my mind and tired of eating sand up in the gun turret on top of a PeaceKeeper—you know, a hardened Humvee."

"Yeah, I know what a PeaceKeeper is."

He took another drink of his whiskey and admired the amber liquid swirling in his glass. "This is good stuff. What is it?"

I looked at mine. "It's really good bourbon, but I don't who made it. It's from Kentucky, though. There's no doubt about that."

"Wherever it's from, it's good. Where was I?"

"Eating sand in a gun turret in Saudi."

"Oh, yeah. So anyway, I'd been up there all day with nothing and nobody to shoot at. I was hot, tired, thirsty, and pissed off that the Army couldn't find anything better to do with a badass Airborne Ranger like me than to stick me guarding some two-bit reserve unit or whatever they were. So, I crawled down, and this specialist, an E-four fresh out of Ranger school, said, 'Hey, Sergeant Johnson, do you mind if I man that gun for a while?' I'd never heard a better idea in my life, so I shoved that kid up through the hole and took his nice comfy seat behind the driver. I'd never been happier to be inside a vehicle instead of on top of it."

I leaned in, intrigued.

"I guess it was twenty minutes later, I was almost asleep. I'd drained two bottles of water and finally started feeling human again. That's when I heard the loudest noise I've ever heard. My driver swerved right, and my head crashed into the window. I'd taken off my helmet, like an idiot, and it rattled my brain pretty good. Before I could shake it off, the light coming through the turret went black, and the Humvee that had been in the lead landed upside-down on top of my PeaceKeeper. I grabbed that kid's leg who'd just gone up on the gun and tried to pull him free, but he'd been crushed between the two trucks, and everything was on fire. I twisted the handle on my door, but it was jammed. The impact of the other Humvee landing on us had me trapped in the back seat. I remember looking up at that kid's body crushed between the top of our vehicle and the burning Humvee on top of us and hating myself for coming down off that gun. If I had stayed up there another twenty minutes, that kid would still be alive."

I stared down at my feet, not knowing where else to look. "There's no way you could've known."

He raised his glass toward me. "Exactly. There's no way I could've known. Just like there's no way you could've known that kicking Salvatore D'Angelo's ass would end us up in the mess we're in right now."

I huffed and took another long swallow. "So, how'd you get out?"

He squeezed his eyebrows together. "Huh?"

"The PeaceKeeper. How'd you get out of the vehicle?'

"Oh, one of the National Guardsmen was a fireman or something back home for his real job, and he came through the door and pulled me out. Both of my legs were broken, and I couldn't hear a thing. We lost five Rangers that day."

I was in awe. "What caused it?"

"That's the worst part. You'll never believe it, but it was a Russian anti-tank mine left over from the eighties when the Russians were fighting the Arabs down there. The lead vehicle clipped the mine with its left front tire. It cooked off and sent the Humvee flying. They sent me to a hospital ship in the Persian Gulf and hung a bunch of medals on me. All of that for getting a young kid killed because I was tired of eating sand." He gazed at nothing in particular, as if he were watching the moment replay right in front of him. "It should've been me."

"I had no idea. I don't know what to say."

"You don't have to say anything. Just let me finish. I spent weeks on that hospital ship, the USS Nightingale. They put me back together, and I was ready to quit. I was done. I was coming home and getting a job as a cop or a fireman or something—anything but staying in the Army."

"But you—"

"Shut up and listen," he insisted. "One night I was on the deck of that hospital ship, talking to this SEAL who'd gotten cut by some jihadi from his ankles to his ass on both legs. This dude could barely stand up, but he was up there on deck, smoking a cigarette, lying on his side, and looking up at the stars. I told him how I'd ended up on the ship and how I was done." He emptied his glass and slid it across the desk toward me.

I poured three more fingers, slid it back to him, and waited for the story to continue.

"You know what that old SEAL said to me?"

"No. What did he say?"

"He said, 'Who's gonna keep that shit from happening again if you don't?'" He swallowed half of the whiskey. "Man, that hit me hard. I went home on convalescent leave when I was well enough to travel, and every night when I'd lie down to try and sleep, I'd hear those words over and over again. And he was right. No matter how much I wanted to run away, I kept thinking, who's gonna keep that shit from happening again if I don't? So, I went back, and I went to Special Forces training and traded in my black Ranger beret for a green one. Because who's gonna do it if we don't?"

Chapter 27

Skipper Was Right

We finished our drinks in silence, letting our thoughts circle our heads like stars, reminiscent of Tweety Bird hitting Sylvester with a skillet.

Someone had to do it, so I broke the silence. "What did your dad have to say? Did he tell you where he is?"

Clark shuddered like he was shaking off a bad dream. "I almost forgot. I told him everything that happened, and he seems to think it was a good thing. Well, not that Garret getting shot was a good thing, but if Giordano believes he killed Antonio, that means he's stopped hunting for him."

"I didn't think about that, but you may be right. The only problem is that I'm his next target. If he was good enough to get into those woods and take a shot without you picking him up, what's keeping him from doing the same thing to me when I least expect it?"

Clark rubbed his head and groaned. "I don't know, but something tells me he's running someplace safe. He knows we're on him. He killed Garret because he knew, and there's no way he missed the fact that I was chasing him across the Rickenbacker Causeway at a hundred miles an hour. If I were him, I'd head for my safe place and let things cool down before coming after you. We'll know soon enough. Garret's team—well, what's left of it—is confident they can find him, and they'll call us the second they do."

"That's what I was about to recommend. Skipper said Garret's team was good, so she had the same idea as you—to keep them on the job."

His crooked smile showed up. "That girl's coming along nicely, Chase. You've got a good one there. She's going to be one hell of an analyst."

"She already is," I said, "and she keeps getting better every day. She says everything is going well on the cruise except for a couple of things. Her gut is telling her something isn't right about Kaminsky. She says she can't nail it down, but there's something about him that bugs her. I think she hit on him and he shot her down."

"Uh-huh. What's the other thing?"

I chuckled. "Paulina is seasick, but she's getting better."

"I knew somebody would get sick. I had Kaminsky pegged as the puker, but I can see Paulina being the one. Where are they?"

"She gave me her position. Does your dad have a Western Caribbean chart lying around?"

He pulled one from a bin and laid it out on the desk.

I plotted the latitude and longitude Skipper had given me. "Right there."

Clark scowled. "I thought they'd be further along."

"Penny is intentionally dogging. Skipper said they're making nine knots. The boat will do fourteen in good wind, so she's dragging it out to give us more time."

"There's another good one you have. How is it that you surround yourself with all these amazing people? Penny is great on the boat. Elizabeth is quickly becoming a top-notch analyst. And, best of all, you've got me—an all-around badass."

I laughed. "That's what I love about you. Your modesty."

Clark measured the distance from *Aegis's* plotted position and Georgetown on Grand Cayman. "It looks like they've still got five hundred miles, so that's two-and-a-half days."

"Yeah, but I don't think she'll take the most direct route. She'll split the distance between Cuba and the Yucatan Peninsula, and sail south until she makes the same latitude at Georgetown before turning east. I told her to try staying at sea for a week, but she can't get too crazy with the route. Mario's wife is smart enough to figure out what's going on if Penny plays around too much. There's more to Gloria than meets the eye."

He rolled the chart and stuck it back in the bin. "I agree."

I finished the remaining whiskey and held up my empty tumbler, allowing the light from the window to play through the glass. "You know, the world looks a lot different when you look at it through an empty whiskey glass."

Clark turned his glass over, letting a final drop trickle out. "Maybe it's the missing whiskey that makes it look different."

"You may have a point," I said. "So, we could guess where Giordano is headed and try to beat him there."

"You're grasping at straws, young Jedi. All we can do now is wait for Garret's men to do what they do best and report back. We can be anywhere in Florida in three or four hours and anywhere in the world in twenty-four hours. There's no reason to go chasing our tails."

"Why do you think Garret called me that...young Jedi?"

"I don't know, but I wish I had thought of it first. It fits you. Chase Skywalker. That's got a nice ring to it."

I pointed an imaginary lightsaber at my partner. "I'll ring you, Chewbacca."

"Chewbacca?" he protested. "Why can't I be Obi-Wan Kenobi?"

"Because you're hairy, and I can't understand what you're saying most of the time."

He rubbed his bare arms. "I'm not hairy, but I do smell like an ape. I could use a shower."

Dominic Fontana's office was more like a bachelor pad for a sixty-year-old lady's man than a yacht broker's office. We each got a shower and changed clothes, making us feel almost human again.

Maria *accidentally* came through the door while Clark was drying off and made a show of surveying her prey. "Oh, good, Papi. I'll make reservations since you're getting ready to take me to dinner."

Clark, never one to shy away from being naked in front of a

beautiful woman, glanced at me and shrugged. "Why not? Can Chase come?"

Maria attempted a smile, but her real answer came through loud and clear.

"You two go ahead," I said. "I've got some work to do, and I need to relax and recharge."

This time, her smile was genuine and radiant. "Your dad's closet is through there. Dress nice, Papi. He has some things I'd like to take off of you later."

She did that salsa-dance walk of hers as she returned toward the front office.

I wonder if that's something all Cuban girls do naturally, or if they go to school for that.

Papi and Maria caught a cab and headed for South Beach while I made use of Dominic's lair to put away a little more of his good bourbon and ponder life. I found a classic rock station on the stereo and kicked back. Thirty-Eight Special belted out "Hold on Loosely."

Maybe that's what was happening to me. Maybe I was holding on to all the wrong things in my life. Maybe spending time seeing the world with Penny was the thing I should've been clinging to. Maybe all that saving the world, one bad guy at a time business wasn't what was most important after all…maybe. I drifted off to sleep with Styx singing "Come Sail Away."

I don't know how long I'd been asleep, dreaming of sailing away with Penny and our puppy, when my chirping phone dragged me awake.

"Yeah, this is Chase."

"Chase, it's Penny. I need you awake and coherent."

I shook the cobwebs from my mind and sat bolt upright. "What is it, Penny? Is everything okay?"

"No, Chase. Everything is not okay. Somebody hit us."

"They hit the boat?"

"No. Listen to me. Six guys in a go-fast boat hit us about thirty minutes ago. They were pros. They took down the security team, put one in Mario's chest, and made off with the lawyer and Marissa."

I couldn't fathom what she was telling me. Who could it have been, and why would they take the prosecutor?

"Are you and Skipper all right?"

"Yeah, we're good, but the boat's in bad shape. She has a couple dozen rounds through each engine, and they slashed the sails up."

By then, I was wide awake and in full tactical mode. "Slow down. Give me a sitrep on each soul on board, one by one."

"What's a sitrep?"

Sometimes it was easy to forget that Penny was a dust-bowl girl from North Texas and not a trained operator. "It's a situation report. Run down the list of people left on board and give me their status."

"All of the security team is dead except for Clay. He's still alive, but he lost a lot of blood. Skipper started an IV, and she's pouring fluid into him as fast as he'll take it, but we're going to run out of IV bags soon. Mario took a through-and-through in his upper right chest. He's unconscious, but we've stopped the bleeding, and we're giving him fluids just like Clay. Gloria is holding it together and playing nurse. She may have some broken bones in her face, but she's not shot."

"Penny, slow down. I know it's overwhelming, but let's make sure we cover everything."

"I know. I'm sorry. I don't know what to do."

"Calm down. You're alive, and the boat isn't sinking…right?"

"Yeah, yeah, the boat's floating. I just don't have an engine, and they cut the sails to pieces."

"Listen to me. Are you and Skipper hurt?"

I could hear her trying to control her breathing through the poor satellite phone connection.

"Yeah, we're all right. Some scrapes and bruises, but no broken bones and no bullet holes."

"Can you describe any of the attackers or their boat?"

"Yeah, I even got a picture of two of them and two pictures of the boat."

"That's why you're the captain," I said. "Way to go."

"I don't feel like much of a captain. I've got two dead bodies on board, and another one who won't make it through the day if we don't get him to a hospital soon. I lost an attorney and a three-year-old girl to kidnappers."

Clark apparently heard the urgency in my tone and came through the door, wiping the sleep from his eyes. "What's going on, man?"

I held up one finger and pressed the speaker button. "Give me your position."

"I don't know exactly," she said. "They shot up the nav gear. When they hit us, we were almost halfway between Las Tumbas on the western coast of Cuba and Cancun."

Clark was immediately fully awake and grabbed a pen and pad.

I tried to bring him up to speed as quickly as possible. "Two dead, two critical with GSWs, two kidnapped, Penny and Skipper are unhurt, and *Aegis* is badly crippled."

The warrior that lived inside my partner took immediate control. "I'm on it. I'll find an asset in the area, if we have one. If not, I'll notify the Coast Guard. Is she sinking?"

Penny responded over the speaker. "No, she's afloat but crippled."

Clark scribbled furiously on the pad. "Who was taken?"

Penny answered before I could. "Marissa and Kaminsky, the attorney."

"Shit! Elizabeth was right." He yanked his phone from his pocket and headed back through the door.

I tried to organize the thoughts in my head, but everything kept coming back to the realization that I had, once again, thrown the woman I love into a pit of vipers, and I was powerless to pull her out.

Even though I couldn't immediately do anything to save her, I had to do everything in my power to head the situation toward a resolution. "Let's go through the asset list. What *is* working on the boat?"

Penny took a deep breath. "She's floating. That's good. I still have a storm sail and the spinnaker. The wind is out of the southwest, so I can turn back for Key West, head for Cuba, or maybe make the Caymans if the wind doesn't shift. Making it upwind to Mexico with just the storm sail would take forever. The generators are still working, so I can make power and run the water makers. I have the sat phone—"

"The sat phone! It knows your position. Scroll through the screen and find your lat and long."

"I should've thought of that," she said. "Hang on. I'll look."

She came back on the line at the same instant Clark burst through the door, waving his phone at me. I held up one finger, asking Clark to hold his information so I could write down Penny's coordinates. She blurted out the lat and long, and I jotted down 21.5070 North by 85.8873 West.

Clark peered over my shoulder, reading the coordinate to whomever he had on the line, then listened intently. "Stand by," he said, and then looked at me. "I've got Captain Stinnett from the Research Vessel *Lori Danielle*. He's off the coast of the Yucatan Peninsula and steaming toward *Aegis* at full speed. He's yelling at the navigation officer to give him an ETA."

"Did you hear that, Penny?"

"Yeah, I heard him, but who's Captain Stinnett?"

"It's a long story, but for now, consider him a mobile trauma center that's headed your way."

"ETA seventy-one minutes!" Clark said.

"Penny, help is on the way. Now we need to know details about the hitters. Which way did they come from, and which direction did they leave?"

Her one-word answer sent a chill down my spine. "Cuba."

I'd been to Cuba twice in the previous two years, and both times I left a trail of dead bodies in my wake. The first time, I shot a Russian oligarch and billionaire in the shoulder and killed one of the world's deadliest assassins, Anatoly Parchinkov, aka Suslik, the gopher. The second time was with Clark when we killed a pair of soldiers and "borrowed" a Russian mini spy submarine. I wasn't welcomed back on that particular island, but welcomed or not, I would get Marissa back, and then I'd make her abductors pay for their sins.

Chapter 28
No Time to Teach

We focused with laser-like intensity on the new task at hand. I briefed Clark on the details Penny had given, and he listened in silence, occasionally taking notes.

"We're going after Marissa," he said.

It wasn't a question.

"Absolutely, but it looks like they took her to Cuba."

Clark grimaced. "I'm not so sure about that. I doubt the D'Angelo family is on Castro's Christmas list. My bet is they're running back for the Keys."

"I hope you're right. I've had all the Cuba I can take for one decade, and I doubt they're waiting to roll out the Cuban red carpet for you, either."

He nodded. "Let's hope I'm right. We need more help."

"What do you have in mind?" I wasn't excited about bringing anyone else into an operation that had already cost too many lives and gotten far deeper than I ever imagined it could.

Clark yelled for Maria, and she came stumbling through the door atop impossibly high heels. "I have to talk to my dad. Get him on the phone ASAP."

Obviously sensing the urgency in his tone, Maria gave no argument and disappeared back toward her desk. Seconds later, she yelled, "Your padre on uno," in some mash of Spanglish.

Simultaneously, my phone chirped, and I stepped out of the room. "This is Chase."

"Chase, it's Elizabeth. I've got 'em."

"You've got who, Skipper?"

I'd given up on trying to call her Elizabeth. She'd always be Skipper to me.

"I've got the bandits. Since they didn't destroy the generators like they did the engines, I've got good power, and I re-tasked a satellite with the uplink you had me install."

"When did you learn how to re-task a satellite?"

"Ginger taught me, but that doesn't matter. I've got a live satellite track on the go-fast boat. They're headed straight for the Marquesas. At first, I thought they were headed for Key West, but I've been plotting their course, and there's no question about it—they're definitely bearing on the Marquesas."

Relieved, I sighed. "You're the best, Skipper. Keep watching them. Are you okay?"

"Yeah, I'm just pissed."

I couldn't help smiling. "I'm sure you are, but stay focused, and keep watching that boat. Clark and I will get the girl back."

"I know you will, and I won't lose them, I swear."

I cleared my throat. "While I have you, tell me the truth. Is Penny all right?"

"Yeah. We're both fine. They weren't interested in us. They just wanted to put the security team down, kill Mario, and make off with Marissa and that son of a bitch, Kaminsky. He was in on it the whole time. He's the one who gave them our position. They were real careful not to shoot him when they came on board. I told you I didn't trust him. I knew there was something fishy about him the whole time. I told you. Didn't I?"

"Yes, you did, and I should've listened. Your instincts were spot-on, but there's nothing we can do about it now. We're heading for the Marquesas. The ship steaming your way is a big gray research vessel named the *Lori Danielle*. They should be there soon. The captain is a guy named Stinnett. He's grouchy, but he's retired CIA, and he's definitely one of the good guys."

Her sigh made it clear that Captain Stinnett's credentials made her feel better. "Thanks, Chase. I'll be in touch when the cavalry gets here, and I'll keep you posted if the bad guys change course."

I headed back into the office where I'd left my partner, and he was hanging up as I came in.

"I've got some good news," I said. "Skipper re-tasked a satellite —whatever that means—and she's tracking the go-fast boat that took Kaminsky and the girl. She's practically certain they're headed for the Marquesas."

"Perfect," he said. "We're headed for the Keys, right?"

"You know it. What did your dad have to say?"

"He's on a boat in The Bahamas near Marsh Harbor. He's still got Antonio, and he's standing by to do whatever coordination we need and task any additional help we want."

"That's great, but, with Skipper in command of the eye in the sky, that gives us a huge advantage and the element of surprise. I think we've got this without dragging anyone else into our mess."

He eyed me warily. "That's what we thought when we tried to trap Giordano, too, so don't get too confident yet."

He was right, as always, but it finally looked like things were turning in our favor.

Not wanting to abandon Dominic's hundred-thousand-dollar Range Rover at the Miami Seaplane Base, we took Maria along so she could drive the truck back to the boatyard.

"When you coming back, Papi? You still owe me dessert." Seduction dripped from every syllable.

Clark almost blushed. "I'll see you again soon, Chica."

She blew him a kiss and disappeared into the Miami traffic.

We loaded our arsenal of firearms aboard the Caravan and had the preflight inspection done in minutes. As we were about to start the engine, Elizabeth called.

"Captain Stinnett arrived ten minutes ago, and you were right about everything—especially the grouchy part. There's no doubt who's in command when he's around. Anyway, they have Clay and Mario on board, and they're working on them. The doctor says Mario is going to make it, but Clay is touch-and-go. They say he wouldn't have made it through the day if we hadn't gotten him to a hospital."

"That's great news, Skipper. How about the boat? Are they still on course for the Marquesas?"

"Yeah, no change there. Are you on your way?"

"We were about to light the fire when you called. We'll be airborne in less than ten minutes."

"All right. I'll call if anything changes. Please be careful. Those guys are good."

"I will. Keep me posted."

Clark spun up the turbine, introduced the fuel, and watched the internal turbine temperature rise. Seconds later, we were taxiing down the ramp into the main channel beside the row of constantly changing cruise ships. I couldn't resist believing it was a sign. Everywhere I'd been in the last week, there was at least one cruise ship. Maybe Penny and I were destined to spend time with someone else driving the boat while *Aegis* got new engines and sails.

"You have the controls," Clark said as he removed his hands from the yoke and throttle.

"I have the controls." I executed the takeoff run just as he'd demonstrated and described. My technique needed some work, but we were soon airborne and climbing out over Fisher Island. A seaplane rating was definitely in my future.

We overflew Key West under an hour later and headed for the Marquesas Keys. Seaplanes routinely overflew the tiny grouping of islands on their way to and from the Dry Tortugas and Fort Jefferson, so if the kidnappers were there, they wouldn't have any reason to be concerned about a seaplane overhead. My hope was that they hadn't had time to make the nearly three-hundred-mile run. Even in a boat capable of incredible speed, the pounding they would take at full speed on the open ocean would be too much for almost anyone to bear.

As the Marquesas came into sight, Clark leaned forward to look for our bad guys. "It doesn't look like anybody's down there. Take the islands down the left side so I can get a better look."

I turned the plane slightly to the right, allowing him a mostly unobstructed view of the smattering of small islands. The huge pontoon would make the job harder, but a few rocks of the wings and some creative rudder work gave Clark the sight picture he needed.

"Yep, it's empty. There's not a living soul down there. I've never seen the place completely abandoned like that before."

"Let me take a look," I said. "You have the controls."

"I have the controls," he said, and turned the big, lumbering airplane through a two-hundred-seventy-degree arc, putting the islands beneath my side. He was right. It looked like a ghost town.

"Get on the horn with Elizabeth, and see where that boat is. I've got an idea."

Generally, I liked Clark's ideas, so I did as he said and slid the earpiece of my phone beneath my headset.

Skipper answered on the third ring. "Yeah."

I wasted no time with pleasantries. "Are you still tracking the boat?"

"Yeah, I've still got them, and they're twenty miles southwest of the Marquesas. Where are you?"

"I'm zero miles directly above the Marquesas," I said. "We're in the Caravan, and Clark has a plan."

"Ooh, I like it when Clark has a plan. Should I call when they're five minutes out?"

"No, that's not necessary. Knowing where they are now is good enough. I'll be in touch when the dust settles."

"Be careful. I mean it, Chase. Those guys are well trained and seriously good."

"I've got that. We'll be careful, I promise, but Clark and I aren't bad at this sort of thing, ourselves."

"I know, but I don't want anything to happen to you guys. Captain Stinnett has us in tow, and we're headed for Isla Mujeres."

214 · CAP DANIELS

"The Island of Women," I said. "You'll fit right in. I'll call you when the lead stops flying."

I hung up and turned to Clark. "They're twenty miles out from the southwest. They'll probably be here in less than thirty minutes. Maybe way less if they're pushing it hard."

He nodded and pointed the nose of the big seaplane toward the ocean. We were soon plowing through the water, headed for the beach on the northeastern side of the islands. Clark had the yoke pulled full aft and plenty of power applied to the turbine engine. We beached the plane aggressively, and he shut down the engine before we stopped rocking.

He threw off his seatbelt and headset and started for the back of the plane. "Help me with the camo netting."

"Camo netting? I didn't know we had camo netting."

"There's a lot you don't know, College Boy, but I don't have time to be teaching you anything right now. Let's get this shiny airplane covered up so we can hold on to what little element of surprise we have."

I didn't argue, and we soon had the plane almost invisible from the sky. I hoped the bad guys would continue approaching from the southeast and not swing around to our side of the islands. Not even the camo netting would keep them from seeing the plane from the water.

We armed ourselves with a pair of Colt AR-10 308 rifles, a pistol each, and all the ammo we could carry. Running as fast as our legs would allow under the weight of our gear, we scouted the island, hoping to find where the go-fast boat would enter the protected harbor, and to find a spot from which we could assault the team of well-trained operators. With the element of surprise on our side, we could easily mow down the bad guys, but we had Marissa to consider. We would do nothing to risk harming her, and we had to make certain that little girl spent the following night in her mother's arms, no matter what it took.

"There!" Clark pointed toward the only reasonable cut in the islands where a heavy boat could enter without risking running aground.

"Yep, that's the spot. And this looks like the best ambush site we're going to find," I said. "We've got what high ground there is, and plenty of cover and concealment."

After surveying the area around us, Clark quickly agreed. "Let's get dug in. They'll be here any minute, and I don't want to give them a chance to get settled into a position they can defend. I want to hit them hard and fast as soon as we have a clean angle."

"Agreed," I said, "but, no matter what happens, we can't risk hitting Marissa."

"Definitely. But what about the lawyer?"

"Let's keep him alive if we can. I've got a few questions I'd like to ask him, but if he gets in the way, I've got no qualms about putting him down."

Clark began digging himself a hasty firing position, and I moved about fifty yards to the south and did the same. The Army taught Clark to dig a fighting position, but I was left pawing at the loose sand like a dog burying a bone. The angle between us would make for a deadly fan of fire and give each of us a unique perspective if the other couldn't get an angle on our enemy.

Clark yelled, "They'll be shooting back as soon as we send the first round downrange, so keep your head down, and take out the most available target first. I'll work from the right, and you cover the left."

"Got it!" The butt of my rifle found its place against my shoulder as if were made just for me. A glance into the chamber reassured me that a round was ready to put an end to another evil that had no right to continue breathing.

Chapter 29
Like a Man

The powerful, thundering boat announced its arrival, and there was no question it was our target. I set my sights past the inlet, waiting for it to come into view, but I didn't have to wait long.

As they approached, the bow of the fifty-foot boat rose as the man on the throttles reduced the power. When the bow settled back toward the water, I saw four heads, but no sign of Marissa.

They idled through the inlet and pointed the bow at a wide section of beach—the perfect position to become my target. Once they beached the boat, one of the four men leapt to the sand. A second tossed a heavy Danforth anchor overboard. The jumper picked it up and walked backward up the beach until he found the spot he was looking for. He sank the anchor into the sand and yelled, "Anchor's secure!"

One by one, the remaining three men I'd seen during the approach hopped from the boat. My trigger finger was twitching, but I had to wait until I could see all six guys—and Marissa—before opening up on the men. Clark and I could easily cut down the four on the beach, but that would leave two more holed up inside the boat. Not knowing where Marissa was, I wasn't willing to start pouring lead into the boat. So, I waited.

Seconds felt like hours, but seeing the men unconcerned about being watched kept my heart rate under control. They clearly weren't expecting trouble. Maybe they weren't as well trained as

Penny and Skipper thought. Any quality operator would set a perimeter defense, even if they thought there was almost no chance of an attack. These guys appeared relaxed and unconcerned.

After the driver and anchor thrower relieved their bladders after the long, torturous boat ride, the remaining crew finally showed their faces. A muscle-bound beast of a man picked something up from the deck and threw it overboard. It only took an instant for me to identify what he'd thrown as Marissa. He'd tossed the child over the gunwale of the boat, and she landed with a tumbling thud on the wet sand. She cried as the pain of hitting the ground collided with the fear she had to be experiencing. My blood ran cold.

Marissa made no effort to get up, and I prayed she didn't break one of her legs in the fall. Seeing her lying there, terrified and hurting, was a sickening feeling, but the fact that I could see her gave me some measure of hope. I wouldn't be shooting blindly and hoping to miss her. I knew exactly where she was, and exactly where I could shoot.

Muscles, and a tall, thin man hit the sand almost simultaneously.

The gym rat who'd thrown Marissa overboard started barking orders. "Get on the horn, and get those choppers out here. I don't want to spend all day exposed like this. We've got to get back to the mainland. Get the lawyer out of the boat. And somebody shut that damned kid up. I'm not listening to her cry all afternoon."

I sighted in on his skull. *You're right, asshole. You're not gonna listen to her much longer. As soon as I see Kaminsky, you're getting a bullet in the eye.*

The tall, skinny guy pounded his fist against the fiberglass hull. "Hey, Kaminsky! Get out of the damned boat!"

The lawyer's head popped out of a hatch near the bow, and he scurried over the side, landing on his butt near Marissa.

The recoil of the rifle pounded into my shoulder the same instant the man who'd been barking orders collapsed to the sand with his head turned to a pink mist. Two cracks of Clark's rifle sent two more men to the beach and on their way to Hell.

The anchor setter hit the beach facedown and drew a pistol. He squeezed off six or seven rounds at Clark's position, and I watched sand and tree bark fly maniacally around my partner. I expected Clark to return fire, but it didn't happen, and I didn't have an angle on the gunman. The sixth man sprinted for the protection of the massive boat, and I sent three rounds in his direction. His body convulsed as the beach behind him turned to crimson.

The sole remaining gunman was still firing at Clark's position, but my partner's gun was silent. I rolled to my left and glanced to where Marissa had been lying in the sand, but she was gone. Kaminsky had grabbed the girl and pulled her to his chest, rolling into a ball beside the boat. I guess even he had enough humanity to instinctually protect the little girl.

Still without a shot at the anchor man, I scampered to my left, trying to open up the angle and get a line of sight on the man who may have just shot my partner in the head. His boots came into view, and I dived forward, landing in a prone firing position with my rifle ahead of me. I opened fire on a spot four feet up the beach from the man's boots, and his pistol went silent.

Keeping my eyes trained on the spot where the anchor man's body should've been, I slowly rose from my fighting position with my rifle still at the ready. It only took five strides for me to see that my barrage of fire had cut him nearly in half, just above his belt.

Another glance toward the boat reassured me that Kaminsky and Marissa weren't likely to move, so I sprinted toward Clark's position.

"Clark! Are you hit? Clark!" Running through the powdery dunes felt like trying to run in wet concrete. The thought of my partner lying atop the dune with a bullet in his brain made the slow progress even more agonizing. "Clark! Answer me! Are you hit?"

If he was answering me, I couldn't hear him through my panting and the ringing in my ears as I tried to catch my breath. I kept my eyes on his fighting position and prayed I'd see him stand up, but there was no sign of motion. The closer I got to where Clark should've been, the more I panicked.

I fell to my knees beside the fighting position he'd dug in the sand, and found it empty. Relief filled my mind when I saw no blood in the sand, but where was my partner?

Scrambling back to my feet, I glared across the dune and saw the most beautiful sight I'd ever beheld. Clark Johnson, badass Green Beret, was kneeling in the sand, spitting, gagging, and clawing at his eyes.

I scampered down the backside of the dune and landed on my butt in front of him. "Are you all right? Are you hit?"

"No, that son of a bitch put half a dozen rounds right in front of me and filled my face with twenty pounds of sand. I couldn't see, so I wasn't going to risk hitting that baby. Are you hurt? Did you get 'em all?"

I couldn't contain my laughter. "Yeah, College Boy got 'em while Special Forces was back here wiping his eyes."

He shoved the butt of his rifle into my chest, sending me sprawling backward. "I'll show you Special Forces. You try taking a bucket of sand in the face and see how you like it."

"Come on, Sandy. Let's go check on Marissa and have a chat with Lawyer Boy down there."

As we topped the dunes and started down the other side, we saw Kaminsky kneeling in the sand and holding Marissa against his chest. I wasn't sure if he was armed or how he'd come to fall into league with these guys, but I kept my rifle at the ready in case it became necessary to forcefully control him.

When Marissa saw Clark and me, she broke free of Kaminsky's grasp and ran toward us like the scared child she was. She was running straight for me, so I lowered my rifle and glanced at Clark.

He raised his weapon to his shoulder. "I've got Kaminsky. You get the girl."

Marissa leapt from the sand and into my arms, clinging to me as if her life depended on it. "I knew you'd come, Mr. Chase. I knew it. You're my hero, and I love you!"

I held her against my left side, away from my rifle. "You're my hero, Marissa. You've been through a lot today, and you protected Mr. Kaminsky while we were fighting with the bad guys."

She giggled. "Yeah, I guess I am kinda a hero, huh?"

Clark, in typical freight-train-on-Main-Street fashion, pressed the muzzle of his rifle to the attorney's throat and forced him onto his back.

"Talk, asshole!"

Terror beamed from Kaminsky's eyes. Through trembling lips, he blurted out, "They've got my mother. I-I-I didn't want to do it, but they said they'd kill her. I'm—"

Clark tapped the man's trembling chin with his muzzle. "All right, calm down. We're gonna check out your story, and if it's true, we'll get your mother back. But if you're lying.... Do you see those six dead bodies scattered on the beach? Seven is my lucky number. Capiche?"

"I'm not lying! I'm not!"

"We'll see. Now, get up and act like a man."

Marissa pinched her eyebrows together and held up a fist. "Yeah, act like a man. Like Mr. Chase."

Once again, I couldn't contain my laughter.

We trekked our way back across the dunes to the Caravan and found it right where we'd left it, still covered with the camo netting and resting solidly on the sand.

"How are we going to get her off the beach?"

"Oh, yeah," Clark said. "I didn't look that far ahead. Why don't you and Marissa go back and get that big powerful boat while Mr. Man and I start digging out the pontoons?"

I carried Marissa back across the dunes, intentionally taking the long way so she wouldn't have to see the bodies scattered on the beach. There was no way to avoid seeing the man who'd been running for the boat.

As we passed his corpse, Marissa held her nose. "That's gross."

"You're right, Marissa. It sure is, but he was a bad man and wanted to hurt you. I couldn't let him do that."

"That's why you're my hero, Mr. Chase."

"Instead of *Mister* Chase, how about you just call me Chase?"

She shook her head. "Nope. My mommy says I have to call you Mister Chase 'cause you're old."

I chuckled. "Okay, Mister Chase it is...since I'm old."

I tossed the anchor back on the boat, and we climbed aboard. We idled our way through the inlet, then I brought the throttles up and made my way around the south side of the islands.

When we arrived at the plane, Marissa looked up at me. "Can I let Charlie out now?"

I wasn't sure I'd heard her correctly. "What do you mean?"

She pointed toward the hatch leading to the cabin of the boat. "Charlie's down there. Can I let him out?"

"You bet," I said, opening the hatch.

The slobbering, high-energy pup was bouncing around like a rubber ball. When he saw Marissa, he ran toward her as if she were his long-lost best friend.

She grunted as she labored to pick him up. "See? I told you it was going to be okay, Charlie."

The puppy licked at her face and squirmed like a tiny tornado in her arms.

After successfully pulling the Caravan off the beach, we buried our arsenal of weaponry in the sand, tightly wrapped in plastic bags for later retrieval. Pirates aren't the only men of the sea who bury treasure.

I started one of the four engines of the boat, slipped the transmission into gear, and stepped overboard. The boat idled slowly southward. I didn't know much fuel we had or how long the engine would run, but if the boat didn't change course, she'd make landfall on the Cuban coast in a few days. I considered that a fair trade for the submarine I took off their hands the last time I was on Cuban soil.

With Marissa in the copilot's seat, "driving the plane," as she called it, I sat beside Kaminsky as he pondered his future and I thought about Penny Thomas, who was somewhere between the Marquesas and the Mexican Island of Women.

Clark leveled off at a thousand feet over the Western Caribbean Sea with the nose pointed into the sun. It would take us under three hours to reach Isla Mujeres off the coast of Cancun, but we'd beat the RV *Lori Danielle,* with *Aegis* in tow, by several hours. I'd soon see Penny, and I vowed never to put her in harm's way again.

Chapter 30
Birds of a Feather

An hour before sunset, we splashed down on the western side of Isla Mujeres, then taxied to the marina. We'd never clear customs with a dog, a lawyer with no passport, and a toddler with no mother, so we made no effort to go ashore.

I called Penny and told her about the gunfight and how Marissa had protected Kaminsky. She wasn't surprised, but she was happy to hear that we'd won the fight and survived unscathed.

"There's a twenty-five-year-old Italian mom who'd love to hear her daughter's voice if you could make that happen," Penny said.

I handed the phone to Marissa. "Your mommy wants to talk to you."

She grabbed it and began her long, animated tale of the boat ride and the gunfight and the airplane ride and the puppy and a dozen other exciting things I couldn't understand. When her epic tale of adventure had finally ended, she paused, and then said, "I love you too, Mommy."

* * *

We spent a long night aboard the Caravan at anchor, but shortly after daylight, I watched Captain Stinnett motor into the channel on the northwest side of the island where the enormous ferries from Cancun ran several times a day. He launched a tender to retrieve the four of us, and we were soon having breakfast aboard the RV *Lori Danielle*.

The reunion of daughter, mother, and grandmother was an emotional event for everyone. Gloria didn't cry, though. She remained stoic, though obviously happy to see her granddaughter again.

Penny and I descended the ladder over the side of the ship to get my first look at *Aegis*. The damage was just as she'd described. The engines and sails were destroyed and would have to be replaced. The sturdy boat that was my home had endured her first face-to-face encounter with true evil and lived to fight another day. I was proud of her…and her captain. I made sure both of them knew exactly how I felt.

She and I sat on the trampoline, holding hands and talking about the events of the past several days.

"I'm never going to put you in a position like this again, Penny, I swear."

She placed her hand against my face. "You didn't put me in this position, Chase. I volunteered. I figured out a long time ago that life with you was going to be an adventure. If I weren't up for the challenge, I wouldn't have said yes when you asked me to marry you back on the dock in Saint Augustine."

I furrowed my brow. "You didn't say yes. You didn't say anything. In fact, I didn't get the chance to finish asking. The fake cops arrested me before I could finish."

"No, Chase. That's not what happened at all. The fake cops did show up, and they did arrest you as soon as you got down on one knee, but you seem to forget that women don't communicate the same way men do. The fact that you got down on one knee was all the asking you had to do, and I said yes a thousand times even though you couldn't hear me through everything else that was going on. So, to me, you asked, and I answered."

She held up her left hand and wiggled her ring finger. I stared at the gleaming diamond and then into her beautiful eyes.

"It's perfect, Chase...just like you. You're terrible at hiding things, though. I know the combination to the safe. I'm the captain of this boat, and the captain always knows, you dingbat."

I held her in my arms and listened to the sea birds squawk and squeal overhead. "It's not over yet."

She leaned back and looked into my eyes. "I know. You've still got a hitman to catch. I'm gonna stay here to get the boatyard started on the repairs, and then I'll fly back to Florida. We can come back together and get our girl when all of this is over and she's seaworthy again."

Back aboard the research ship, I asked to speak with Captain Stinnett privately. He took me to his cabin, and I laid out the whole story. I owed him that much. I told him about the hitman in Florida I was going to find and capture. After I laid out my intentions with Giordano, Captain Stinnett's eyes lit up.

"Count me in!" he said.

Until that moment, I didn't know he was capable of smiling, but my plan brought out the twelve-year-old adventure-seeking boy in him, and he was instantly on board.

He shook my hand and clasped my shoulder. "You and Clark get back on that seaplane of yours and go catch a hitman. I'll take care of the rest of these folks and get Penny and Elizabeth on a plane back to Florida. Don't you worry about a thing, young man. As soon as I get everything settled here, I'll head north and meet you in Cumberland Sound."

"I can't thank you enough, Captain. You've been a lifesaver more than once."

"You don't have to thank me, boy. I'm having a lot of fun watching you do your thing. It reminds me of when I first started trying to save the world. Don't ever forget that it's worth saving." He winked at me. "I'll see you up north in a few days."

I stopped by the infirmary to check on Clay. Dr. Shadrack worked another miracle, just like he did for me when I got blown up on the bottom of the Panama Canal. Clay was going to live, and he was in good spirits. So much so, that I couldn't get him to stop telling me dirty jokes. I promised to check on him again and see that his buddies got the proper, honorable burial they deserved.

He thanked me and wished me luck in hunting down Giordano. "You know, if I could, I'd go huntin' with you."

"I know you would, Clay, but I have a feeling our paths will cross again before long. Something tells me I'm stuck with you."

He chuckled. "Yeah, you know what they say about birds of a feather."

I shuddered. "Don't put that on me, you sick joker."

Clark and I rode the tender back to the Caravan. We took off from the water and landed less than two minutes later at the airport on Isla Mujeres. It was the shortest flight I'd ever been on.

"We need fuel," Clark said as we taxied toward the pump.

I paid the attendant in American hundred-dollar bills and laughed at his toothless grin. Of course he couldn't make change, so he kept the leftovers.

The flight back to Key West was uneventful except for the pandemonium that seemed to be happening on the Marquesas as we flew over.

"Would you look at that?" Clark said. "I briefed my dad on what happened out there, and he said he'd get the right guys on it."

I scanned the action below. "I don't know if those are the right guys, but there seems to be plenty of them. I wonder how long it'll take them to sort out what happened down there."

"If our friend, the U.S. attorney, is any indication of the competency of the Justice Department, I'd say they'll be scratching their asses over that one for years to come."

We landed at Key West International for a bathroom break and something to eat. It had been too long since we'd had either of those things. As we shut down the engine, I checked my voicemail to find thirteen messages. They were all from Garret's team, so instead of listening to every message, I simply called them back.

"Where the hell have you been, man? I've been calling you for two days."

"It's a long story," I said, "but we had our hands full with a gun-fight in the Marquesas and then some trouble off the coast of Cuba. We were in Mexico overnight, but we're back in the Keys now. Tell me what you've got."

"Holy smoke, man. You've been busy, but so have we. We've got your boy pinned up in a trailer house south of a town called Abbeville, Alabama."

I covered the mouthpiece. "Clark, they have Giordano in southeast Alabama."

He flashed the thumbs-up.

"How long has he been there?" I asked.

"We tracked him here last night. I figure this is where he goes when he needs to let things cool down. I can see why. This place is out in the middle of nothing."

"Can you sit on him another couple of days?"

"We can sit on him as long as you're willing to write checks."

"My pen's got plenty of ink, so keep him in your sights. Let me know if he makes a move. I've got at least a day and a half, and probably two days before I can be there."

"You got it, man. I don't think he has any idea we're tailing him. He's settled in here for a few days, but you do know he's coming for you as soon as the heat is off in Miami, right?"

"Yeah, I know," I said. "I'm actually counting on that. Just keep me posted. Check in every eight hours if nothing changes, and anytime he makes a move, got it?"

"Sure, I can do that, but answer your phone when I call. I'm tired of leaving messages."

"I promise to answer if it rings, but it doesn't work in Mexico."

He scoffed. "All right, amigo. I'll be in touch."

I briefed Clark on the conversation and decided it was time to let him in on my plan with Giordano.

He sat back in a chair in the pilot's lounge and slapped his forehead. "That's brilliant. And you got Captain Stinnett on board?"

"Absolutely."

"You're a genius, Chase Fulton, and I'm proud to have you for a sidekick."

"Hey, wait a minute. *You're* the sidekick."

"Whatever you say, young Jedi. Whatever you say."

We ate lunch from an airport vending machine and blasted off into the sky for the hour-long flight back to the Miami-Opa Locka Airport where we'd left Cotton's Lake Renegade.

Clark negotiated arrangements to park the Caravan on the ramp at Opa Locka until we could have someone take it back to the Miami Seaplane Base for his dad. As I expected, the smitten girl behind the counter wasted no time agreeing to do whatever Clark "Baby Face" Johnson wanted.

"I'll never understand it," I said, shaking my head.

He feigned innocence. "Like I told you in Riga three weeks ago, it's a curse. But's it's a cross I'm willing to bear."

I laughed. "*You're* a curse. You know that?"

"We all have our penance to pay. Maybe putting up with me is yours, College Boy."

"Maybe you're right. Now let's see if Cotton Jackson has my airplane back in one piece."

After flying the Caravan for a week, the Renegade felt like a go-cart. It was far less capable than the turbine-powered Caravan, but it burned a lot less gas. Clark, as he tended to do, sat in the back so he could catch up on some "much-needed sleep." Since I wouldn't be landing in the water, I didn't need him up front with me.

We made the flight back to New Smyrna Beach in two hours. When I checked in with the tower and reported ten miles southwest of the field, the controller told me, "Make straight in for runway seven, report five-mile final. You're number two following a Cessna One-Eighty-Two on a maintenance test flight on a six-mile final."

I hoped that Cessna was mine. "Roger. I'll report five-mile final, and I'm looking for the One-Eighty-Two."

The instant I released the push-to-talk button, Cotton's voice came over the radio, "Hey, Chase. Is that you? I've got your old girl as good as new."

Obviously, the tower controller wasn't happy with Cotton's abduction of his air traffic control frequency. He keyed up and said, "Cessna Two-Charlie-Foxtrot, this is New Smyrna Tower. How about letting me use this frequency—if you don't mind?"

Cotton chuckled when he answered. "Sorry, Tower, but that's my buddy in my Renegade back there, and this is his airplane. I just wanted to say hey."

The tower controller wasn't amused. "Cessna Two-Charlie-Foxtrot, the wind is zero-five-zero at six, runway seven, cleared to land."

Cotton said, "Two-Charlie-Fox is cleared to land on seven. We'll see you on the ground, Chase."

It was in their genes. Cotton was the male version of Earline, and that made him all right in my book.

I keyed the mic. "Tower, Renegade Six-Charlie-Juliet has the One-Eighty-Two in sight, and we're five-mile final."

"Renegade six Charlie Juliet, wind zero-five-zero at six, cleared to land runway seven, number two behind the Cessna."

"Roger, we're cleared to land number two behind the Cessna, two Charlie Juliet."

I taxied the Renegade to the ramp behind Cotton and shut down the engine just as Clark was stirring from his well-deserved siesta.

"Wake up, honey. We're here."

He yawned and stretched. "Nice landing, Jedi. I still have some teeth left in my head. You didn't knock them all loose."

"You could sleep through a hurricane," I said. "I know my landings won't wake you up."

"Your landings—if that's what you call those controlled crashes—could wake the dead."

We climbed out of the Renegade and met Cotton halfway across the tarmac.

"Welcome back, boys. How was the trip? Did you do anything exciting?"

I shook the mechanic's grease-stained hand. "No, it was nice and relaxing. We did some sailing, a little flying, and even spent a couple of days in Mexico."

Cotton's eye's widened. "Mexico? Well, you boys have had quite a week."

He pointed toward my airplane. "Well, there she is. Better than new. I put eleven hours on the new engine, and she's humming like a Singer sewing machine. I did the oil change after ten hours, and there wasn't a speck of metal in what came out of her. But boy oh boy was that other motor a train wreck. I ain't never seen one blown apart like that. You were lucky to make it out alive."

"Yeah, I guess we're just the lucky type. Maybe I should buy a lottery ticket."

Cotton grinned. "Yeah, I reckon you should. Well, come on, take a look."

Cotton ambled toward my plane, wiping his hands on a filthy rag from his back pocket. "I can take the cowling off if you want, but I assure you she's better than she was when she left the factory back when they built her. I put all new baffling in. She's ready to go."

Cessna installs spring-loaded doors on the cowlings of their small airplanes. I opened the hatch to peer inside and realized Clyde Cessna must've had the smallest hands in history if he thought that tiny door was a good idea.

"It looks good to me, Cotton. I can't thank you enough. I guess I need to pay your boss."

He looked toward the hangar. "Yeah, I guess you do. He likes to get paid."

I signed the credit card slip and grunted at the final bill, but it had to be done.

Cotton handed me the logbooks for the plane as I headed out the door. "All the work is detailed in there and signed off by the IA. We did the annual inspection while we had her torn down, so you won't be due again for another year. If you have any trouble out of her, you just let me know. I can always come up to Saint Augustine and take care of it up there. Besides, that'd give me a chance to see Earline. Boy, she sure speaks highly of you."

I shook his hand again. "I'm sure it'll be fine, Cotton. Thanks again for everything, and especially for letting us use your Renegade. That's a great plane."

He looked across the tarmac. "Aw, it's something to fly every now and then."

I patted him on the shoulder and slid seven hundred dollars into the pocket of his coveralls.

He pulled the money out. "What's that for?"

"That's for taking such good care of my airplane and for letting us use yours."

"No, I can't take this. It's too much."

I took the bills from his hand and stuffed them back into his pocket. "If you don't want it, you can give it to somebody else, but I'm not taking it back. Thank you for everything."

"You know, Earline's right about you. You're something else. I'm glad I could help, and you call me anytime you need anything. I mean it. I'm your airplane mechanic from now on. Like Earline tells you about them motors on your boat, don't you go lettin' nobody else mess around on that motor in your airplane."

It was impossible to resist laughing out loud at the family resemblance. "I wouldn't have it any other way."

Chapter 31
Green Beret School

"What's the plan, Stan?"

I stared at Clark. "Oh, now you're a poet. Is that it?"

He laughed. "No, I just figured you were tired of hearing me call you Jedi or College Boy, so I decided to switch it up."

"I've got a name, you know."

"Yeah, I know," he said, "but your name's a verb, like *run* or *jump* or *sit*. What kind of name is Chase anyway?"

"You never cease to amaze me. Sometimes I wonder how that much crazy gets inside one person's head."

"It's a gift. Don't be jealous."

"Jealousy isn't what I'm feeling. It's something closer to pity."

He ignored the jab. "Let's get back to Saint Augustine. I'm tired. We've got a lot to do tomorrow, and we need a good night's sleep."

"What? You slept for two hours in the back seat of the Renegade."

"Yeah, but that was airplane sleep. It's not the same as good quality bed sleep."

I did a thorough preflight inspection, and once my airplane checked out, we headed north for the short flight back to Saint Augustine.

"Hey, Clark. Where are we going to sleep tonight? My house is in a boatyard in Mexico getting new engines and sails."

"Looks like you're springing for a hotel. I'll buy dinner. It's the least I can do."

We landed at Saint Augustine, and drove to our favorite restaurant, the Columbia. Elizabeth, the waitress we'd come to love, danced up to our table with a bottle of wine in one hand and a broken plate in the other. "Hey, guys! Where've you been? I haven't seen you guys in weeks." She elbowed me in the shoulder and winked. "And where are the ladies?"

"We've been on vacation," Clark said. "You know, a little trip to Eastern Europe, and then a jaunt down to the islands. It's a tough life, but somebody has to do it."

"Geez, I wish I had to suffer through life like that. You guys have got it made. But seriously, where's Penny and the other Elizabeth?"

"They're working," I said. "Somebody's got to support my and Clark's adventures."

"You're lucky to have them," she said. "Now, what can I get you to drink?"

"It's gonna be mojitos tonight."

"Comin' right up. And I know you won't be ordering your own food. I'll bring you whatever I think you'll like. Just like always."

"You're too good to us, Elizabeth. How ever can we repay you?"

"Taking me on one of your adventures would be a good start."

Clark waved his hand in the air. "Ah, you'd be bored to tears. All we do is read and people watch."

"That sounds like the life to me."

She vanished and reappeared in no time, going to work making her magical tableside mojitos. She delivered food we couldn't identify, but as always, we scarfed down every bite. She never failed to deliver something amazing when we let her do the choosing.

After two hours at the Columbia, we settled into the Casa Monica, one of Saint Augustine's finest resort hotels. I didn't want to risk Clark missing out on his quality bed sleep.

Garret's team checked in right on time. "Nothing's changed," he said. "He's still in that trailer. He comes outside twice a day, walks the perimeter, then goes back inside."

An idea hit me. "Does he do his walk at the same times every day?"

"Yeah, why?" asked the PI.

"Just make a note of the times," I said. "We'll be there tomorrow morning before lunch. Is there an airport in Abbeville?"

He scoffed. "Well, if you can call it an airport. It's really just a strip of concrete out in the middle of a cotton field. There's a good airport in Dothan, about twenty miles away, and another one in Headland between here and there."

"The Abbeville Airport sounds perfect. I'll call you in the morning with a good ETA. Can you pick us up when we land?"

He paused for several seconds. "Well, yeah, I can, but that'll leave the other guy here without wheels. What if your man runs while I'm gone?"

"That's a risk we'll have to take," I said. "Call me if anything happens overnight. Otherwise, I'll call you when we leave here in the morning."

I walked into Clark's room to brief him on the plan, but I was too late. He was naked, on top of the cover, and snoring like a lumberjack.

I took a shower, trying to get the vision of Clark's naked butt out of my mind's eye, and crawled into bed, wishing Penny were with me. I dialed the satellite number and hoped she'd answer.

"Hello?"

"Hey, it's me."

I could almost hear her smiling. "Hey. I was hoping you'd call. Is everything all right?"

"Yes, everything's fine. I got the airplane back, and it's as good as new. We're at the Casa Monica. We had dinner at the Columbia, and Elizabeth says hi. How's everything there?"

"It's good. Skipper and I are in Cancun. They pulled *Aegis* out of the water today and removed the starboard engine. There's a pair of new Volvo engines here at the yard, so they'll have them installed tomorrow. The sails are a different issue, though. A sailmaker is coming in tomorrow afternoon, but it may be a month or more before he can get them ready."

"That's not so bad. That'll give us time to do some other things while we're waiting. Why don't you catch a plane home? I'll book this room for you."

"We'll do that. I miss you, Chase. How's it going with the other thing?"

"If by 'the other thing,' you mean Giordano, it's going fine. The PIs from Panama City have him hemmed up in Alabama. We plan to pick him up tomorrow and spend some quality time together."

"Just be careful. He's a dangerous man."

"I know, Penny, but so am I. I love you."

"I love you, too. Thanks for calling."

I fell asleep in no time and dreamed of nobody shooting at me, wishing, even in dreamland, that my dream would someday come true.

* * *

The Abbeville Airport was as the PI had described—literally nothing except a long barren strip of concrete surrounded by cotton fields. We landed before noon and called for a ride. The PI who'd worked for Garret showed up in a plain white Jeep Cherokee, just like the one his boss died in.

I slid into the passenger seat, and Clark hopped in the back. "Thanks for coming," I said. "How's it look today?"

The man stared straight ahead. "It looks the same as it did yesterday. Nothing's changed."

"Consistency is a good thing most of the time."

He didn't respond.

"You never told me your name," I said, mostly to break the awkward silence in the jeep.

"You never asked me *my* name," he said. "I figured you didn't want to know, so I never brought it up."

I liked his style. "So, are you going to tell me?"

He shrugged. "Not if you don't ask."

I laughed. "So, what's your name?"

"Jude."

"Well, Jude. It's nice to finally meet you. I wish it could've been under better circumstances."

"Me, too, but now that my dad is dead, I guess you'll be dealing with me if you need our help again."

I stared at the man who couldn't be much older than me. "Garret was your father?"

He pressed his lips together and bowed his head.

"I'm sorry, Jude. I didn't know. I would've never—"

"You couldn't have known. This is how Dad would've wanted it. He wouldn't want us to quit doing what's right just because he's dead."

We drove for ten minutes in silence, mostly on red clay roads through thousands of acres of pine trees and what would be cotton and peanut fields when springtime came. We pulled off the dirt road, through a thicket of dense pines where Jude parked the truck.

"The trailer is through there about a thousand yards. He walked the perimeter at ten after nine this morning, and he'll do it again at four thirty this afternoon."

Clark surveyed the area, taking in every detail. Wooded environments found him at his best, and I could see the wheels turning in his head.

We crept silently through the pines until we came to a pile of rotting brush.

"Welcome to home sweet home," Jude whispered. "We've been nestled right in here, watching your man for three days."

Clark nodded his approval. "You picked a nice little nest, Jude."

"Thanks. It's pretty much what we do."

I kicked the twigs around and flattened them, subconsciously trying to make his temporary living quarters more comfortable. "If you can stand it one more night, we'll snatch him up tomorrow morning, then you can head home—wherever home is for you. I know you've got a lot to deal with."

"This *is* home for us," Jude said. "We live a hundred miles south of here."

"Where's your partner?"

Jude stared at me for a long moment. "I've never really thought of him as being my partner. He's my brother, and he's watching the trailer about a quarter mile from here. He'll be back before the dude starts his afternoon walk, though."

"Your brother?" I said.

"Yeah, it's a family business, you might say."

Jude motioned for us to follow him, and we eased silently forward about thirty yards then lay down in the pine straw.

In an even softer whisper, he said, "There it is. That's where your boy's hiding out."

The trailer was tucked beneath a stand of pines that kept it well hidden from anyone who happened to be flying overhead, and the dilapidated condition made the trailer blend in perfectly with its surroundings.

"It'd be hard to see if you weren't looking for it," Clark whispered.

After watching the trailer for a half hour, Clark said, "I'll meet you back at the brush pile. I'm gonna have a look around."

Jude looked over at him. "I'll call my brother and tell him not to shoot you."

Clark leapt to a crouch. "There's no need. He'll never see me."

"Suit yourself, but he doesn't miss much."

As if he were invisible, Clark vanished into the pines, then reappeared at four fifteen. "There are a lot of ways out of here, but they all lead into open fields."

"Holy shit!" whispered Jude. "Where'd you come from?"

Clark just smiled, and two minutes later, Jude's brother crept into position beside the brush. Introductions were quietly made.

"He'll be making his walk in about five minutes," Jude said.

"I'm going to follow him," Clark said as he pressed himself to the ground. "I'll meet you back here as soon as he's finished."

He low-crawled toward the trailer, and just as before, disappeared into the trees.

My watch showed four thirty, on the nose. I heard the door of the trailer close, and the man who tried to kill me twice strolled down the rusty stairs and across the yard as if he didn't have a care in the world. The outline of a pistol was clearly visible under the man's sweatshirt as he turned to the east. I thought I caught a glimpse of Clark moving through the trees, but I wasn't sure. Giordano walked a hundred yards from the trailer, then turned left.

"He'll walk around the trailer at that distance like he's going for a stroll or something, and then he'll head back inside. It's always the same."

I nodded in acknowledgment.

A few minutes later, Giordano appeared on the west side of the trailer and continued walking in a slow arc toward us. When he was between our location and the trailer, he turned and looked directly at us, cocking his head as if he were listening for something. Then he leaned forward into a crouch and began inching forward.

Steadily, I moved my hand toward the pistol on my right hip. On the verge of my second gunfight in one week, this time I was at a marked disadvantage: I wasn't dug in, I didn't have the high ground, and I was armed with a single forty-five automatic instead of the thirty-caliber rifle I had in the Marquesas.

Just as I solidified my position in the dirt, Giordano lunged forward like a cat pouncing on its prey, and quickly stood erect with a writhing, four-foot snake in his hand.

He lifted the reptile and spat in its face. "You thought you were the scariest animal out here, but you were wrong."

He drew a knife from a scabbard on his left hip and sliced the snake's head off, tossing the carcass into the trees and heading back for his trailer.

I exhaled a relieved breath. "Whew, that was close."

"Never fear, young Jedi. I had you covered." Clark was inches away with his pistol drawn, still covering Giordano as he climbed the steps back into the hideout."

"I guess they taught you that at Green Beret school, huh?"

"Ah, we all have our strengths. You got the book smarts. I got the how-to-blend-in-and-move-silently smarts."

Chapter 32
Welcome Aboard

I sent the two brothers into Abbeville for the night and told them Clark and I would hold down the fort. They deserved a break and a night in a real bed. They didn't love my plan, but I was paying the ticket, so they finally relented.

"Try to be back by daybreak," I said. "We'll take him on his morning walk."

"You're the boss." Jude led his brother toward the jeep.

Clark and I took turns standing watch and sleeping. We would need our strength and wits when we nabbed Giordano the next morning, but we couldn't risk both of us sleeping at the same time.

Just as Jude had said, nothing changed overnight. There was never a light on inside the trailer, and Giordano didn't make another trip outside.

As the eastern sky began to turn orange, Jude and his brother snuck into the brush pile.

"Welcome back, guys. Did you get some rest?"

"Yeah, it was nice to sleep in a bed for a change. Anything new here overnight?"

I shook my head. "Nope. Still the same."

"Jude," Clark said, "you're one hundred percent certain he takes the same path every time?"

"Absolutely. It never changes."

"Then here's the plan. I'm going to dig in right in front of the trailer. When Giordano walks out and gets just beyond where I am, I want Chase to stand up and say something friendly—anything to get his attention."

Jude held up his hand. "Wait a minute. This guy will drill a hole in you if you try that."

"No, he won't. He won't have time. I'll take him down before he can draw. I just need you to get his attention for half a second. I'll do the rest. Got it?"

Jude raised his eyebrows in disbelief. "You guys are insane. This is never going to work."

Clark locked eyes with him. "We underestimated this guy once, and your dad paid the price. We won't let that happen again."

Without another word, Clark crawled away and set his plan in motion. He took position beyond the right front corner of the trailer as I crawled forward to watch for our prey. At precisely ten minutes after nine, the door opened, and Loui Giordano stepped outside. I counted his strides, watching for any change in his movement or difference from what he'd done the day before.

Three steps down the rusty, metal stairs, left foot first. Eleven strides toward me and a turn to the east, just as he'd previously done. Six strides across the front of the trailer, and he flinched. Something caught his attention. Clark was less than four feet away from the hitman, and I had to do something.

I hopped to my feet. "Hey! I didn't know anyone else was out here."

That was all the distraction my partner needed. Giordano spun to face me, drawing his pistol in rapid, well-practiced precision. I reached for mine, but before I could get the barrel clear of the leather holster, Clark hit Giordano like a defensive lineman crushing an unsuspecting quarterback. The hitman went down, but he didn't stay down. He moved like a panther and leapt to his feet to face my partner.

I moved in with every ounce of speed I could muster, my pistol pointed at Giordano's head, but Clark caught my eye and shook his head. He knew how badly I wanted Loui Giordano alive. The assassin advanced on Clark like a striking cobra, but he hadn't anticipated my partner's combat reflexes.

Clark sidestepped the attack and sent a hammer fist exploding into the back of Giordano's head. He grabbed the man's right wrist and spun in a violent arc, sending the hitman in an accelerating flight toward the corner of the trailer. He raised his left arm to block the collision, but it was too little too late. His body careened into the rusty metal and slid down the side, landing in a heap at Clark's feet. Clark sent a boot heel to his temple, making certain the second deadliest animal in the yard wasn't going to be getting up anytime soon.

I yanked the boots from Giordano's feet, then bound his hands and ankles with the laces. Clark laced the hitman's belt around his neck and into his mouth so there was no risk of him waking up and trying to bite either of us.

I should've anticipated what happened next, but I'd let the humanity of the scenario pass without a second analytical thought. Any reasonably competent psychologist would've seen it coming, but I suppose I didn't fall into that group.

I heard the hammer cock on a pistol inches from my head, followed by Jude's cold tone. "This is for our dad, you son of a bitch!"

Thrusting upward with all the speed I could generate from my position, I struck at Jude's gun hand, knocking the pistol free from his grip. Clark stepped in front of Jude's brother with blinding speed, preventing him from drawing on the unconscious hitman.

I took Jude by the collar and pulled his face to mine. "I understand what you're trying to do, but this is *not* the place. Killing your father was only one of his many sins. He's got a lot to pay for, and I'm going to make sure that happens. You'll have to trust me on that."

Jude clenched his teeth. "I don't care about anything he's ever done, but I'm gonna make him pay for killing my dad."

I released his collar and patted him on the chest. "I'm going to make him pay, I swear it, but not here. Not now."

Jude didn't waver. "He'll get some sleazy lawyer and plea bargain, and he'll never really pay for what he's done. The only justice for people like him is a bullet in the head."

"I completely understand, Jude, and you're not wrong, but look at me." I stared intently into his hatred-filled eyes. "I'm going to make him pay. No court, no lawyers, and no plea bargains. Now, bring the Cherokee as close as you can. We'll carry him the rest of the way."

Jude pointed his finger directly into my face. "If he doesn't pay for what he's done, it's on you, and you'll have me as the worst enemy you could ever dream up."

Reluctantly, the two brothers headed toward the jeep. Jude glanced back twice but made no further effort to carry out his own brand of justice on his father's killer.

Clark said, "We probably should've seen that coming. If the roles were reversed, I'd have the same thoughts those two are having."

"I know. Me, too."

Forty minutes later, at what qualified as an airport in Abbeville, Alabama, we were loading the hitman's unconscious body into the back seat of my airplane.

I handed Jude thirty thousand dollars in cash. "If that doesn't cover the bill, you know how to reach me."

Instead of saying a word, he simply pocketed the money, and that seemed appropriate.

The flight to Saint Augustine was interesting. Each time Giordano stirred, Clark nailed him with a punch designed to send him back into the spirit world. The man was going to be badly bruised and sore by the time we landed, but that was the least of what he had to fear over the coming days.

Back at the hangar, I pulled my car out, and we shoved the Cessna inside. Thankfully, no one was roaming around the airport with curious eyes.

A call to my old friend, Captain Stinnett, yielded a welcome surprise.

"We're abeam Daytona now," he said, "and we can be off the coast of Saint Augustine in two hours. I'll send a tender and a couple strong young men to help you get our cargo aboard."

I was amazed. "How did you make it up the coast so quickly? How fast is your ship?"

"It's fast enough. There's a place called the Oceanview Lodge just north of the Saint Augustine inlet. Do you know the place?"

I had no idea how Captain Stinnett could know so much about so many places, but he'd obviously been around. "Yeah, I know the place."

"Good. My men will meet you there in two hours. Don't be late."

I'd stashed a few doses of the ketamine I used when Penny and I nabbed Salvatore D'Angelo. Fortunately, I'd stored a couple extras in the refrigerator at the hangar. That relieved Clark of the necessity of pounding on Giordano every time he woke up. I doubted Clark minded hitting the man, but I was going to need his hands in good shape.

Captain Stinnett's men walked up the beach exactly two hours later. We folded Giordano in half, stuffed him into a giant duffle bag they brought, and hefted him down the beach and onto the tender. We were underway and cutting through the surf before I could find a place to sit.

The crew of the RV *Lori Danielle* were the epitome of professional efficiency. With all of us on board, they hoisted the tender as if they'd done it a thousand times, and placed us in the cradle on deck without so much as a thud.

Giordano landed in the ship's brig, and Clark and I landed on the bridge.

"You two are a real pair of cowboys, you know that?"

I considered that a high compliment from the captain. "Maybe it takes one to know one, Captain."

He winked. "Maybe it does. Now let's go find some sunken treasure. Whaddya say?"

* * *

The ship dropped anchor in twenty-five feet of water an hour before sundown, and Dr. Shadrack, the ship's doctor who'd saved my life in Panama, joined us for dinner. Over the chef's five-star-restaurant-worthy Caribbean lobster and grilled shrimp, the doctor filled us in on the happenings of the previous two days.

"While you two were playing in the woods, we delivered Mr. Kaminsky back to his office in Miami, and the FBI raided the house where his mother was being held against her will. You'll be happy to know she's alive and well, but still pissed off."

"Well, what do you know? The lawyer was telling the truth," I said. "That's rare for an attorney."

"Antonio is in the custody of the Justice Department, and your old friends, the Righettis, are tucked away neatly in our protective custody until the case goes to trial. Like you, we don't trust the Marshals Service to keep them alive long enough to testify, so we've got that issue under control."

"You guys are too much," I said. "We couldn't have done it without you."

Captain Stinnett adjusted his hat. "It's all in a day's work. We've got a couple more surprises for you, but we'll save them for tomorrow. We'll have divers in the water at sunup. Are you two going in with 'em, or did that incident in Panama scare you out of the water for good?"

Clark came to my defense. "It's gonna take more than a case of the bends and a few pounds of plastic explosives to scare Chase out of the water. We'll be suiting up with your divers at daylight."

* * *

I slept like a log and hit the water as soon as the first rays of sun beamed through the trees of Cumberland Island. Two hours later, the massive crane aboard the *Lori Danielle* was hoisting our prize from the muddy bottom of the sound.

Four men with high-pressure hoses had the relic spotless in no time, and the crane lowered it gently into the largest tender the ship had. Though the research vessel was constrained by draft and couldn't navigate the shallow waters up to the dock at Bonaventure Plantation, the tender had no trouble making its way to the dock alongside Judge Huntsinger's center-console fishing boat.

It took eight men to carry the relic from the tender to the gazebo in the judge's backyard, and two more to handcuff Loui Giordano to it.

When I knocked on the front door of the plantation, I expected to see Judge Huntsinger's granddaughter open the door, but instead, the most beautiful woman I'd ever seen, wearing the most beautiful engagement ring I'd ever bought, was standing in the foyer of the antebellum mansion.

"Penny! What are you doing here?"

"Are you kidding me? I wouldn't miss this for the world. Besides, Captain Stinnett says you'll need a ride home. He's had enough of you on his ship."

I hugged her. "Is the judge here?"

"Of course. He's in the parlor waiting to see you."

She led me through the house and into the parlor where Judge Huntsinger was beginning the first steps of hefting himself up from a two-hundred-year-old sofa.

"It's good to see you again, young man. I hear you've got something to show me."

I reached for the man's hand before he could push himself from the antique. "Yes, sir, I do. But I need to talk with you first."

"Is this some elaborate scheme to get me to marry the two of you? Because I can do that sort of thing, you know."

Penny's eyes lit up in what anyone could see was the epitome of school-girl excitement.

"There's no one I'd rather have perform the ceremony for us, but that's something we can discuss later. Right now, I have something quite different to show you."

The look of utter disappointment on Penny's face was impossible to mistake. I silently vowed to never again allow myself to be the source of that look from her, but that day, what lay ahead for the judge would leave no room for a wedding ceremony.

I allowed my eyes to echo Penny's disappointment, silently reassuring her that our wedding day would come. I hoped she'd soon understand why that particular day in December of two thousand one could not be the day.

"Judge," I began, "I have two things to show you. The first is a gift for the kindness you showed me and my partner, Clark, when we visited you a couple weeks ago. The history lessons you taught that day were not only fascinating but also unforgettable."

The judge beamed. "Son, I didn't do any of that expecting anything in return. Those were just the ramblings of an old man thrilled to his soul to have somebody to talk to. I don't want any gift. I merely enjoyed your company, and, as a matter of fact, I'd like to extend an open invitation for either of you, and of course Miss Penny here, to come back anytime you'd like. You're always welcome in my home here at Bonaventure."

Penny beamed with the smile that is unique to women of certain parts of the south—the smile that expresses a thousand sincerities without uttering a word. At ninety, I assumed the judge didn't see the beautiful Penny Thomas in the same lustful light men of my age perceived her, but it was clear he was no less smitten by that smile than a man of any age would've been. I believe he almost blushed.

"Judge, I can speak for the three of us when I say we look forward to spending a great many hours here at Bonaventure and hearing hour upon hour of your delightful stories. Again, your kindness seems to know no bounds."

He waved a dismissive, wrinkled hand in my direction. "It's just hospitality, my boy. Something that seems to be escaping this world faster than my old body. And that's a damned shame. Pardon my profanity, won't you, Miss Penny?"

"Nothing to forgive, Judge." She flashed him an exaggerated wink.

I cleared my throat, unsure how to bring up the rest. "Judge, the second thing I have for you is less of a gift and more of a twenty-five-year, past-due delivery."

His brow fell, and the delight consuming his aged face vanished in an instant, replaced by a combination of intrigue and uncertain curiosity. "What are you talking about, son? What could I possibly have been due for a quarter of a century?"

Believing for the first time that what I'd done may have been an unforgivable mistake and result in nothing but anguish, I said, "I truly don't know how to tell you, Judge, but I've come too far to turn back now. Would you join me out by the river?"

Side by side, I walked with the man who'd spent his life in service to others and lived by every rule the law had laid before him. As we approached the gazebo, the judge stopped in his tracks, standing in silent awe of the sight in front of him.

I placed my hand on his shoulder. "We pulled that cannon from the mud on the bottom of Cumberland Sound this morning, right where you told me Captain Abraham Massias burned those British ships. And that man handcuffed to your cannon is Loui Giordano. This isn't the first time he's been to your house, Judge. He's the man the D'Angelo family has dispatched to do their unthinkable deeds for thirty years. The last time he was here, he found your wife standing in that kitchen behind us. It was that night in nineteen seventy-eight when you were confronting Antonio D'Angelo in the county lock-up. Sir, I thought you might like to have a word with him."

About the Author

Cap Daniels

Cap Daniels is a sailing charter captain, scuba and sailing instructor, pilot, Air Force veteran, and civil servant of the U.S. Department of Defense. Raised far from the ocean in rural East Tennessee, his early infatuation with salt water was sparked by the fascinating, and sometimes true, sea stories told by his father, a retired Navy Chief Petty Officer. Those stories of adventure on the high seas sent Cap in search of adventure of his own which eventually landed him on Florida's Gulf Coast where he owns and operates a sailing charter service and spends as much time as possible on, in, and under the waters of the Emerald Coast.

With a head full of larger-than-life characters and their thrilling exploits, Cap pours his love of adventure and passion for the ocean onto the pages of The Chase Fulton Series.

Visit www.CapDaniels.com to join my mailing list to receive my newsletter and release updates.

Connect on Facebook www.Facebook.com/WriterCapDaniels

CPSIA information can be obtained
at www.ICGtesting.com
Printed in the USA
LVHW022304040819
626504LV00002B/167/P

9 781732 302488